Eddy, Eddy

Eddy, Eddy

KATE DE GOLDI

CANDLEWICK PRESS

First US edition 2024
First published by Allen & Unwin (New Zealand) 2022

Library of Congress Catalog Card Number 2023944036
ISBN 978-1-5362-3282-0

SHD 29 28 27 26 25 24
10 9 8 7 6 5 4 3 2 1

Printed in Chelsea, MI, USA

This book was typeset in Centaur MT.

Candlewick Press
99 Dover Street
Somerville, Massachusetts 02144

www.candlewick.com

For Sally Zwartz
and in memory of Jenny and Fra,
who gave us the books and the songs

Marley was dead: to begin with. There was no doubt whatever about that. The register of his burial was signed by the clergyman, the clerk, the undertaker, and the chief mourner. Scrooge signed it: and Scrooge's name was good upon 'Change, for anything he chose to put his hand to. Old Marley was as dead as a door-nail.

—Charles Dickens, *A Christmas Carol*

SEP
TEM
BER

1

"Marley was dead: to begin with. There was no doubt whatsoever about that."

Eddy's uncle got to the immortal words first. It was a quotation begging to be said that day. One of them had to say it, Eddy supposed. Brain grabbed the moment.

Funny, really, since Brain was a slow thinker and mover most of the time. But he spoke the second they settled into the car. Then he shut the passenger door softly—a full stop. Brain did most things carefully, even delicately. This sometimes made Eddy itch.

Maybe he'd been waiting years to say it. Maybe, all that time ago, he'd named Marley just so he could say the line when Marley died. Only now he said it wrong.

"No doubt whatever," said Eddy. Really, for a research librarian, Brain could be surprisingly imprecise. He often fluffed song lyrics and quotes. "No 'so.'"

"Are you sure?"

"Positive."

Brain looked at Eddy: his baffled-animal look, the raccoon eyebrows bending inward. He seemed to be staring at Eddy's forehead as if trying to make out the words etched there or something, proof.

"Marley was dead:" Eddy paused.

"Colon," said Brain, with a wan smile.

"Marley was dead colon: to begin with. There was no doubt whatever about that."

There really wasn't any doubt. Marley was in the back seat, head resting on her old pillow with its stains and holes and sprouting kapok.

She was wrapped in the Kaiapoi Pure Wool blanket. The blanket was Eddy's sole inheritance from his unknown maternal grandmother. He'd donated it to Marley when she was a pup, and it had been her bed rug for as long as anyone could remember. It was all felted from years of washing, spattered with ragged holes from Marley's unclipped claws. She liked to rough up the rug before she slept; she pawed at it, bunched it into little hillocks, then thumped down onto it, exhaling noisily, her long nose between front paws.

"Memories of snow," Brain told Eddy all those years ago. "The reptilian brain remembering Labrador—you know, all the snow, how they paw into the snow for warmth.

"Labrador. Where Labs come from," said Brain unnecessarily. Every moment a teaching moment. Labrador habits. Dreamtime lore. The Jesuits' misdeeds in China. Lines of poetry—misquoted probably, now that Eddy thought about it. The arguments for and against veganism. The meaning of thanatology . . . It had been all right when he was young, Eddy supposed. He couldn't stand it these days.

Marley's old rug would go with her now, into the ground beneath the wattle tree in the backyard, where she had lain in the shade all the hot afternoons of Eddy's life.

He'd already prepared the hole, spent half the morning marking out the plot and digging, manufacturing a decent sweat. It was sweltering by 11 a.m., a breathless, pressing heat, though it was only September. Eddy had derived a grim enjoyment from the liquid gathering under his cap, leaking unpleasantly down his neck and back. He imagined it glistening in the sun, a moist and manly rebuke to Brain. One of them was practical, the sweat said. *One* of them had borrowed the spade from next door and prepared the grave.

Not that Brain had been watching. He was inside with Marley, contemplating the animal soul. Saying a prayer, no doubt.

In the car now, Brain still stared, dwelling on the quotation, listening to it in his head. Everything in Brain's head happened at adagio.

"Marley was dead: to begin with," he said again. *"There was no doubt whatever about that."*

Eddy had been there at the death. Brain, too, but only Eddy watched. Brain laid a big white hand on Marley's flank but stared fixedly at the poster on the otherwise bare clinic wall: an image of a gadfly petrel, aslant against a blue sky.

Eddy held Marley's shabby left forepaw. It had troubled her for years; she couldn't manage a run longer than 3 km without developing a limp—a Marley limp, graceful and apologetic. He massaged the furless patch on the side of the paw with his thumb. He watched Marley's face, the grizzled muzzle all slack now, her lovely eyes gummy with sickness.

At the same time, from the corner of his eye, he watched the vet expertly filling the syringe.

"It's very quick," the vet said. "And completely painless." Eddy doubted the vet knew this for sure, not being a dog. It was Fat Vet. He was in practice with his brother Thin Vet: Fat Bob and Thin Tim.

Yeah, but shut up, Fat Vet, Eddy thought. Don't talk.

He liked Fat Vet well enough. He liked him much better than Thin Vet, who was terse and kind of bitter. But Eddy didn't want Fat Vet talking, not while Marley was getting the needle. He wanted it just to be Marley's sounds, her little snuffles and wheezy exhalations, the occasional tail *thwomp*, pathetically tired. He wanted to hear her breathing right to the end.

Fat Vet obliged. He said nothing more. He felt around with his competent sausage fingers for the soft gap in Marley's neck and slid the needle neatly into the cavity, and Marley was as dead as a doornail. In less than a minute. No doubt whatever.

"Except," said Eddy now, "it isn't 'to begin with.' It's the end. The end of an era. The Marley Era. Marley was dead. Full stop. The End."

He started the car and pulled out into the road, pitted and hummocky like so many of the roads in the area; even at normal speed, the going was bumpy. Today the traffic ambled, befuddled by the heat. The air was hazy, filled with spores. This city is comatose, thought Eddy. He imagined flooring it, frightening all the dozy motorists, driving somewhere at great speed. He pictured the long straight roads north of town, the magical vanishing point. But really, you couldn't floor a Suzuki Alto with any conviction.

"Marley was dead to end with," said Brain, trying it out.

Eddy felt the familiar spike of irritation with his duffer uncle, with Brain's over-deliberate enunciation, his ponderous—as he called them—*cerebrations*. He felt the evil little urge that visited him sometimes to pinch Brain someplace painful.

"To begin with is better," said Brain, oblivious. "God closes a door, opens a window."

If he closed his eyes, thought Eddy, they might end up in the river, sink into the silted-up bottom, let the water close over the Suzuki Alto, their banana-colored coffin, Amen, Amen.

"Lift up your heads, oh ye gates!" sang Brain through the windscreen, into the suburban middle distance.

2

The month of Marley's death was the two-year anniversary of the first earthquake. Which meant it was exactly two years since the death of Brain's mother. She had probably died during the long shaking, though no one could say for sure. Bad heart. They had found Doris in her narrow bed when they went around to check on her, an hour after the quake. Could have gone at any time, the doctor said. It might have been the quake.

"Frightened to death," said Brain mournfully, but Eddy doubted it. Doris was quite the termagant. Mostly, people were frightened of her. He had frequently witnessed her admonishing tradies and shop assistants, hapless passersby. In church she recited the prayers at an uncomfortable volume, in competition with the rest of the congregation. Once, she had barked out her disagreement during the sermon. Heads had turned, but the priest plowed serenely on, used to Doris, no doubt. Eddy, ten years old at the time, had gone hot and horrified. He refused to accompany his grandmother to Mass ever again.

This weekend, Brain had arranged for the Modern Priest to say an anniversary Mass for the repose of Doris's seized-up little soul. In their living room, on a Saturday evening. The Modern Priest loved a house Mass; he grieved for the 1970s when everyone and their aunt apparently took up homestyle worship.

"Count me out," said Eddy, even as he automatically helped Brain push the couch across the room to make space for the temporary altar trestle. Eddy had not been to a church since the quakes, and before that he'd gone solely to sing in the Cathedral choir. The choir loft was sufficiently far away from the priest and the progress of the Mass to make it feel like you were uninvolved, practically elsewhere, which suited Eddy fine.

He'd finally let his friend Thomas More talk him into the choir. Toss More was an inconsistent theist, but he had unshakable faith in music of all kinds and the glory of voices raised in chorus. Eddy had resisted joining because Brain was the deputy choirmaster, but Toss More worked on him, wore him down like a faltering surface under a power drill.

In fact, Eddy loved singing just as much as Toss. He loved singing *with* Toss. They'd been in every school choir together since primary school, had formed countless short-lived bands, all with satisfyingly abstruse names. Their last band (Steal Away) had been barely a band: just the two of them, harmonizing Toss More's increasingly strange secular spirituals—Toss liked a paradox.

"Ginge will be here," said Brain. He smoothed the woven runner carefully across the tabletop.

Eddy was very fond of cousin Ginge, a bachelor like Brain, with a houseful of cats (last count, six) instead of a nephew. Cat-love on Ginge's scale was possibly pathological, but Eddy approved of it: if not for Ginge's interventions, the moggies were destined for the prick in the paw. Ginge was a union organizer and sometimes as dufferish as Brain, but he was a committed communist and very droll. Also an atheist, though (more paradox) he went often to Mass, in his ancient army coat and Doc Martens—for old times' sake, he said. If you considered Brain and Ginge with a cool eye, you could not fail to conclude that the Smallbone genetic makeup was peculiar. And coming to an end. Any reproductive glory was up to Eddy.

"Bridgie's coming too," said Brain. He placed the pottery candlesticks at either end of the trestle. Next, he would get the oval Temuka pottery bowl for a makeshift chalice. Eddy just knew Brain was imagining himself as an early Christian preparing for the Eucharist in a Roman atrium.

Well, Bridgie. Bridgie was wild. She was Eddy's godmother, though she believed in neither God nor mothering. She taught piano and viola and played in the symphony orchestra, had in fact played in two of his and Toss More's five-minute bands. Bridgie dressed extravagantly and pursued a dangerous line in conversation. She sometimes inquired after Ginge's and Brain's peckers: Had they shriveled and fallen off yet, due to long-term lack of use?

The quartet's friendship was a mystery to Eddy, but they went way back. Back through the mists of time to Our Lady of Perpetual Succour, their hallowed primary school, where fragrant and beautiful nuns had cast an unfathomable spell, and when the Modern Priest (chief altar boy) had answered to the name Christopher Mangan. They had all regularly played at Masses in Chris Mangan's bedroom and, in Eddy's view, they were playing still.

"When I was a child, I spake as a child," said Eddy, watching Brain fold the lily-white table napkin he kept especially as a purificator to wash out the pottery chalice. Brain was pretending he hadn't heard.

"But when I became a man, I put away childish things."

"King James?" said Brain.

Eddy pretended he hadn't heard. They sometimes did this. It was 1:50 p.m. He had a pickup in forty minutes.

"I'm off," he said.

9

3

He walked to Paparoa Street, a zigzag route that dodged the worst of St. Albans's chewed-up footpaths. He had a bike, but lately a disturbing thing happened whenever he swung his leg over. Slowly, terribly, he felt himself turning into Brain. He felt his arse spread and his fingers plump up. His scalp itched as his hairline seemed to recede. The pedals moved as if through porridge. He could have cycled naked, but still it would have felt like he was wearing a navy blazer, wheat-colored corduroys, and polished brogues.

This sort of horror had happened at intervals throughout his adolescence, especially once his voice had broken and settled in the same baritone range as Brain's. Eddy had been violently alarmed by the first of these episodes, bursting from Toss More's sleekly appointed sleep-out into a cold June night. He'd leaned against the roughcast exterior wall, his breaths short and his scalp prickling on the inside.

Wtf? said Toss More by way of his eyebrow when Eddy finally came back inside. Had he sounded like Brain? asked Eddy.

Toss thought about it. "No more than usual," he concluded. Eddy was appalled. "It's the vocabulary," said Toss. "How many fourteen-year-olds say *concatenation*? And, you know, the *sound*—same timbre as Brain's." Thanks for nothing, thought Eddy. And btw, how many fourteen-year-olds said *timbre*?

He'd tried to keep watch on vocabulary after that, suppressing Brain-type words. Interstices. Adumbrate. Desuetude. He would lead a two-syllable life. He tried to speak in less well-formed sentences, too, use a more bass voice. It was hopeless, of course. He'd been a sitting duck; fourteen years with Brain was a full-scale colonization. He would never escape his uncle's words, his grammar and tone, his *cerebrations*. Occasionally Brain's voice even narrated passages inside his head while he was reading. Did this happen to everyone at some stage—their parents or caregivers taking up passive-aggressive occupation inside them, a desperate stakeout just before their offspring left forever?

Not that Eddy was leaving anytime soon. The quakes had seen to that. The city's housing stock was gutted. Rentals were thin on the ground or beyond his pocket. But also, in his many interior fantasies of Moving Day, there appeared always a reduced and stoical Brain helping him lug furniture, pressing household linen and appliances on him, waving a brave farewell from the front porch. Eddy couldn't do it to him. He might just have done it while Marley was still alive—he could have trusted Brain to Marley's care. But that ship had sailed.

As it was, on most days they were both engaged in elaborate delaying tactics, re: arrival home from their respective jobs. It was the silence that came down the path to greet you, the lack of hustle and operatic whimpering. And being alone in the house. Nothing, nowhere, felt as it should. No dribbling dog-love when Eddy slumped on the couch. No slavish companion padding alongside him down the hallway or curled like a conch beside his bed. He didn't like going to the fridge or the pantry, the dog-roll and the half-full bag of Eukanuba staring back at him, all sad and unemployed. He meant to take them next door for Pluto the Maltese but somehow never got round to it.

Brain, for his part, had suddenly organized extra choir rehearsals. He'd dreamed up new parish good works: taking Communion to the elderly, writing material for the parish bulletin, visiting lonely parishioners. Dusting the bishop's miter, for all Eddy knew. They were in a figurative slow bike race: seeing who could be last to the home finish line and claim victory. He couldn't leave Brain to the Ghost of Marley and the accusing dog-roll. It was infuriating.

Which was why he made his way now to Paparoa Street, where a new entry in his portfolio of pet-minding jobs awaited him. So far he had four dogs (walking), two cats (feeding while owners away), and a shifting miscellany of tropical fish, guinea pigs, and budgies, also Rhode Island Red hens, who were prodigious layers. The best way to continue living with Brain, Eddy had concluded, was to live with him as little as possible. Evening and weekend employment was essential.

He'd moved through a number of jobs since leaving school two months before the first quake. In the dizzying days after his abrupt departure, he'd signed on as a builder's laborer. His grandmother had been infinitely sardonic.

"From cloth cap to cloth cap in four generations," said Doris. She seemed almost pleased, as if Eddy had proved some private thesis. But his grandmother had always been grudging about him—ungrateful, Eddy thought: he was her only grandchild, after all. It was because he'd been born out of wedlock, an antique notion to which Doris still subscribed. Sometimes, Eddy thought he could see the word *bastard* shimmering above his grandmother's head, a malign aura, emanating toxins. It was hardly his fault. If anything, it was *her* fault. She was the one who'd reared a feckless son.

Eddy's great-grandfather had been a railway laborer and his grand-father a doctor, a socially upward leap in Doris's eyes. Brain's job—librarian—was something of a comedown. Jobbing builder's boy was beneath contempt. Except Eddy'd had the last laugh, hadn't he? Because now there were building sites all over the city with every man and his dog wanting a job on them. It was the new gold rush.

Except, really, he hadn't had the last laugh because he'd broken his foot six months after the February quake, and the delicate bud that was his building career had withered and died. A shame, because hefting two-by-fours, sawhorses, and bags of tools—really, his building career was just lifting, carting, and digging—had provoked some embryonic upper-body muscles.

On the other hand, though the sudden release from uniforms, timetables, earnest teachers, and the need to memorize myriad facts had been initially thrilling, by the time the June quake rolled around, ha, Eddy had begun to feel that builder's laboring was not for him. It was interesting only up to a point. He wasn't really *making* anything. This had been his pitch to Brain—the pleasure of seeing something solid, something *material*, come into being, he'd said. What had he been thinking? He hadn't, of course. He'd become allergic to thinking. Thinking made him *sick*, he told Brain, he was sick of reading, writing, researching, and regurgitating. He was sick of being inside his head, being a swot and a nerd.

No, he wasn't making anything, or rather *he* wasn't making anything. Cullen & Kelleher Homes was doing the making—and pretty ordinary it was, too. If anything, he was unmaking, Eddy thought. Digging holes, for instance, that was an absence of something, a pit, an abyss. He wound himself into a bitter little state every so often dwelling on this. Clearly laboring didn't completely obviate thinking. Plus, it was tiring—no, exhausting. He was mostly too whacked to go out at night, and when he did, he regretted it the next morning, rising in the dark at 5 a.m. He loathed the alarm.

It was exhaustion that made him break his foot—exhaustion and Toss More's effete boots. He'd worn them home after a night in the sleep-out composing an anti-disaster-capitalist rant, "Eat My Aggregates," which Toss was planning to perform outside the earthquake recovery authority offices, if he could ever make it out of bed. The boots were too narrow for Eddy's feet, which meant that when he climbed the gate at Snorebins Park's east exit and dropped as carefully as possible to the ground, the left boot rolled disastrously and somehow this had broken two metatarsals. He was laid up for a week with a monstrously swollen foot, the pain throbbing throughout his body, and only a pile of Brain's Inspector Wexford novels to divert him. He read them helplessly, one after another, and was brought very low by this further evidence of Brain-creep.

Thereafter he'd hobbled about with crutches, then crutchless but jobless, then finally with just an imperceptible favoring of his left foot. Occasionally a twinge still surprised him if he encountered a treacherous footpath eruption.

Doris would have cared little for his broken foot—she had been a famously heartless nurse, heedless of anyone's sore stomachs or headaches. "Go to the toilet," she said in answer to every complaint.

"She was forged in different times," said Brain.

And actually out of iron, thought Eddy. He learned to shut up.

"Doris was born crabby," Bridgie told him once. "And then there was Vincent."

Well, Eddy conceded, a dead drug-addict son was a bummer for sure.

4

Paparoa Street had done okay in the quakes, Eddy thought. He assessed all parts of the city in this way: Avonhead, scot-free; Papanui, surface wounds; St. Albans, broken limbs; Dallington, six feet under.

Paparoa Street was bungalowed, big-sectioned, abundantly gardened, deciduously treed; high-sided trampolines and swing sets were ubiquitous. Number 62 was two stories, the wood exterior pristine white. The job was for a Josie Mulholland. They had two dogs, she'd emailed, a spoodle (of course, the dog du jour) and a golden retriever. Thank God. A retriever offered some gravitas amidst his doodle-dominated charges: thus far, two spoodles, a cavoodle, and a completely insane chipoo with overactive tear glands. He had turned down a peekapoo, ostensibly because its owners lived outside the parameters he'd determined—no more than 5 km in each direction from home—but really, it was one ridiculous cross-breed too many. He was hanging out for something noble: a border collie, a boxer, a standard poodle. Even a German shepherd. No Labs though. Or not yet. Eddy felt a terrible ache around the heart each time he saw one, which was often; since Marley's death, the suburbs seemed riddled with Labradors.

He couldn't imagine having another dog himself. A replacement companion. Some people acquired new pets with impunity—his old friend Ollie, for instance. That family's pooches were always getting run over, or poisoned, or falling prey to bizarre medical conditions. But Ollie and his brothers shed their dog attachments with ease. They found new puppies speedily, like necessary household items, a kettle or toilet seat, and life went on as usual. Until the new dog met its inevitable end, providing more compost for their vegetable garden and the chance for a bit of a ceremony. Eddy had attended at least three dog funerals in Ollie's backyard.

These pet-care jobs—when did a cluster of jobs become an actual business?—they filled an emotional hole. He was dog-adjacent but not fully involved. Hands-on but no strings. Was this how early childhood caregivers felt? Or teachers? He could certainly do with the kind of variety a nursery of children provided. At the moment it felt like he was in charge of a dispersed multiple birth—all skittish and hairy. Bring on the retriever.

It was 2:30 p.m. Eddy pressed Josie Mulholland's doorbell.

The Mulhollands' house was large. Its décor would be the opulent sort he knew from his ex-girlfriend Hazel's and her friends' houses on the west side of town. Marble benches, leather sofas that sucked at your skin, vast beds with oppressive numbers of pillows and cushions, everything conspicuously clean, tucked up, and tidy.

The boy who answered the door was conspicuously unclean. He wore ancient jeans and a manky, spattered hoodie. Sparse hair sprouted hopefully from his chin. He was barefoot and sizable and said nothing. A wave of fruity sweat met Eddy.

"Eddy," he said, stepping back. "To see Josie about the dogs."

"She's out." The boy looked past Eddy, his face expressionless. Eddy turned to see what was behind him. Nothing.

"You can just take them," the boy said. He turned and lumbered down the hallway. A *big* lad, as Ginge would say. Eddy followed, feeling slight and tubercular, as he always did around substantial people.

"In there," said the boy, pointing to a door. He pushed through another door and was gone.

In there was a kind of conservatory, Eddy supposed, sun-filled and awash with shiny-leaved plants. A girl dressed in white sat in a rocker, a dog in her lap, another by the side of the chair. He was suddenly in a Tennessee Williams play. But then the dogs rushed him (undisciplined!), and it was the inevitable first-meeting mêlée. He gave them the love, of course. Oh, the old doggo slavering, it never disappointed; even if you didn't know the dogs, out went your hands involuntarily and back came their paws and tongues, the snuffling, the trembling bodies. It was another language, and he was fluent. You stayed patient and attentive, and their frenzy eventually settled, the sniff test sorted on both sides.

"I've been trying to train them," said the girl. "But it's not working. We went to a class, but Dad hated it." She was young—nine, ten? He could never tell kids' ages. Was she wearing an enormous nightie? Stick arms and legs poked from it like a scarecrow's. Her hair was like straw.

"Don't you mind?" she said, watching the maul.

"Love it," said Eddy.

The spoodle was mental, wanting full lip kisses already. "Hey, you! Not on the first date."

She giggled. "Rizzo's needy."

"What's this one called?" The retriever sat now, earnest and aquiver. Eddy gave him an approving pat.

"Waffle."

"Because?"

She sighed. "He's kind of *toasted* like waffles. I was only four when we got him. I'd probably call him something different now. Like Henry or Toby. A proper dog's name. My dad had a German shepherd once called Norman."

Clearly the talker of the family.

"We got Waffle from the pound. He had a terrible life. But Rizzo was from a dog breeder. Two thousand dollars Dad'll never see again. That's what he said. She was my present for sleeping in my own bed for a month."

And where did they get you? wondered Eddy.

"I'm Delphine," she said.

"Eddy." He held Rizzo firmly away from his face, waiting for her to slacken.

"I know. Eddy *Smallbone*. And you're a dog walker."

"Amazing no one's made that joke before."

"That was my brother who answered the door. He hates doing it, but I'm not allowed. In case of kidnapping. I'm not making that up. Dad says it could happen to anyone."

Pity the kidnapper, thought Eddy. She was like a brat-sprite, precocious and invasive, all angles and ghostly skin and a high, insistent voice.

He gave in to Rizzo then, tired of disciplining. He knelt properly and her nose went straight into his crotch. Delphine looked at him askew.

"In case you're wondering," she said, "I have a wandering eye."

"All good."

She rocked a little in the chair, looking at his ear. "Sometimes I have double vision. I could see two of you."

"Twice as much fun," said Eddy.

"Our last walker was a failure. He lost Rizzo; he was a student. We had to make signs and put them on lampposts. It was three days before we got her back."

Eddy stood, looking for the leashes.

"Is dog walking your actual *job*?" said Delphine, pitching forward, holding the rocking chair in place with her bare feet.

"Mum said you walk lots of dogs. She found out about you from her friend Erica. She's got a spoodle, too, but she calls it a cockapoo? She used to have a Maltipoo. Two *poos*." She laughed maniacally. "Did you know there's a designer dog called a whoodle?"

In fact, Eddy did know this, having been driven to doodle sites on learning there was a breed as risible as a chipoo. But he'd had enough of Delphine. He took the leashes from the arm of an overstuffed chair.

"Well, *is* dog walking your job?" She rocked herself up and out of the chair.

"It's one of them," said Eddy.

"What are the others?"

"Grave digging and dentistry."

She stared at him, the eye roaming. "Can you tell me about the grave digging?"

"No," said Eddy, clipping a leash to Rizzo's collar. Waffle stood at attention. Good boy. Sorry about the name.

"Mum says they need a long one and there are poo bags in the kitchen drawer. They're compostable." She trailed Eddy from the room.

"I wish I could come. I used to go with Dad, but he's moved out now. But I'm having a nightie day because I didn't go to school. Do you have those? Or a pajama day?"

"No," said Eddy. He never wore pajamas. Brain wore pajamas. Pale blue striped ones from Ballantynes, bought every three years since the Bronze Age.

"Mum's at the gym. And Jasper never goes out if he can help it. Except sometimes at night. Like a bat."

"What about school?" He opened the front door.

"Correspondence," she said, looking up at his face, more or less.

"I'll be about an hour," said Eddy.

"Mum said she'd be back."

He felt her eyes as he went down the path, drilling a hole in his spine, or thereabouts.

"Careful," he called. "Kidnappers!"

The door slammed and the dogs pulled him through the front gate.

5

"There are two really good things about dog walking," Eddy had once told Toss More.

"Let me guess," said Toss. He languished pale and wasted on his bed, like *The Death of Chatterton*, only without the lilac trousers. "There's the dog. And? Oh yes, of course, the *walking*." Illness had greatly increased his satirical tendency.

"It's much more nuanced than that," said Eddy.

"Do tell."

But, really, he couldn't adequately express the deep pleasure and comfort of dogs plus walking, except that it had something to do with the rhythm of footsteps and his wandering mind, the great green stretches of parks, the scents on the air, whatever was coming through his earphones, and the eternal entertainment of pooches and their mysterious distractions—a sensory world, an intelligence, to which he had no entry. Toss could never understand anyway; he'd renounced pets since catching salmonella from his two red-eared terrapins. He'd lost a third of his body weight and was still recovering months later, tired all the time.

Eddy missed the turtles. He'd spent much time lying in front of their tank, staring at their Yoda-ish necks and old eyes while Toss went on and on. Sickness did not dim his monologues, scurrilous and interminable.

It took just minutes to discern the personalities of new dogs. By the time they'd walked the back streets of Papanui and Merivale and explored a couple of parks, Eddy knew that Waffle was keen to please and Rizzo wanted medicating. Neediness plus attention deficit plus no sense of consequence. A potential topic of conversation with Brain next time he was home for dinner.

Brain liked to hear about Eddy's various charges. There had always been cats and fish and birds in Eddy's young life, and Brain had fed him a steady supply of animal books. For his sixth birthday, Eddy had asked for a blue-tongued skink and a frilled lizard, both in a book of Australian animals. Brain had explained in his tirelessly instructional way that these were not animals for houses or cities. Their fullest and happiest life could only occur in their natural habitat.

Despite Eddy's current irritations, creatures remained a point of connection between him and Brain. In the fortnight following Marley's death, they had by unspoken agreement rewatched every episode of *The Life of Mammals*, Eddy's fiftieth birthday present to Brain. Sunk in the couch with him, Eddy had been both consoled and tormented by their mutual need. It was spring in their wrecked city and he was nineteen, but it was also every Friday night of his life for as long as he could remember: cheese and chutney toasties, ice cream sandwiches, a wildlife documentary, and his wheezy, softhearted uncle at hand.

6

Delphine waved madly from the bay window of the front room as Eddy ushered the dogs back through the gate. Rizzo immediately lay down on the warm path.

"Vanquished," said Eddy. He jerked the leash gently, but she wasn't having it, so he gathered her up and carried her to the front door, Waffle in lockstep beside him.

Josie Mulholland answered the door. She was still in her gym gear, her face pink, hair piled on top of her head. The child was on tiptoes clinging to her mother's back.

"Eddy, I presume." She held out her hand. "Don't crowd me, *please,* Delphine."

"I told you he had a man bun," said Delphine. "And a tattoo."

"It's a low bun," said Eddy repressively. He shook Josie Mulholland's damp hand.

"Seventy minutes," he told her. "They're good and tired, especially this one. And wanting water."

"Mum says you're too young to be a dentist!"

"Enough, Delphine," said Josie. She took the child by the shoulders and steered her toward the plant room. "Let me talk to Eddy."

"Did your tattoo *hurt?*"

"Delphine."

The child lolled against the door, gargoyling at her mother.

"Just ignore her," said Josie, taking Rizzo from Eddy. "You have time for a coffee?" She nuzzled the dog's neck. "A big walk, eh? We like a tired Rizzo. And please take off my nightie," she called to the child, though not with much conviction.

"I have another job at five thirty," said Eddy. "But coffee's good."

"Some grave digging probably," shouted Delphine after them. "For *coffins.*"

"Sorry about that," said Josie in the kitchen. Glass-fronted cupboards, a half wall of wine bottles, high stools, and acres of bench. She filled the gleaming espresso machine with water. The dogs drank furiously from grand aluminium bowls.

"They go okay?"

"All good," said Eddy. "Rizzo needs a tight leash, but the big boy's a sweetie." No outright criticism of your charges' behavior, he'd learned. Owners never failed to take it personally.

"Milk?"

"Thanks." Eddy sat on a high stool, watching Josie Mulholland. He studied mothers habitually, auditioning them for a role in his past. There was a show reel in his head: his friends' mothers, teachers, the pet owners, retailers, strangers—all alien and a little alluring.

Josie Mulholland was one of the quietly efficient ones: coffee brewed, cups filled, bench wiped, biscuits from a tin, all smoothly done. Not a chatterer.

"Bought, I'm afraid," she said, holding out the plate of biscuits. "I used to bake, but what good does that do?" Eddy took a biscuit.

"Bran," she said. It looked unnervingly like Marley's dinner biscuits.

"I wanted to ask, I know you're in demand, but could you possibly manage every weekday? If I begged hard enough?" She blew on her coffee. "Things are tight right now. My husband was the dog walker, but we've recently separated." She paused, as if this information surprised her. "I'm hoping he'll take Waffle eventually, but right now he's in a no-pets town house so I can't push it."

Eddy scrolled his mental timetable. Did he want to interface with Rizzo five days a week? On the other hand, he could do some decent training. And Waffle was a lovely soul.

"I could do four days," he said, hating the bran biscuit. It was like eating hay. "An hour. I'd play fetch with Waffle, too." He'd read up on retriever muscle health last night. "You have a Frisbee?"

"Hardly. Not an outdoor household. And I'm—what's the phrase? Time poor."

Eddy was unsurprised. But why did these people have dogs? It maddened him. On the other hand, feckless dog owning was proving lucrative. Against the grain of the times, his work life was gathering steam.

"I should get one, anyway," he said. "A tool of the trade."

"You really couldn't stretch to five days?" said Josie Mulholland. Mascara flaked in the soft wrinkles under her eyes. "I'm happy to pay more. Do I sound winning?"

"Sorry, can't at the moment." He was a bit sorry. She seemed nice and kind of harried. "Are afternoons good with you? Do I need a key?" He was used to all the details now, knew what to ask for. People gave him their key box codes or spares. He had a little collection on his Our Lady of Guadalupe key ring, a present from Hazel.

"You know I can only use this ironically," Eddy had told her.

"Our Lady believes in you, even if you don't believe in her," Hazel whispered into his neck with hot little accompanying kisses. They'd broken up soon after that, but Eddy was attached to Our Lady anyway, to her sorrowful face and the holy rays springing from her sides like anteater spines.

"Jasper's here every day," said Josie. "But he collects Delphine in the afternoons, so a key might be good." She took one from a drawer and handed it to him. "You'll keep me in mind, if you get a space? I don't suppose you cook or clean?"

Well, yes, actually, he did both very competently thanks to his uncle's training over the years and the job before last at Wilbur and Orville's Café. But no thanks. For sure they'd be gluten free or dairy free or egg allergic. Or grain intolerant. Needing three different meals. He'd cooked for a family very briefly in the winter, businesspeople on and off planes all week. One kid ate only chicken nuggets, the other no meat at all, but the parents did the full nutritional range. A nightmare. He'd deleted cooking from his résumé.

"Full book, sorry," said Eddy. He waved his phone vaguely.

Delphine was at the front door as he left, still in the nightie.

"Upstairs now, please," said her mother. "No arguing. Take that off."

"Are you coming back?" said Delphine. She took backward steps toward the stairs, not looking at her mother. He wasn't sure where she was looking.

"Monday," said Eddy. He felt sorry for her, her wacko vision and irritating personality. That spindly little frame.

"Happy grave digging," she said, continuing in reverse up the stairs.

"That was a joke," said Eddy. "My other job's at New World supermarket."

"Fah-la-la-la-*lah*," bellowed Delphine, turning away, waving upside down behind her back.

7

It was a forty-minute walk to the supermarket. He was thrashing his sneakers these days, what with pooch walking and this new bike phobia. He tried not to drive the Suzuki in daylight. The car had been Doris's, left to Brain with the rest of her modest estate, but Brain had never had a license, never learned to drive. He'd been riding his bicycle— he always called it a *bicycle*—for almost fifty years, and now, in this globally warmed, earthquake-ridden universe, the incurably uncool, rule-abiding Brain had become both an eco-conscious exemplar and a wily gamer of the traffic queues endured by their city.

"Think of the car as yours," said Brain generously, once Doris's estate was settled. But was a yellow car really a generous gift? Briefly, Eddy contemplated a paint job. But it would still be a Suzuki, a flimsy toy car. Toss More occasionally refused to get in it.

"It compromises my masculinity."

"What masculinity?"

"True," said Toss. "But still."

They'd been preparing for a clothes-shopping expedition. Following the salmonella curse, all garments hung limp and baggy on Toss's reduced frame. Naked, he resembled St. Sebastian, minus the arrows. His mother had given him her credit card to reclothe himself, instructing him to go only to decent shops. But his mother's definition of decent was irretrievably bougie, Toss said. Instead, they headed for the thrift shops, dispersed now around the suburbs.

"Also, I want more bang for my buck," said Toss.

"In fact, your mother's buck," said Eddy.

Toss had never had jobs, part-time or otherwise. His parents believed he should rest during the school holidays, rest before university, rest after the salmonella. They rewarded this resting with regular deposits in his bank account. Toss squirreled away the money, enjoying it piling up.

"What for?" Eddy inquired, wanting a new keyboard for Steal Away.

"Rainy days, rainy days," said Toss. Eddy had argued more than once that receiving what amounted to a stipend from rampant capitalists (the Mores had a large property portfolio) was inconsistent with Toss's alleged anti-capitalism. Toss had various florid counter-arguments to this charge, but the truth was he didn't give a rat's arse about consistency. His relationship with capitalism was as incontinent as his relationship with God.

In relation to New World, Toss was an anarcho-activist. Or a thief, depending on how you viewed these things. He regularly stole fruit, sweets, and craft beer. It was anarcho-activism, apparently, because supermarkets were virtual monopolies that exploited producers, paid their labor force crap, and held consumers wretchedly captive to price and supply. And by the way, their increasingly cunning surveillance systems not only raised privacy issues, but they also would soon be putting hardworking shoplifters out of business.

Yes, yes, thought Eddy as he walked westward, listening to Alynda Segarra, enjoying the soft wind on his bare arms. It was all true, or most of it—could kleptomaniacs really be styled as hardworking? Maybe. In their own way. But he had developed an instant and profound affection for New World and all who worked there. He had banned Toss More from this corner of food retail under sentence of severed friendship. In exchange, he weathered regular denunciations of the place and its people.

He'd avoided derision from that terminal employment snob Doris, at least. By the time Eddy's foot had mended and he'd scored the job, his grandmother had been six feet under for some months. Although even Doris might have conceded that the combined effects of the quakes and the recession made the securing of any job, however cloth cap, a small triumph. But it was really an old-school tie, he supposed. Dirty luck. Hazel's parents owned the supermarket.

In principle, Eddy maintained a mealy mouth toward the west side of town—it had largely escaped crippled houses, fissured roads, mud baths, unreliable sewage, fused schools, no-go parks, bulldozed shops, insurance bastards. But he'd needed the job. And Hazel's mother— Judith—felt sorry for him because he was an orphan saddled with a duffer uncle who was a librarian. Probably Hazel did, too. Hazel was a law student now and had acquired a new law-student boyfriend named Anzac who wore suit jackets with jeans and was, by Toss More's pungent reckoning, an immense twat. Eddy agreed. He and Hazel didn't have much to say to each other these days. She was, it turned out, uncomfortable with an ex-boyfriend at the checkout.

And Toss was fully wrong about the supermarket: it wasn't a terrible place—it was *marvelous*, a great clockwork universe with dozens of moving parts, a glorious, edifying cooperative, a . . . new world! It was an alternative family at least, encompassing multitudes, unlike his own extended family, which now comprised just an uncle, a first cousin once removed, and a second cousin who lived in Timaru. They were an etiolated clan barely worthy of the name.

His supermarket family, though—it was full and fabulous, thrillingly ordinary *and* lunatic. Brad the butchery apprentice, for instance, who could rap lyrically on lamb and beef cuts, mincing methods, and the underappreciated beauty of offal. And Bernardine, tiny and wrinkled, who moved like a windup mouse; she worked every possible shelf-filling shift to get away from her husband and could provide in-the-moment coded commentary on high-maintenance customers. Alefosio, the bakery manager; whenever they saw Eddy, they enveloped him in a lengthy hug and begged him to join the New World touch rugby team. Marcus, the liquor manager, of indeterminate age, shy and prone to stuttering, who had blurted to him one day last December that he was flying to Wellington to hear the *Messiah*. Eddy had been astonished on so many counts. And Shamura in the deli, beautiful as the day. Sometimes Eddy bought ham slices or Scotch eggs just to watch her wielding the tongs, weighing and wrapping, handing over packages with a gloved hand and spectacular smile.

Plus the trolley boys. He watched them on his coffee breaks. They were fierce and determined and wrenchingly humorless. Each had his own collecting system and strange navigational path around the car park. They were almost balletic with their trolley trains. And long-suffering with the ruder clientele, who roared across their paths in high-up cars. Not a flicker crossed the trolley boys' faces. They'd been schooled—they all had—never to show the slightest exasperation, even to the most imperious of matrons, of which there were plenty, btw, on the west side of the ragged city.

As for Eddy's own in-store duties, these were unexpectedly diverting. Take shelf filling. It was *interesting* to learn about new lines of products—artisan cracker biscuits, say, or yet another paleo-muesli brand. Or to wonder about the price differentials in caper or prune or coconut milk brands.

After he was shifted to checkout—a promotion!—Eddy perfected the art of packing a shopping bag, the proper weight distribution and layering of goods. He was curious about what people bought, too. He liked to watch the unfolding contents of a trolley and imagine the various snacks and meals they might turn into, the people who ate them. The west side of town, he noted with a newly alert sociological eye, ate fully and well. A lot of vegetables and protein. Moderate sugar and fat intake. Much alcohol. He was forever raising his hand for one of the managers to okay a wine purchase, a practice he never failed to find humiliating.

Generally, interactions with a manager had a humiliating edge. They were all women and perfectly pleasant—it was their overt motherliness that made him bristle. They patted him or gave his back proprietary rubs. Maureen, not even old enough to be anyone's mother, had once squeezed his cheek in a hearty and presumptuous way. Judith had doubtless been sharing his history. She was the worst: caring eyes and a certain tone and her glance straying regretfully to the quotation tattooed the length of his right arm.

Eddy looked at his arm now. It always pleased him to see the words, the way they seemed to rear and rebuke. He'd had to cover up once he was on checkout.

"But it's biblical," he'd argued, just for the sake of it.

"Possibly offensive to customers," said Judith, and the warped truth of this was perversely satisfying. But he dutifully wore the long sleeves, he tied his hair back in a bun, he joked with the customers. And sometimes when he saw Judith on her rounds, he imagined stopping suddenly in front of her and intoning a different though equally scolding quotation: *"for ye pay tithe of mint and anise and cumin, and have omitted the weightier matters . . ."* That was the great thing about the Bible. It had as many apposite quotes as *Friends*.

8

Eddy caught a ride home on the back of Reuben from accounts' motorcycle; Reuben carried a spare helmet for potential passengers, which said something about him. He lived in Sydenham, so Eddy's was out of his way, but nothing was a bother. Eddy put a pilsner in his saddlebag as thanks—accounting gave you a powerful thirst, Reuben said. Eddy had marveled at this thirst during last year's Christmas party when Reuben and Sylvester from inventory had put away three dozen beers between them. His own capacity for beer was extremely limited. "Pitiful is the word," said Toss More when three beers had once laid Eddy out. "If you must do it at all, do it properly."

This made no sense to Eddy, but he hadn't been in any condition to argue. Toss himself drank only sometimes and only purloined beer. He was always mortifying the flesh in one way or another—fasting, praying naked on frosty mornings, swearing off stimulants, having ice-cold baths—even in his semi-atheist phases. "A young man of troubling extremes," the Modern Priest had pronounced one evening after five glasses of wine: Eddy had counted. These days he believed scarcely a word that fell from the Modern Priest's mendacious lips. Even *and* and *the* were suspect, as the saying went. But he had parked that comment.

Annoyingly, when he arrived home, there was the Modern Priest ensconced in the reordered living room. Eddy had been looking forward to the trace of snuffed candles, a melancholy comfort. Instead, the pervasive aroma was chili beans. Ginge and Bridgie had dug in for the evening as well. There were three empty bottles of wine and another half-full amidst the dinner dishes on the coffee table. Dinner. He hadn't eaten since Josie Mulholland's horrible bran biscuit.

"Hail, Eddy!" said Ginge, picking up the bottle. He, too, had a prodigious thirst and was helplessly convivial, loving nothing more than to pour large glasses for everyone else. The Smallbone family tree was weighty with drinkers.

"A glass of red, Ed? You deserve it, working for the man from dawn to dusk."

Well, it was half-true. And he had been up at 6 a.m. to feed the cats, in Edgeware and Richmond, respectively, and then to take Bunny the chipoo to the vet. More drops for the lachrymose eyes.

"Sure," said Eddy, checking the state of the bean dish. Plenty. Brain always provided for an army; before library training, he'd cooked for a youth remand facility. Eddy filled a bowl, drowned it in cheese and sour cream, and thumped down on the couch between Ginge and Bridgie.

"How are you, George?" said Bridgie. "How are you, *really*?"

This was a joke between them, the *really* both serious and not. Bridgie had also been calling him George for years, for no reason Eddy could determine.

"Not so bad." Sweet Jesus, the ultimate Brain phrase, communicating nothing. The chili was excellent, though. Fire in the digestive tract. Nice wine, too. A Chilean grape no doubt. Or Argentinian. Ginge had been on a South American jag since the quakes, reading up on anarcho-syndicalism. He read and drank in quantity, and only red wine, the proper Marxist libation, he said.

"In your eye," said Eddy, holding up his glass, not looking at the Modern Priest, though he knew the Modern Priest was looking at him, at his tattoo Eddy hoped, uncovered now, out and proud.

"Alla vostra," said the Modern Priest. He'd spent years at the Vatican; he dropped Italian phrases like dog doo.

"Cent'anni!" said Bridgie, leaning into Eddy, giving him a smacker on his cheek. She was well-liquored, smelled comfortingly of her smoky perfume. Brain looked sleepy, though he generally nursed a single glass through an evening.

"Edmundo! I have another customer for you," said the Modern Priest.

He detested the Modern Priest calling him Edmundo. But it was an uncomfortable fact that the foundations of his pet business (surely eight clients constituted a business?) had come through the well-oiled connections of Father Chris Mangan, onetime Cathedral administrator, now disgraced. The Cathedral lay in ruins, the parish was scattered, the choirmaster had lost a leg, and the Modern Priest had been removed from his position. Yet he carried on regardless, glad-handing, spreading god-dust, shepherding an invisible flock.

"Much obliged," Eddy said, and shoveled a forkful of chili, keeping his eyes on the bowl. Expunging the Modern Priest from his emotional universe, though, without making it too obvious, sometimes drove him to act and speak like a lowly character from Dickens.

"In Phillipstown," said the Modern Priest. "The owner's in Vietnam for three months. His frog needs feeding. Live flies—"

"True?" said Brain. "It's getting heavy, Ed."

Eddy granted his uncle a smile and a nod. This was, for some reason, always easier when the Modern Priest was around. Context was everything.

"You should be keeping a journal," said Bridgie. "Rhode Island hens, guinea pigs, frogs and flies . . . It's *My Family and Other Animals.*" A quotation slid across Eddy's brain: *smooth blue muscles of wave*. Brain had read him that book when he was nine years old and then, night after night, he'd listened to a library CD of the story, too, understanding only half of it but gathering that crazy family around him like a giant blanket.

"To frogs and flies—and cockapoos—*of cabbages and kings*," said Ginge, raising his glass, too swiftly this time. A wavelet of wine broke over the edge and splashed his nose. The other three laughed immoderately.

The moon was shining sulkily, thought Eddy. Brain had regularly recited "The Walrus and the Carpenter" too. For a long time, Eddy had squinted at full moons, trying to make out their aggrieved faces.

"You'd better stay, Ginge," said Brain. He always said this, but Ginge would not leave his cats alone overnight. Sometimes Eddy drove him home, sometimes Bridgie, though she was certainly over the limit right now. If only he could stop reflexively monitoring their intoxication levels.

"I can take Ginge," said the Modern Priest, somehow reading Eddy's mind. Most unpleasant. "I'll leave the Phillipstown details."

"Right you are," said Eddy, standing, picking up the empty bottles from the table. "Mercy Buttercup. Kia ora, homies."

"Right *you* are, Eddy," said Ginge, thrusting his glass up again. "Workers of the World Unite!" Indulgent chuckles all round.

Jesus wept. They were like a bad '80s sitcom. Eddy felt a scream might suddenly burst from him.

Instead, he took refuge in his long-serving rage repellent: he began to whistle as he mooched from the room. It was the patter song from *The Pirates of Penzance*, a great favorite of the Modern Priest's. He had once played the Modern Major-General to Brain's Frederick in a school production. They were surely the last two Gilbert & Sullivan devotees on earth. Sometimes after several glasses of wine, the Modern Priest got down on Brain's old vinyl, and it was all "Take a Pair of Sparkling Eyes" and "Poor Wandering One." Against his will, Eddy had, over the years, become familiar enough with the loathsome G & S repertoire, just as he was conversant with an entire antediluvian alternative culture unknown to his peers: the Father Brown stories, great tracts of T. S. Eliot, Vaughan Williams's choral music, and the spiritual songs of the Medical Mission nuns. He was somehow simultaneously an Edwardian and a child of the 1960s, though he'd been born in 1993.

"What do you expect?" said Toss More. "Your adoptive uncle-father was a born great-granddad." Well, quite.

The patter song parody had been Eddy's idea. He and Toss had written the lyrics in an afternoon, gleefully rehearsing until they had it all by heart. Of course, its full glory would only ever be performed to themselves, but Eddy had whistled the tune many times in the Modern Priest's company, softly or with rude heartiness. It was a disguised insult, a dagger to the heart under cover of camaraderie—though perhaps he had once or twice seen unease flit across the Modern Priest's handsome face . . .

He rinsed the wine bottles and put them in the recycling box, whistling adagio. The song should be up-tempo, but he liked to hit the notes in their true tuneful middle, hear the lyrics clearly in his head: a perfectly camp caricature and a bitter lament.

I am the very model of a modern man of Goh-hoh-hod
I catechize, I weaponize the armies of the Catholic squad
I'm liturgically forward, I have earned the name of Father Mod
I baptize, I sermonize, I steer my peeps from birth to sod . . .

OC
TO
BER

9

Eddy had walked nearly the length of Barbadoes Street toward Phillipstown. It was a sorrowful pilgrimage and he took it regularly, needing somehow to give witness to the rubble piles and empty lots, the boarded-up windows, the toppled and broken headstones of the old cemetery, and, finally, the great open wound of the Cathedral, domeless and gutted, a still life of vomited stone. He stopped now and considered its misshapen countenance against the pale spring sky. *Here let us stand, close by the cathedral. Here let us wait.*

In the weeks after the February quake, Toss More had plotted a secret assault on the Cathedral ruins. They would sing sacred songs in the debris-strewn nave, he declared, howl at the stars for the lost dome. They would intone a chorus from *Murder in the Cathedral* after all. They would tenderly collect glass shards from the Trustrum window, gen-uflect before the Summers' Stations. Also, they must film everything.

Eddy knew this would only ever be a theoretical sortie, since Toss was enfeebled by the salmonella, and the army patrolled the red-zone boundaries, and there were sizable fines for trespassing miscreants. But part of him wished they *could* observe some grand obsequies for the sad old place. His eyes had swum, hot and furtive, when he'd first seen it after the quake, the sun blazing carelessly, and the Cathedral cowed like an injured animal.

Eddy had written a list of the hymns they would sing; he loved a list after all. Thank you, Brain. He texted various mates with video cameras. He and Toss argued chorus excerpts. But then a southerly storm arrived and Toss suffered a prostrating spasm of nausea, and thus they were delivered from the burden of action. They stayed in the sleep-out and wrote a song about the statue of the Virgin that had once presided over their rehearsals in the choir loft.

The next day Eddy had texted his tennis friend, Harry, whose property boasted a rare court with undamaged turf. A blinding tennis workout and half an hour of purposeless chat with Harry was sometimes necessary after a sleep-out session with Toss, and this urge caused Eddy to dwell yet again on the peculiar place T. B. More occupied in his life: Toss was his best and oldest friend, but one kept almost entirely separate from his other mates. Eddy sometimes felt bad about this, though he doubted Toss gave a rat's arse. The truth was, Toss was monumentally disinterested in most people and the ordinary things they did—hanging out, chewing the fat, playing sports, living in the everyday beat of popular culture. Their bands had all been short-lived because Toss was a tyrant who made no effort to win hearts and minds. On the rare occasions he did cross paths with Eddy's other friends, he uttered only enigmatic non sequiturs or stayed thunderously silent. Toss was altogether best kept private. "Like wanking," said Toss when Eddy confessed this. They could say anything to each other. That was the point.

10

It was his fourth visit to the Phillipstown frog. In fact, Arbuckle—
a solid name in Eddy's estimation—required feeding only once every
three days, but Eddy fretted about him, alone in his tank, no one to
talk to him or admire him through the glass. He was a lovely specimen,
a slim and shiny golden bell, but Eddy detected a lingering wistfulness.

Since Arbuckle's house was between Bunny the chipoo and a new
prospect—a cockatoo, plus some chores for the owner who was temporarily discommoded (Brain word)—Eddy had decided to call on
Arbuckle every other day. The frog's owner, Justin, had left him a
friendly note with instructions on Arbuckle's little ways, plus an open
invitation to snack, play the grand piano, borrow any books he fancied.

It was odd at first, roving freely in a stranger's house. Eddy had
moved tentatively from room to room. He noted the books and paint-
ings and the few personal photos, peered into each of the bedrooms; to
frankly investigate seemed impolite. Before leaving, he sat at the piano,
lifted the lid carefully, and stared for some time at the creamy keys.
Then he closed the lid, said goodbye to Arbuckle, and left.

But today he had lost all reserve. Scanning Justin's bookcase, he
had found a copy of *Murder in the Cathedral*. The same edition as the one
from Year 13 drama. This was eerie and unnerving. He stared at it for
a minute, then stuffed it back between two other slim volumes, but a
second later he took it out again. He went to the kitchen and made
green tea in the Japanese teapot, assembled a plate of crackers and
cheese, and sat in Justin's reading chair in a pool of sunlight, one eye

on Arbuckle. He'd been right about the frog: company suited him. He became a little frisky; he jumped in and out of his small pool—*plop, thud*—as if to entertain his new friend. It reminded Eddy of something, though he couldn't think what.

The reading chair was extremely comfortable, chrome and padded leather and just the right amount of concavity for his back. There was a matching footstool that he judged unmanly, but in a minute his feet were planted there anyway and something close to contentment came over him.

How very good it was to sit in a plush chair in an empty house with only a princely frog and a book for company. He felt about forty-five years old and fully sagacious. It was the sitting that did it; at home he lay down to read, on his bed or the couch, or along the window seat, or in front of the wood burner—like a child. And even if Brain was out (choir, SPCA, te reo class, book group, and other improving activities), he was still somehow there—in the very weave of the hearthrug and the Anaglypta wallpaper and the view from the window seat: a great linden tree that Brain liked to contemplate through all seasons.

What shall we do in the heat of summer . . . The words of the play still had the old, familiar charge, though Eddy never could shake the idea that *Murder in the Cathedral* represented his last sorry schoolboy testament, thrill and repugnance in one.

If he closed his eyes, he could summon those heady readings that final term in drama class, the Modern Priest, austere and mesmerizing, briefly seducing them all with his delivery of the Archbishop's ghastly sermon.

But Eddy had declined the role of the Archbishop and the knights' roles, all of the solo speaking parts. He wanted only to be one of the chorus.

"A Woman of Canterbury!" he said, itching to provoke the Modern Priest.

"What do you mean?" said the Modern Priest, quite unable to compute this.

"Part of the collective," said Eddy. "The *ladies'* collective."

"Don't be crass," said the Modern Priest. "This isn't pantomime."

But Eddy had dug in, and in a while the rest of the guys, naturally seditious, stood with him. A storm of feelings showed on the Modern Priest's face: disgust, petulance, anxiety. Eddy watched him straining for patience. But they had all suddenly become deaf to his cherished persuasive powers.

"This play," said the Modern Priest, not quite shouting, "is not the platform for a statement about contemporary gender politics."

"Why not?" called Roberta O'Brien from the back of the room. They'd all turned to look at her. She was perched on a stack of bench seats, legs swinging.

"Why can't we comment on the play as well as perform it? Make a point about women and power. I'm up for the sainted Becket. Who wants to be a knight?"

Every girl raised a hand. The Modern Priest had lost them. Now the girls demanded all the solo parts, and the guys were delighted to agree. When the Modern Priest stonewalled, a very testy debate about clerical misogyny and the ordination of women broke out, students and priest locked in dislike. Cold and furious—and thoroughly bested—the Modern Priest had walked out.

"What danger can be for us, the poor, the poor people of Canterbury," Toss chanted ironically in the days after the second quake. The two of them had laughed bleakly in the sumptuous sleep-out. It all seemed so long ago now, and the words of the play, the Modern Priest's incarnation of Thomas Becket, and Eddy's awful exit interview with The Venerable all collided and merged, a sour music in his head. Sometimes—as a kind of penance, he supposed—he opened The Venerable's office door just a crack and replayed that last meeting in his head.

11

"You are a tabula rasa, Smallbone," The Venerable had said. He persisted in calling male students by their surnames. "A blank slate waiting to be written upon. *Your* choices, *your* actions determine the writing."

Eddy only half listened, distracted as usual by the titles on The Venerable's bookcase. They were an odd mix: theology and ancient history, both predictable, he supposed, for a Brother and a classics teacher. But there was everything from poetry to crime, too, and, confoundingly, *How to Win Friends and Influence People* by Dale Carnegie. A self-help book—*the* foundational self-help book—seemed to Eddy a dead peculiar read for a religious Brother. But surely The Venerable hadn't actually read it—or, if he had, he'd never taken the slightest notice of it. Eddy had checked out the book at the library, and the first thing he'd read under the heading "How to Win People to Your Way of Thinking" was avoid arguments. Let the other person do the talking. Or something like that.

"You really are a weasel and an idiot, Smallbone," The Venerable had said with great weariness. "I'd like to personally eviscerate you."

"Sorry about that, Brother."

"Like hell you are."

He'd wanted a cigarette, Eddy could tell. The Venerable was an ardent smoker, fifty-plus a day. Perhaps the last great smoker in the world, outside Serbia. The only place he didn't light up was in church, but he must have decided an exit interview should be smoke-free, too. He rubbed his eyes lengthily instead.

"What are you going to do?"

Eddy heard the wet suck, suck of his eyelids.

"Get a job, Brother."

"Good. Boys like you shouldn't be idle."

"Boys like me, Brother?"

"Thinkers, Smallbone." He looked at Eddy again, the skin around his eyes munched up like one of Toss's terrapins.

"I'm more of a doer, Brother."

"You only *think* that!" He gave his smoker's laugh, all grumble and phlegm.

"Yes, Brother."

"And you can stop that pseudo-respectful crap right now. For God's sake!"

Now he was opening the top drawer of his desk and getting out the makings anyway, Zig-Zag and a packet of Champion Blue. Their encounter was plainly impossible without the assistance of tobacco.

Eddy had seen The Venerable roll his own many times. He was famous throughout the school, if not the diocese, for his one-handed agility. Eddy watched it now, already nostalgic. It was probably the last time: a small conjuring wonder.

The Venerable stared sourly at him as he rolled. He jammed the cigarette between his teeth and struck a match, fierce and fervent, hungry for the business. It was nearly lunchtime and the ashtray in the middle of his desk was almost full.

"I don't know," said The Venerable, his head in his hands suddenly, his exhalations billowing around him. "Where did we go wrong?"

"Not your fault, Brother."

"Easy for you to say."

He raked his hands through his hair. It was gray, streaked with black; there was a swatch of yellow brown in the front where wandering smoke had done its work over the last fifty years. Like all people in religious orders, he seemed of indeterminate age, not young but not quite old, either. Eddy figured mid-sixties, which meant he'd probably been in the Order for forty-odd years. He tried to picture him as a twenty-year-old: Brother Bede O'Brien. Black-haired and full of energy. Full of faith, too, and idealism. Rangy and striking, like a bird of prey.

"I suppose—" Eddy had the oddest urge to throw him a bone. A small bone (ha). He suddenly wanted to give a crumb of comfort to the guy. Or to that fire-eating young man who hadn't yet become The Venerable, crusty old relic, the last remaining religious principal.

"Don't insult us both by trying to explain, for Chr—" The Venerable bit off the word and glared at Eddy. He drilled his cigarette into the ashtray. There was a long silence.

"You've driven me to blasphemy, Smallbone."

"Sorry about that, Brother."

The glare slackened minutely.

Eddy counted the butts in the ashtray. Seven. One for every year he'd been at Champagnat College.

"Is this all part of some adolescent Oedipal melodrama?"

"Oedipal, Brother?"

"You know perfectly well what I mean; you're doing bloody scholarship classics. *Were* doing it," he amended.

"I don't want to kill my father, Brother. He's already dead."

"Your father substitute, you smart arse. Oh, bugger off, before my language heads irretrievably for the gutter."

Eddy tried to think of something to say, by way of goodbye. It bothered him how wound up The Venerable was. "I'm—"

But The Venerable cut across him. "It is a terrible thing to waste God-given talent."

His voice was stark, his eyes a little shiny. "Sinful. But you probably don't believe in sin."

Eddy couldn't keep looking at him. He looked down instead at the famous beach stones on the desk. They were graywacke, flat and unpolished, scored with fine white lines. The Venerable's version of an executive toy: he fiddled with the stones, rearranged them constantly, made little cairns while he smoked or took notes or talked on the phone. You knew it was a bad interview if he left them alone. Today the stones remained unbothered, silent in their three small columns. Father, Son, and Holy Spirit, thought Eddy, with all due wryness.

"Where are those stones from, Brother?"

"What do you care?"

"Just curious."

Eddy took a quick look. The eyes were back to normal.

"Blaketown Beach," said The Venerable. "Where I grew up."

"Nice," said Eddy, absurdly.

They were silent again.

The bell rang for lunch. In a moment a great rough chorus would break out: six hundred chairs thrust back, doors bursting open, six hundred girls and boys shouting and shouldering their way out into the fresh afternoon.

"You'd better go," said The Venerable at last. He stood, his face wintry. Then he held his hand out over the desk.

Eddy was so surprised, the heat rushed to his cheeks. But his own hand went obediently for The Venerable's and they shook, almost shyly.

"Good luck."

"Same to you, Brother."

He headed for the door, trying to outpace a surge of shame.

"God bless you, Eddy," called The Venerable as Eddy closed the door behind him.

12

The morning sun had crept across Eddy's cheeks, singeing him along with the memory. Tabula rasa, eh? Was he still a blank slate, though? He felt pretty heavily written upon these days. The weight of experience, ho, ho, blah.

Plop, went Arbuckle. *Look at me!* His eyes bulged hopefully toward his audience of one, and Eddy knew immediately who the frog was like. That crazy Delphine. His new best friend.

She was in his face from the moment she clocked him, watching breathlessly at the bay window whenever he arrived back with the dogs, spattering him with questions, bursting to communicate some marvelous thought or thing. Occasionally she was oppressively silent, staring wonkily until he was properly unnerved and driven to say something, though this only encouraged her. Yesterday it had been one of her interminable stories he must read. He sat down in the plant room—Delphine's preferred stage set—and tried in vain to decipher the words. Her handwriting was bonkers.

"How about you read it to me? It's good to hear your own work aloud."

She was delighted. "Jasper hates me reading out. And Mum gets distracted."

It was a kidnap story: victim Delphine and a bizarre collection of goofball abductors who mismanaged everything and were outwitted by the heroine. Eddy sank into the cushions as the child declaimed this wacko narrative. What a model of tact and patience he was. He should get a medal. Or babysitting wages.

It was impossible to get out of the Mulholland house in under an hour. Delphine all but clung to his T-shirt; she was utterly deaf to a curt or withering tone. He was caught each time, feeling sorry for her again, left to her own devices every afternoon, unsupervised by the semipeculiar Jasper, and her mother always at the office.

". . . and then the battish man came roaring from the crepuscular room!"

Eddy burst out laughing. *"What?"*

"What what?" said Delphine. "You're not supposed to laugh. It's scary."

"Crepuscular?"

"It's not just *your* word—anyone can use it." She was very offended.

He smiled now, remembering. Days before, she'd dragooned him into a tour of the house, during which he'd heard the provenance of almost every object in every room, including a chronological history of Delphine's bed linen and soft toys. They'd finished at the door to Jasper's room.

"Knock, knock!" shouted Delphine.

"What *now?*" said Jasper, opening up, looming. The curtains were closed and the room dimly lit. There was the smell of dirty socks, takeout, and other things Eddy preferred not to imagine.

"Apologies," said Eddy. "I'm getting a tour. We'll move right along."

"Welcome to my den," said Jasper unexpectedly. It was the longest sentence Eddy had heard from him. "Feel free to check it out."

Eddy obediently did so.

There was a king-size bed piled with clothes, magazines, and take-out detritus strewn around the floor, and a comprehensive technology suite along one wall: a winking desktop computer, PlayStation 3, Xbox, a hinge-mounted LCD screen, two pairs of state-of-the-art head-phones. A poster of Kurt Cobain.

"'Smells Like Teen Spirit,' eh?" said Eddy, and some distant cousin of a smile passed over Jasper's face.

"Jasper Bat," said Delphine.

"Yes," said Eddy, "in his crepuscular cave."

"Hrhurgahh," said Jasper, which might have been a laugh. "You play *Fez*?"

"Strictly a dabbler," said Eddy. He'd played a bit with Sylvester from inventory, but his game was sadly adagio.

"We could do it sometime," said Jasper, looking away.

"Sure." Though, please open a window.

"Adieu," said Jasper, closing the door.

Delphine's eyes popped at Eddy all along the hallway. "He *never* asks other people," she whispered. "He really likes you." She said it like a prayer.

But how? Eddy wondered. They'd exchanged fewer than thirty words.

Delphine had written *crepuscular* in her school notebook—she was building a word bank, apparently. You're so very welcome, Eddy did not say. From the brain of Brain to me to you. Pet minding was expanding in ways he certainly had not anticipated. Some vexatious act of God was turning him into a version of the parental Brain he was trying furiously to get away from. Cripes.

Plop, plop. Arbuckle surpassed himself with a double hop. That, and an effortful stretch for his thrice-weekly live fly, was about the limit of his aerobic activity. Golden bells, Eddy had read, were more lookers than doers, though lengthy contemplation of Arbuckle's limited repertoire certainly had its charms. The silky throat purse, ceaselessly throbbing. The alien toe disks. Those fastidious little leg swishes in the shallow pool. Gymnastic stuff was for tree frogs. Or Surinam toads. Those babies were bananas—seconds after birth they were somersaulting. From *sombresault*, Old French, Eddy remembered, because the *sombre* had always seemed strange given the joyfulness of head-over-heels—as he still thought of it.

He recalled very clearly his own moment of head-over-heels mastery, the rush and terror of his feet leaving the ground, the miraculous velocity of his turn. It had been in Snorebins Park, where he and Brain went every weekend when Eddy was small, Ginge and Bridgie in faithful attendance. The men were strictly standing duty—pushing Eddy on the tire swing; twirling the merry-go-round; waiting beneath the climbing frame, anxious and hopeful—but Bridgie cavorted with him on the spinning bucket and the seesaw, hurtled them both down the slide, screaming with pleasure. It was Bridgie who taught him airborne head-over-heels, while the men looked on, slow clapping in wonder. Brain's and Ginge's childhoods, Eddy learned in time, had been largely *mens sana*, very little *corpore sano*.

Well, *bicycling*.

His fifth birthday party had been at the park, too, with a cake shaped like a dog bone, constructed painstakingly by Brain from a children's party recipe book. There had been an egg-and-spoon race and a treasure hunt, Marley herding and patrolling the children with soft growls. Eddy had thought all this quite marvelous at the time, so charged and exultant, he'd been unable to fall asleep that night. Now it seemed yet another weird outtake from an out-of-time childhood. One with three childless parents. Plus a bad-fairy priest, *in loco avunculus*.

And wtf with this outbreak of interior Latin? Thoughts of The Venerable, Eddy supposed. The Venerable was gone now to the head office in Auckland, holding the line amidst lotus-eating and commerce, cleaving to the Five Pillars, watching the clerical world through slitted eyes. Smoking himself to death.

Arbuckle returned to his usual ruminative position on the flat rock. Eddy studied the cover of *Murder in the Cathedral*, the bloody title banner, the font grand and severe as befitted the intransigent prelate in his Gothic cathedral. He had read up on Canterbury Cathedral years ago, fantasized about going there and seeing the Wax Chamber he'd read about in one of Brain's childhood books. Truthfully though, the world seemed impossibly distant, possibly even fictitious—at its most real in novels and history books. Their holidays had been in campsites around the country, walking adventures amidst native bush and wildlife or along the coastline, a little gas cooker and reading in the *crepuscular* summer nights. Often with Ginge, if he could secure a live-in cat minder.

He skipped the scene with the three priests and the Messenger— oily tosspots (Ginge word)—and went straight to the second women's chorus. *Here is no continuing city, here is no abiding stay . . . We are afraid in a fear which we cannot know . . .* Rousing, gloriously dark. Of course he was deliberately misreading, planting his own town and soul in the text, but surely everyone did that. Eddy had recognized the chorus the instant he'd read it; it had felt like *his*, human-size and of the material world, but existentially fraught, too: *the small folk drawn into the pattern of fate, the small folk who live among small things.*

He checked out the Archbishop's repellent sermon once more, to enjoy his contempt all over again—*the true martyr is he who has become the instrument of God, who has lost his will in the will of God . . .*

"Ugly, life-denying bollocks!" Eddy had shouted at the Modern Priest during their post-drama-class showdown. He'd been summoned to the presbytery parlor, an arid space despite the Vatican tat spattered about—Virgins, bleeding hearts, a photograph of Cristoforo and Il Papa, in their respective black and red robes, beaming down the camera lens.

But only a stiff smile from Cristoforo that day in the presbytery.

"What the devil's got into you?" he said.

"You really want to know?" said Eddy, loathing the parlor that smelled of old carpet and boiled potatoes, and loathing the Modern Priest in his bespoke dog collar from his favorite clerical tailor in the back streets of Rome.

"I'm fucking sick of this antediluvian death-cult crap," said Eddy. He badly wanted the Modern Priest to lose his temper.

"This is a *play*, Edmundo. It's a medieval worldview we're examining."

"And you *love* it, you shitless reptile!" spat Eddy.

The Modern Priest obliged. He lost his temper spectacularly. At the time Eddy had found it very satisfactory, indeed.

It was 10:30 a.m. He should get moving. He put the book down and went to the piano, playing the first thing that came into his head, which was, regrettably, "Younger than Springtime," his very own semipermanent earworm—thank you, Brain, who la-la-ed it per-petually, even in the depths of winter. He played with a wide and indulgent rubato, thinking of Bridgie, who had been his piano teacher until he was fifteen and taught him countless songs. She could still make him laugh, impersonating A Great Pianist, distorting and swell-ing accompaniments, swaying and plunging toward the keys. Eddy swayed and plunged himself now, pushing aside the specter of a stern God and his priestly avatars. Music, he and Toss More had agreed again and again, was the one truly reliable faith, no intermediaries, just you and the properly holy harmonies. Oh yes!

So much for swearing off sentimental show tunes. Hopeless.

13

Sue, the discommoded cockatoo owner, lived within view of Church Square in Addington. Socialist Addington, as the Modern Priest liked to say. He, who had grown up mostly in Tory Merivale. Eddy shook his head vigorously in the hope the Modern Priest might fall out of his ear and break apart on the footpath. He *must* take control of these internal ramblings.

The Square was dependably picturesque, a swath of spring leaf and lawn today, bouncing green. Eddy had picnicked and played here as a child with the kids of Brain's friend Adrian. Where were those kids now? he wondered. Probably Brain had told him—he kept assiduously in touch with all friends, updated Eddy regularly, but these days Eddy barely registered these monologues, and if he did, he instantly deleted them.

It was unkind, he knew it, a passively belligerent resistance, but he couldn't seem to stop; it was involuntary, he told himself. At least he stayed in the room. Toss had described to him how he'd trained his parents in this regard: whenever they mentioned a friend and their colossally uninteresting doings, he either left the room or held up his hand and intoned, "Can't hear you." In short order, his parents had stopped bothering. But Toss was eye-poppingly rude to his parents. Brutal. It made Eddy breathless.

"Pure survival," said Toss in defense. "Only children have no choice."

He wasn't an only child, but his sister, Meg, was years older and had left for Australia when Toss was five. She visited every couple of years,

a comet from another stratosphere crashing splendidly to Earth—
her energy and sociability in inverse proportion to her brother's—
and because of this, in the summer Eddy turned thirteen, he had developed a sudden and consuming crush on her. It had something to do
with her supple, muscled body, often on display in the Mores' sprawling back garden, and her dark eyebrows (eyebrows—who knew?), but
also how readily she lounged in his and Toss's company, greatly amused
apparently by their habits and conversation, dreaming up names for
their band at the time.

Eddy's squeezed heart did not, alas, escape Toss More's mordant
eye. He knew Eddy too well, could read his careful nonchalance, his
newly spritzed dialogue.

"She's getting married," Toss informed him. "To a screenwriter."
(Meg was a lighting designer.) The screenwriter had stayed in
Melbourne to write his absurd screenplay, which would never be
filmed. His name was Bevan. A terrible name, they both agreed. But
Eddy didn't care. The coordinates of his relationship with Meg—an
entirely solid thing in the storybook of his head and the privacy of
his bedroom—remained the same. Both Bevan and the twelve years
between Eddy and Meg collapsed, along with all other pesky hurdles.

One of the great romances, thought Eddy fondly, staring now at a
patch of daffodils waving perkily from the Church Square green. And
then—all gone, poof! Nothing, *nothing* there the next time Meg came
over the ditch. Amazing. He'd seen her again this last July and she was
heavily pregnant—*torpid*, Toss had muttered, contemplating a photo:
Meg beached semi-naked in her bed, a startling mound rearing from
her middle. In July, Meg had hugged Eddy hard, and he had tried not
to dwell on the creature between them. "Lying in wait," said Toss.

14

Sue Lombardo's house was on Dickens Street. There was a whiff still of the nineteenth century in Addington—the vanishing remains of brick factories, workers' cottages, the faded glory of rail, and Great Men all over the street signage—Emerson and Macaulay and Disraeli and Ruskin were just around the corner. By great good fortune, hooray, hooray, Eddy knew both his Dickens *and* that old windbag Macaulay because Brain, if not a broad contemporary traveler, nevertheless journeyed lengthily in the written past. Brain had pressed various essays by Macaulay onto Eddy, but the only thing he could remember was the little start he'd experienced reading the phrase *some traveller from New Zealand.* Presumably Macaulay Street was the windbag's reward for acknowledging the vulgar colonials at the bottom of the world.

Dickens was different. Eddy had read his way through much of Brain's *Complete Dickens* the summer he was twelve, and—it pained him to think of this now—as a birthday present for Brain, Eddy had recited the opening page of *Bleak House.*

Brain, who regularly mourned the lost art of recitation, had been wet-eyed with joy. When winter fog settled over the city, one of them was sure to say to the other, *Fog everywhere. Fog up the river . . . fog down the river . . . Never can there come fog too thick . . .*

Fog creeping into the cabooses of collier-brigs, Eddy thought now—his favorite line, though he hadn't known what collier-brigs were at the time. And literary fog was all very well; the real thing quite another matter.

The dank days of the recent winter came queasily back to him, the city drear and bowed down. In the clinging fog and sclerotic traffic along Fitzgerald Avenue, Eddy had experienced a moment of terrible bleakness. He'd stared out the car window at the subsided buildings and barren lots, the huge leafless plane trees down the middle of the road. They were like great tired bodies, broken sentries in their ruined city. He had a fleeting glimpse of himself from outside the car, as if through a camera, a moment in a noir film: despondent guy on the brink of despair. Winter could do that, and last winter had been a crock.

But now, here was spring busting out all over Sue Lombardo's cottage garden, a scatter of bluebells and grape hyacinths, jonquils and pug-faced pansies. A buoyant flowering of forsythia flanked one side of the house; a lone cabbage tree leaned toward the other. Eddy went down the west side to the back door as per instructions, knocked, and let himself in.

Somewhere, the *Messiah* was playing. That was a surprise. He followed the music down the passage, *Ev'ry* va-*al-ley, ev'ry* va-*al-ley*, and found Sue Lombardo at her desk, turned and ready to greet him. A pair of crutches was propped nearby. The sun poured through the window and made a dandelion halo of her silver hair. She was straight-backed and lean. Brown eyes, long face, kind of *handsome*. Eddy shook her outstretched hand, smooth-skinned and warm. He was shaking a lot of women's hands these days.

"Tēnā koe, Eddy," she said. "Excuse my not getting up." She patted her hips. "Double hip op. Or bilateral replacement, as the specialists like to call it. They love the big words, those guys. Have a seat in the sun."

She nodded to the window seat where sat the cockatoo, already alert, spreading its lateral feathers. It was an umbrella cockatoo;

he'd done his homework. He sat gingerly, but the bird immediately hopped up to the sill, gave a short, muffled scream, and raised its crest. Impressive. Perhaps he should set his own hair free, Eddy thought, give all due respect, etc. He nodded at the cockatoo instead and it screeched again.

"Easy, Mother," said Sue Lombardo. "Not short for motherfucker, by the way."

"But it's a he, right?" The males had dark eyes.

"Yes, though I didn't know that at first—nor did the person who gave him to me."

Eddy felt the bird inch closer to his head. It seemed to be vibrating.

"He's incubating another scream. I suggest you make us a cup of coffee? Give him time to settle. And then we can talk. Coffee's in the first cupboard on the left. I'm milk, no sugar."

He was also having a lot of coffee with women these days, thought Eddy in the kitchen, heating milk and waiting for the stovetop maker.

Sue Lombardo's kitchen was more modest than his other clients' though, a galley kitchen really, but with a most pleasant view: a good-looking vegetable garden, apple blossoms and a walnut tree on the fence line, spring flowers in clusters about the lawn. A black cat unfolded itself from a clump of jonquils and stepped elegantly across the grass. A little swell of happiness rose in Eddy. It was not unlike the view from his own kitchen window, but mostly it made him think of illustrations from his childhood picture books: crumpled children playing in suburban greenery. Alfie and Annie Rose and co. Cats and dogs and birds and garden geckos. Sun spots and warm stones. The reliability of the story in Brain's voice. The comfort of Brain's bulk.

In the study, they sipped coffee and Eddy basked in both the sun and *Messiah*, which he knew by heart, having sung it several times with the Cathedral choir, and because Brain thrashed it on the stereo through Advent to Christmas. The cockatoo thrummed and moaned beside him. Eddy kept his head very straight and still, though stray hairs maddened his cheek.

"It's three weeks since the surgery, and all's fine," said Sue Lombardo (the two names were now forever yoked in his head). "But I can't drive for several months. I'm hoping you'll do the groceries for me and a bit of this and that. For instance, take Mother to the vet." She paused.

"That sounds slightly sinister now that I say it aloud." She raised her cup in salute. "Good coffee. My car would be yours, of course."

A lady's car, thought Eddy. For sure. Not yellow, he hoped. She did not seem a yellow-car person.

"Sounds good. What's up with her? Him?"

"Constipated! I'm the one who's had surgery, but he seems to have gone out in sympathy. Cockatoos are prone, but once they start straining—that's the little moans—you need the vet. We don't want a prolapse.

"Or do we?" She narrowed her eyes at Mother.

Eddy laughed. "Really?"

"Well. Sometimes I wish him gone. A double-edged present, to say the least. He wasn't well-socialized in his last home; the idea was I would rehabilitate him—but then the surgery came up and he was here too much by himself. I was at my sister's for a fortnight, but Mother wasn't welcome . . . And now he's in a state."

As if to confirm this, Mother screamed directly in Eddy's ear. He shot up and relocated to a chair in the crook of the old fireplace.

"Mother, Mother, Mother," crooned Sue Lombardo.

She had a nice voice, Eddy thought. Seasoned. Probably a contralto.

"He needs a more patient companion. And I need some quiet to get on with work. Otherwise, I'll strangle him. And you know, *Hurt no living thing . . .*"

"*Ladybird, nor butterfly, Nor moth with dusty wing,*" said Eddy, automatically. And groaned inwardly.

"How nice!" said Sue Lombardo. "I don't expect anyone under sixty to know that."

"I am kind of sixty," said Eddy.

She considered him. "The *Messiah*?"

"*Messiah* through to Mos Def. With an occasional weakness for musicals and classic Gospel." His tongue seemed to have developed a mind of its own.

"Commendably catholic tastes," said Sue Lombardo. "Small *c.*" She smiled and her face was almost beautiful. She had very white, even teeth.

"So what do you think? Some errands for me and friendship therapy for Mother?"

They talked details and times and the soprano sang, "*And suddenly there was with the angel,*" and the black cat found its way to the office and copped a screech and a baroque crest performance from the cockatoo but was quite unperturbed and arranged itself prettily at Eddy's feet instead, eyeing his lap, then leaping fluidly and soundlessly onto it. Eddy stroked the muscled back.

"This one has adopted me," said Sue Lombardo. "She was very insistent. I had to put a cat door in. I like cats, but it's puzzling to have two pets one has not actively chosen. She's Puss. A real name seemed too active a commitment."

"A cat door's quite the commitment," said Eddy. Puss purred loudly. What with the sun and the pleasing weight of Puss and the well-loved music, Eddy felt like purring himself.

"So why pet minding?" said Sue Lombardo.

15

Sue Lombardo's vet—Friendly Vet—was at the bottom of the
Port Hills, a drive that would once have taken fifteen minutes from
Addington, but these days nothing was so predictable. A line of the
loathed orange cones vanished overnight from one street and took up
residence next day in another, scuttling route plans, denying access, or
crippling progress. Eddy imagined the transport planners, sociopaths
all, plotting orange-cone incursions and competing with each other to
create ever more prolonged crosstown trips. Now in an interminable
line of cars, and with Mother hissing balefully in his cloaked cage,
Eddy cursed himself for not going on foot. He might have strapped
the cage to his back, joggled the liverish bird into silence. Instead,
Mother squawked and screamed and rattled the cage incessantly.

He turned up Sam Cooke and breathed slowly to calm his
irritation.

He wasn't *intrinsically* impatient. He had been Brain-trained, after
all, had grown up to a slow beat, well-schooled in the pleasures of
deferred gratification. Come to that, he'd been further trained by Toss
More; God knows, *he* required the patience of the proverbial. And
animals required patience, didn't they? Also learning an instrument.
Also a sport. Ten thousand repetitions. He could queue with good
grace, too; he could, if necessary, take himself out of body, tread water
in some null place untroubled by thought.

But a traffic queue—or to use one of Brain's more hilarious cir-
cumlocutions, *slow vehicular progress*—made Eddy edgy and irritable, and

almost afraid, as if his head might blow apart at any moment. Strange how a car could offer both heedless freedom and creeping unease. (*"The incubator of malaise,"* quoted Toss More, after his sole experience of sex—which had been in his mother's car and not at all transcendent.)

In traffic queues, Eddy suffered eruptions of restless legs, a deranging complaint—most common in women, Toss had been pleased to inform him. This made him urgently want to burst from the car and run for the hills, or at least pump furiously up and down on the spot.

Probably no one would care if he did. There was a lot of aberrant community behavior these days, minor league mostly, but sometimes startling. Last week, for instance, a stately Fendalton woman at the checkout had screamed and thrown both her umbrella and not-small bag at the trolley behind her when the guy emptying his groceries had fumbled and three bottles of wine had exploded on the floor.

"My arthritis," said the guy, shrugging; he held up his knobbled fingers pathetically. Rose, the checkout manager, had taken the woman to the staff room for a cup of tea, but the wine guy had hung around, tense and useless, while Eddy and Mel in supervision mopped up the great lake of Merlot and broken glass. "Quake brain, poor old chook, quake brain," said the guy at intervals, wringing his mangled fingers.

In the Botanical Gardens, a man shed all his clothes and climbed a ginkgo on a frigid July afternoon. Balanced precariously between the bare branches, he had sung workers' anthems ever more desperately to a gathering throng, until the police arrived and talked him down. Dominic in frozen foods had described the incident to Eddy while they drank coffee and watched the trolley boys. The cops had covered the guy with a survival sheet, and Dominic, midway through a run, had collected the scattered clothes—the singer had begun disrobing meters away, dropping his garments as he walked and wept. "Weirdest thing," Dominic told Eddy. "The boxers were Brief Insanity with, no kidding, RELAX in big letters across the crotch."

Meanwhile, on Bishop Street, Brain and Eddy's neighbor Loretta Peatling, a perfectly sober citizen of forty-seven years whose house was wrecked but did not apparently qualify for a rebuild, had now become completely maddened by her circumstances, writing letter after letter to the editor, bailing up people on the bus and in the street, railing against the depredations of insurance companies and demanding signatures for a blazingly bonkers petition. Eddy had signed Loretta's petition—who liked an insurance company?—mostly to make her go away; but Brain had invited her over for tea and ginger cake. She came every Saturday afternoon now, for the solace of Earl Grey and baked goods. Brain was big on comforting the afflicted. It was a "spiritual work of mercy." (Thanks to Brain, Eddy could recite the full list of spiritual and corporal works of mercy. The only one he'd ever actually enacted was *visit the sick*, the rubric under which he rationalized spending much idle time in Toss More's sleep-out.)

The car in front moved forward a promising twenty meters. It was a red Toyota Corolla with a smashed trunk and dented license plate: CDGZ222; having stared at it so long, it was now forever and pointlessly in his memory. Eddy inched ahead, too, and the car's movement silenced Mother—for long enough to make Eddy worry. Was he silently prolapsing? A prolapse, he had learned from Sue Lombardo, was the falling out of a body part. In the case of the cockatoo, his rectum. Holy God. What an unattractive word rectum was.

"Hello?" said Eddy. Nothing.

"No straining please."

Silence. Perhaps Mother had fallen asleep, worn out by all his clamor.

More movement up ahead. The car glided forward. Sue Lombardo's car—he could hardly believe this development—was a Merc. It drove like a dream. Theoretically, Eddy was uninterested in cars, knowing only what he didn't like (yellow Suzukis and SUVs, the ludicrously tiny and the offensively large), but along with a torrent of other disposable information, he had also somehow absorbed miscellaneous particulars about classy car models. When Sue Lombardo handed him the car keys—why was this always plural when there was only ever one key?—he couldn't disguise his surprise.

"Unlikely, I know," said Sue, "especially given a vow of poverty, but I inherited it from my older brother. He was wealthy and unattached. He liked to shower me with worldly tat. It is a sinfully nice car."

It certainly was. No doubt whatever. Though difficult to fully enjoy in clogged traffic. Eddy had reveled briefly in its liquid power along Brougham Street, but since then it had been all stop-start. And now the queue was stalled again.

"What's your *problem?*" snapped Mother.

Sue Lombardo had prepared him for this. Despite her retraining efforts—you could apparently, with diligence and patience, teach a cockatoo any number of conversational gambits—Mother had maintained the unsubtle argot of his former life. Eddy should expect some semi-aggressive openers and a salty vocabulary.

"My problem is our current lack of celerity." (Brain word.) At this rate they were still twenty minutes from Friendly Vet.

"What's your problem?" Squawk. "What's your problem?"

"Limited time! Another job at three p.m. I'm a man of many parts.

"Within a limited orbit," he added, and a small frost crept over his skin. He was a man in motion, sure, but to what *end*? He lived with a quinquagenarian, as Toss liked to style Brain. His city was cratered. He had a weird pet-minding business, with social work overtones. And a supermarket job that, despite its odd charms, was almost certainly going nowhere. He could not imagine a sincere vocation in New World. And now he was talking to a gender-fluid cockatoo.

"I guess my friendship group is expanding. Or re-expanding." Did the bird's silence suggest listening with interest?

Eddy had seen nothing of his friends over the winter. He had worked every possible shift at New World and when not there was sleeping off his efforts. There'd been a few nights with Clementine from checkout, a very nice person it was undeniable, but Eddy's heart had not been in it. He hated himself on every score: for getting involved, for insufficient appreciation, for cutting it short. They sidled past each other now, their brief intimacy a scab and a rebuke.

He'd neglected his old choir friends, too; as soon as the Cathedral had fallen, his interest in choir evaporated. Choir, parish, and Modern Priest had been transplanted to an altogether less impressive space: no soaring ceilings, no creamy stone columns and sepulchral side altars. The Modern Priest was far too close now, all his bowing and bending and kneeling, his portentous arm sweepings right up in your face. Eddy had sung just once at the reconstituted Cathedral, in the *Street Requiem* after the June quakes, and with gritted teeth. Then he'd left forever. Amen.

He whistled the doleful incantation from the opening of the *Street Requiem* and waited for Mother to protest. He did not like whistling, said Sue Lombardo. It was really curbing her self-expression.

"Shut yer face!" said Mother. "Shutyerface! Shutyerface!"

"Shut your own," said Eddy, glad to find the cockatoo reliable in this respect, then gladder still because now there was a sustained loosening of the traffic. The Merc could express itself.

The bashed Toyota in front of them expressed itself, too, and, without indicating, did a lurching turn across oncoming traffic and disappeared down a side street, outraged tooting in its wake. Road etiquette had gone to hell with everything else. People did frantic seven-point-plus turns in the tightest of traffic, any lunacy to avoid orange cones glimpsed in the near distance. Eddy turned onto Barrington, and the needle sat on a dreary 25 km. With luck, Sue Lombardo would dream up birdless errands farther afield, and Eddy and the Merc could stretch out on a highway.

She was rather wonderful, Sue Lombardo. Very direct. But warm. Kind of noble-looking, with those brown eyes and dark brows (more eyebrows, hmmm). She had a steady, unthreatening gaze.

The cockatoo was named after Julian of Norwich, she'd told him. Did Eddy know of her? He did not.

"A remarkable woman," said Sue. "A fifteenth-century nun—hence *Mother* Julian. Also an anchorite."

Instantly, Eddy had been visited by a swift vision of Toss More, upright in bed, two duvets wrapped about his scrawny frame, declaiming the virtues of an anchorite life. He had shaved his head, and it shone under the wall lamp, smooth and yellowed like an old rutabaga. This was his response to being deflowered in his mother's car.

"It was whimsical," said Sue Lombardo. "I'd never named a pet before; it felt big! He's a good icebreaker, at least."

"Hey, Icebreaker," Eddy called to the back seat, where the decibels were rising again. "Could you please get a grip?"

"No problem!" shrieked the bird. "No problem!"

Julian of Norwich had apparently written the earliest surviving book in English by a woman. Well, good. And Eddy had learned a number of other things, small and less small, during the conversation with Sue Lombardo.

She was a passable tennis player, when her hips were working. She'd worked in Lima, Peru, for ten years, been home six months. She was studying Jungian psychotherapy. And, of course, liked to whistle, milk in coffee, baroque music fan, deceased rich brother, sister who didn't welcome cockatoos.

They inched toward the hills, Mother blessedly quiet again. On the corner of Moana and Barrington, there was action on the footpath—two dog owners facing off, a woman waving a plastic bag at a squat man, who batted it away with angry hands. Three dogs moved unbothered about their owners' legs, prospecting the ground and each other.

A dog-shit argument, Eddy was sure. Incredible the people who still brazenly left their dog's crap on other people's grass strips. He gave a blast of support on the horn (oddly high-pitched for a serious car), then worried it might be misinterpreted.

"What's the problem?" squawked Mother. "What's the problem?"

"Thoughtlessness," said Eddy after a moment.

For weeks this last winter, Brain had found regular dog deposits at the bottom of their drive when he collected the newspaper. Mostly, Brain was a stranger to irritation or rage. He could be cast down by serious world problems, but in the face of everyday annoyances (toast landing jam-side down, a flat *bicycle* tire, slow internet, mislaid sock— all things that caused Eddy to froth), Brain was composed and pacific. But the trespassing dog doo flicked some dormant switch. His uncle was incensed—for only the second time in Eddy's memory.

"It's the sheer *thoughtlessness*," said Brain, having consigned yet another leaving to the outside bin. "The quantum of things this sort of person refuses to think about makes me . . ." He paused. He wasn't sure what it made him. Mad? Sick? Done with life?

"I would *very* much like to . . ." Another pause. Ring the Council? Put up a sign? Lay poison? Pulverize the owner?

"The sort of person who does this," said Brain decisively, "is the sort of person who steals a library book with impunity. Or defrauds a pensioner. Or persecutes minorities. Or lays waste to Afghan villages with drone strikes. These people start *small*."

Eddy enjoyed this outburst immensely. It bounced him from his winter slough for several days. Never mind the debatable moral equivalences—dog shit to drone strike, anyone? He just loved Brain's fury. Even more, he loved what Brain did next—parked himself behind the mingimingi bush in the predawn for three days and finally caught the morally vacuous (Brain description) dog owner and his Rhodesian ridgeback as they took their pleasure on the driveway. Eddy was there, too, at Brain's invitation, and beheld with wonder his uncle's firm but exquisitely polite dispatch of the pair.

"The terrible thing is that I enjoyed that," said Brain afterward. He was glum.

Eddy had no such misgivings. He regularly reprised the skirmish in the eternal cinema of his head. Brain, hard man of Bishop Street.

"Fuck off!" said Mother.

"True," said Eddy. Brain wasn't hard. But he did have a certain tensile strength. (Building phrase.) Years ago, he had gone very politely head-to-head with Mrs. Evans, Eddy's Year 7 teacher, who had taken Eddy's books—*The Bunny Suicides*—from him in class reading. They were comic strips, not literature, she said, and their subject reprehensible.

"Mrs. Evans reminds me of Sister Duschene," said Brain to Bridgie and Ginge after he'd dealt with the matter.

This had led the three of them to wallow yet again in the legend of their intermediate teacher, long dead but living on in their combined memories, a penguin-suited gorgon of assorted villainies.

Eddy enjoyed a Sister Duschene story—in his mind's eye she was a composite of Miss Trunchbull, Mr. Squeers, and Mrs. Coulter: sadistic, irrational, and tyrannical but demonically clever, too, like a fallen angel. Sister Duschene stories had all the comfortable ghastliness of a scary children's book.

He parked at last outside Friendly Vet. He opened the backseat door and lifted the cage gently.

"Fuck off," said Mother halfheartedly. Eddy adjusted the cloth around the cage so there were no gaps for light.

These days, it seemed, nuns could plow their own furrows—connected to their communities but sometimes living apart. They had jobs; they dressed like other women. They drank espresso. They gardened, whistled, and drove their dead brother's Mercedes-Benz. They swore at their constipated cockatoo.

"Are you a *nun*?" he had asked, incredulous, as Sue Lombardo arranged the cover on Mother's cage. It had suddenly all come together:

Julian of Norwich, *a vow of poverty*, the *Messiah*, and other things less concrete.

"I am," said Sue Lombardo. "But be not afraid. I am robustly normal."

Eddy carried Mother carefully up the steps to the clinic and through the door. He gave Mother's name to the woman at the counter and found a chair in the waiting room. He put Mother on the empty chair to his right.

"Problem?" squeaked Mother experimentally.

"No problem," said Eddy. "We're here now. So shut up and give us some peace."

Which was how I found myself once again seated beside Eddy Smallbone. For the first time in two years and three months.

He looked much the same crossing the room toward me, oblivious: a little taller and his hair scraped back now in the ubiquitous bun. He looked even more like the picture of the loving Jesus on my grandmother's living room wall. Hollow-cheeked, big-eyed, beautiful.

I could have punched him.

Boo

Being perpetually distracted by the hundred-piece orchestra of maunderings in his overstocked head, Eddy didn't register who it was he'd sat beside. He did, after a moment, respond to Possum, mewing pathetically in her cat carrier on the floor.

"Beautiful cat," he murmured, bending down, still not looking my way, animals nearly always trumping humans in his hierarchy of being.

"A Bombay?" He was thinking aloud. I decided not to answer. Also, I was distracted by an elevated pulse and an unexpected heat crawling up my neck. I thought about leaving.

"Or just your good old American shorthair."

The book I'd been reading was open in front of me, but I was wishing it were a different book. It certainly wasn't an Eddy Smallbone kind of book, unless he'd radically metamorphosed over the last two years and become a chick-lit aficionado. Which I doubted. The book was ineffably silly, but sometimes all you want is a dumb book. Unfortunately, it was called *Good in Bed*, not a title you want to brandish if you're about to reencounter someone with whom you've had an erotic past.

But what did I care for Eddy Smallbone's opinion of my reading matter? Not much. I kept on staring at the words and thinking how I'd respond when he finally noticed me. Disinterestedly seemed a good option.

"Black cats are very cool," said Eddy, in that easy way he has with everyone and their aunt. He turned slightly toward me, but my head was bent, hair hiding my face. "The second one I've seen today."

"That's either a double dose of good luck or a double dose of bad," I said, pretending to read. "Depending on your culture. Or your moment in history."

He said nothing, but I *felt* his abrupt stillness, the cogs and wheels of his memory meshing. I decided to hurry things.

"He belongs to my aunt," I said. "Two years old and pampered as hell." I put the book facedown in my lap and turned, finally, to look at Eddy Smallbone.

"Mr. Kleinbein," I said after a well-judged pause. "Still channeling St. Francis, I see." I was pretty pleased with that.

"Boo?" said Eddy very tentatively. He was shocked, indeed. *"Boo?"*

Short history: I arrived at Champagnat College in Year 11 from Hokitika. Lived with my aunt Viv. Sat next to Eddy Smallbone in history, did drama with him, too. Played ukulele in one of his bands until that arch-shit Thomas More made life impossible. We were friends, and then much more than friends, and then not quite friends, though sometimes almost. Then, in August of Year 13, Eddy had a crisis, blew an almighty gasket, and left school. The earthquakes came. I left town. We lost contact: The End.

NO
VEM
BER

16

Eddy lay on his bed watching the sun set pink and yellow behind Loretta Peatling's house. His room smelled of gingersnaps: the baffling conduction of air molecules in their house meant that whatever was being cooked in the kitchen—three rooms, a set of stairs, and several closed doors away—somehow dumped its aromas in Eddy's bedroom. This was, on the whole, not unpleasant—except in late summer when Brain entered his annual preserving frenzy, which included among much else a cornucopia of pickles and the noxious tang of raw onion and vinegar. Tonight Brain was baking for a morning tea at work, to mark his twenty-fifth year at the library: Madeira cake, gingersnaps, shortbread, and club sandwiches—morning tea from 1954.

Eddy tried to imagine twenty-five years in one place of work, albeit two buildings. And now a temporary third, cavernous and comfortless, despite the library staff's best efforts. Perhaps Brain would work in a fourth edifice if a new library was built before he retired, though this seemed a distant prospect. The city innards were being gutted. Disembowelment, or urban heart surgery, depending on how you saw it.

People made the best of it. Eddy had been to a few empty-lot parties—frantic, hopeful affairs, with braziers and portable music and a *cornucopia* of drugs. Back in the winter, at a party in the south city, he'd stepped outside the mass of dancers and had a moment of profound disorientation. Where was he again? He could not remember which street they were on; there were no signal buildings with familiar ornamentation, just the big bowl of the night sky, the heat of bodies, and the cloud of their collective breath. They were a displaced tribe, marooned on some outer planet, charged with rethinking the new world. He had left, almost running, needing to get to a place where some landmarks remained, needing the trees and houses and silted streams of Snorebins, the long rectangle of their backyard, miraculously untouched by all the ruptures.

Eddy had been invited to Brain's morning tea, but tomorrow's animal and human roster was jam-packed. He and Sue Lombardo, his new nunly benefactor, had come to a most agreeable arrangement. The Merc was his as often as he needed it; Eddy, in turn, would relieve Sue of Mother's company whenever possible. Thus, the car became essential to the execution of his packed timetable, because the most efficient way to fulfill all his obligations was to combine cockatoo care with Delphine duty, and the distance between Socialist Addington and Tory Paparoa Street was too great to cover four times daily on foot. He closed his eyes temporarily to this increased carbon footprint. Happily, too, Josie Mulholland had no problem with a regular visitor from the family Cacatuidae. Though it was possible, Eddy thought, she would have agreed to almost anything. She had rung him one evening three weeks before. Eddy had been sitting in the shade of the walnut tree, staring over at the smoothed surface of Marley's grave, wondering how much decomposition of doggy flesh and Kaiapoi Pure Wool had taken place beneath the soil; whether in twenty years another dog might disinter a Marley femur or radius and spend a happy afternoon chewing and sucking before burying it again.

Josie Mulholland was apologetic but determined. Could they, sorry, but could they *please* revisit their arrangement? Eddy knew what was coming; Delphine had prepared him in her apparently guileless way. In short order he found himself agreeing to five days a week and Delphine accompanying him on the dog walks. Delphine-walks then: goodbye contemplative pleasures. But he could not locate sufficient hard-heartedness to refuse.

"She adores you," said Josie. "And Jasper says you're so patient . . ."

Very nice of Jasper.

"And all that extra time. I feel bad not paying you properly. It's childcare now, not dog walking."

True, and how had this happened exactly?

Five more minutes and he had mentally ditched two more New World shifts. Josie offered double the checkout wage if he stayed on post–dog walks till 7 p.m. He was only slightly ashamed of his mercenary calculations.

"I trust you completely, Eddy," said Josie.

Oh really? Based on what? Some old tribal church network? Well, *that* had worked out well in the past, he did not think.

"Delphine doesn't suit everyone. Jasper does his best, but you know . . ."

Eddy did know. Jasper was not quite of Planet Earth. Or not often. He seldom left his room, but for the unavoidable earthly necessities: bodily intake and release and, a rare nonnegotiable of his mother's, collecting Delphine from school.

He was kind to his sister, in an absent, more or less wordless way. Sometimes, if Delphine kept at him, buzzing like a demented mosquito outside his room or, catlike, delivering strange treats to his door, he consented to play a computer game with her. She was freakishly adept at *Mark of the Ninja*.

Occasionally Jasper appeared in the plant room, as if he'd suddenly recalled the rest of the world and a hazy memory of fraternal obligation.

"Oh," he'd say, impassive, seeing Eddy pinned helplessly to some game or convoluted dialogue with Delphine. And depart. The child was quite untroubled by her brother's oddness. She was happily his voice, his translator in the world.

"He hates getting me from school," she told Eddy. "He doesn't like people looking at him. But he has to get vitamin D. Mum insists. She said, 'I *insist*, Jasper.'"

Delphine went to a girls' school in Merivale, all striped blazers and sports uniforms and despotic homework. Eddy had seen the photos and school notices under magnets on the fridge; he had frequently been co-opted into Delphine's homework dramas.

Jasper didn't have homework, Delphine confided. He was very clever and did all his work before lunch. Then he played with his friends online. "He has friends all over the world. The best is Golub Bubanja. Do you love that name? He's from Montenegro, but he's coming here one day."

It was unclear how Delphine knew all this, given Jasper's disinclination to speech. Eddy supposed she simply mosquito-bombed him with questions and eventually he surrendered. Quiet was her enemy. She ack-acked it to death with a fusillade of talk, narrating her thoughts, her activities, the perfidies of the playground, her chaotic dreams. Also, much family detail that Eddy doubted was for his consumption.

From Delphine he learned the facts of the new family arrangement. Dad lived with Claudia now. She was from his work. They had only one bedroom, so Delphine could never stay, but she saw them sometimes on Sundays. Jasper never saw them because Dad wasn't his father. His father lived in Cape Town, too far away to visit.

"Claudia is very pretty," said Delphine. "She has perfectly straight hair and green eyes. And no breasts."

"Are you sure she's a woman?" said Eddy, not thinking.

"Of *course*. What else could she be?"

"Okay."

"She only has *nipples*," said Delphine. "I saw them when we went to the beach. They poke out this far." She demonstrated a preposterous length with her thumb and forefinger.

"What is a parallelogram?" said Eddy, reading from the homework math sheet. He didn't want to think about the unknown Claudia's nipples, let alone discuss them with the child.

"I'm going to bind my breasts."

"Suit yourself. How do you calculate the *area* of a parallelogram?"

"Rosa's sister did that. She just wants to be flat. Forever."

"Concentrate, please. Try this one: What is the formula for the area of a triangle?" Two could play this game.

"Multiplybasebyheightanddividebytwo," droned Delphine. She knew stuff, that was for sure. But mostly she couldn't be bothered.

"Good. Write it down."

She did so with great labor, tearing holes in the paper and snapping the lead several times. Her pencils were either blunt as butter or sharpened to splintered points.

"What is the formula for the area of a cone?"

A very bored look. "Can't remember. But." A sly eye, wandering toward the door. "Have you ever seen a cone *bra*? Back to breasts!" She was extremely pleased with herself.

Eddy had laughed. He couldn't help it. She was undisciplined, theatrical, demanding, and wearying. But sometimes she made him laugh out loud.

Which was the real reason, he supposed, that he caved to Josie Mulholland's entreaties. The truth was, he'd become oddly attached to the little weirdo. A further truth: when Josie said *She adores you*, he had felt something. In his chest. Or his side. Like a pain, or a fright. Holy God.

The addition of Mother to the household greatly excited Delphine. She immediately began trying to make him say Fah-la-la-la-*lah*, both her celebratory exclamation and her rude retort. And Mother brought forth Jasper from the crepuscular cave. The plant room was suddenly crowded—three humans, one foul-mouthed bird, and two dogs in the patch of sun beside the rocking chair, slumped and sleepy after their vigorous constitutional. The gathering of this odd little assembly drove Delphine to new heights of manic happiness, though it did not assist the homework. But the homework was staggeringly pointless. Eddy eventually said so to Josie.

"You think?" she said, immediately anxious. She was never quite confident about anything to do with her children.

"Maybe the equations," said Eddy. "Probably useful to practice them. But those fact sheets are nuts. They're make-work. Random general knowledge questions with no narrative context. You search Professor Google, then instantly forget the answers." He was parroting Brain so exactly it was embarrassing. But what the hell. He shoved his feet right into Brain's figurative slippers.

"She should just read."

"She doesn't like reading. Same with Jasper. Years of reading recovery and tutors for both of them."

"I'll read to her."

In fact, he had already begun. It was the very best way to keep Delphine quiet and sitting in one place. They were midway through *The Midnight Fox*—quite the animal rights lesson, in Eddy's view. Also, an excellent story. Brain had read it to him when he was eight.

"But she'll get in trouble if the homework's not done. *I'll* get in trouble. They're so strict. They phone or send mean emails. They terrify me."

"We'll do it. But more efficiently." He had trialed this new homework approach, too. It was a cooperative enterprise, further detaining Jasper in the plant room. Delphine read out the question, Eddy and Jasper supplied the answer or Jasper found it in ten seconds flat on his phone, and Delphine filled in the homework sheet. The answers were semi-illegible, but the whole thing was dispatched in fifteen minutes.

Then they read. And now Jasper stayed for this; Mother perched on his shoulder or some other body part if he parked on the floor. Sometimes the bird sat inside the cowl of Jasper's hoodie, its crest shiny white against the oily black of the boy's hair. Mother had taken to Jasper—it was his slow bulk perhaps, his spreading quiet.

But reading was balm and lullaby for all of them. Delphine sat close by Eddy, her twitching and darting, her febrile thoughts, stilled and hushed. When matters became stressful for Tom the fox rescuer, she moved tight into Eddy's side, her eyes squeezed. Jasper's eyes were closed throughout, a big breathing boy-island in the ocean of the plant room carpet.

It was all very satisfactory, Eddy thought, reading to this audience of three, despite the voice that fell on the air being so thoroughly Brain-ish in its cadence and emphasis. It was so good to be back in the pages of a well-loved story, in an old friend's life, an imaginary life far from his own time and place, far away from quakes and liquefaction and existential gloom, and *discommoding* shocks. Mother, too, was largely pacified, just the odd squawked commentary on the text, always comical, occasionally apposite.

"*'He took the turkey,' Aunt Millie said*—"

"Shut yer face!"

"'*—never even cracked an egg*—'"

"Shut it!"

Or:

"*I saw Uncle Fred's gun rise*—"

"Holy hell!" said Mother from on top of Jasper's chest, and the boy had begun to laugh, which was so unusual that Eddy felt a stab of anguish.

17

The sun was gone, 8:19 p.m. He had a date. With doom. Or destiny. Or density, more likely.

Never forget, I am your *density*, Boo O'Brien had once joked many, many months ago, sitting astride him in the dark, sublimely naked. She was a *Back to the Future* fan, quoted at will from all three films. An '80s nostalgia thing, which Eddy emphatically did not share, the '80s being Brain and Ginge and Bridgie's (alleged) heyday. He'd had his fill of photos from that bizarre decade, when Bridgie's hair was big and Ginge's army coat a permanent fixture, Brain's wardrobe already old-fashioned. The time when the Modern Priest was in the seminary polishing his white smile, perfecting his pomps.

The Modern Priest was in the kitchen with Brain right now. He often turned up round dinnertime, to score a glass of wine and good cooking, to ply the reluctant Brain with gossip. Brain himself was constitutionally incapable of gossiping, a virtue Eddy alternately admired and regretted, but he was a kind of sponge for the Modern Priest, a safe repository, Eddy thought, rarely caviling or criticizing. What a very peculiar pair they were, the Modern Priest and the antique librarian. *Modern* was a joke, of course, as paradoxical as the rest of Christopher Mangan. The Modern Priest may once have flirted with liturgical dance and other progressive expressions of faith, but *in truth*—a favorite phrase of the Modern Priest's—*in truth*, these days he believed ardently in *the authority of the magisterium and the indissoluble doctrine of a filthy two-thousand-year-old patriarchy!* Or so Boo O'Brien had shouted at him during the great *Murder in the Cathedral* ding-dong. She had been magnificent: righteous and furious.

This memory, successfully repressed for two years, roared back into Eddy's head, stirring and uncomfortable.

In truth, he had never expected to see Roberta O'Brien again.

She had returned to Hokitika after the quakes, the school broken. His own convenient inner narrative had then sent her to Australia, where everyone adventurous eventually lit out for; she had often talked about it. If he thought of her—he had tried so hard not to—he imagined her in Sydney, a dumdum bullet shot out of Aotearoa New Zealand, spraying in every direction.

But there she had been, so shockingly, at Friendly Vet, decidedly herself as ever, and that little mocking sigh on the first syllable of Kleinbein.

Mr. *Klein*bein.

18

The vet had been thoroughly entertained by Mother Julian. The parrot had told her repeatedly to fuck off.

"Fair enough," said the vet, Maxine. "Who wants their rectum inspected?" She was further delighted to hear Mother belonged to a nun.

There was no sign of the cloaca prolapsing, apparently. Cloaca: another deeply unattractive word, thought Eddy, fastening on this instead of thinking just yet about Boo O'Brien.

"Means sewer," said Maxine. "Enough said." She prescribed olive oil and more fruit in the diet. Also, regular scrutiny of the droppings. Charming.

In the car, on a circuitous but unobstructed route home, Eddy could no longer avoid the inevitable. His thoughts were a hot slurry, Boo O'Brien bobbing within like a rogue jack-in-the-box on an unleashed coil.

She had been both different and exactly the same. Older, of course, but subtly—her face grown into itself or something. Her hair was still unruly and the familiar near-scowl hovered. She still navigated conversation with a clenched fist. And there was that old maddening sense of having been outwitted in a contest he'd not actually signed up for. He had wanted instantly to curl up in a ball, fall into a long sleep. The past had reared up from nowhere and kneecapped him.

The last time he'd encountered Boo had been at his grandmother's funeral, a week after the first quake. It had been altogether confusing seeing her in the pew, then in the hall afterward. Eddy was touched and annoyed and remorseful, all at the same time. He'd not once texted her since his grand exit from school, and she wasn't on social media. He'd avoided their mutual friends. He'd shoved Boo into the crypt that existed in the furthest reaches of his brain.

"Thanks for coming," he'd said, hiding behind a sausage roll.

"Burying the dead," said Boo, in her bald way. This made them both snigger. It was a "corporal work of mercy," much practiced by Brain. Boo was officially agnostic, but fully in favor of rituals. She was completely clear about this sort of thing. Eddy's spiritual psychodrama irritated her. She had no patience at all with Toss More's operatic religious extremes. But they disliked each other, Toss More and Boo, for reasons Eddy preferred not to investigate. Predictably, Toss had not stayed for sausage rolls and dutiful condolences.

"I doubt Doris has gone to heaven," said Eddy. He felt pastry flakes clinging to his face, swiped at them. "Not that there is one."

"Doubtless she would have been bored there," said Boo. She had been quite the Doris fan; they'd tickled the hell out of each other. This had confused Eddy, too. He was often confused in Boo's company. Except when they'd been in bed, where, miraculously, all confusion fled, and great purposefulness consumed them both.

She had gone off then and talked to Brain, hugged him hello and goodbye with fervor. No hug for Eddy. Not that he wanted one. He didn't think. He had half raised a hand when she looked around at the door, and that had been it. Adieu. Auf Wiedersehen. Haere rā. Eddy and Brain had driven away in the yellow Suzuki, trailing the hearse— the smallest possible cortège—to a cemetery on the outskirts of town where a plot had been hastily purchased. The cemetery where Brain's father was buried had sunk into the sand during the quake and was closed to new corpses. But at the side of his grandmother's open grave, he had no thoughts of his grandparents, only Boo and her confusing charms.

"Saw Bonobo," said Toss More the next day.

"Don't," said Eddy automatically.

As was his passive-aggressive custom, Toss More had devised his own name for Boo. He was a natural caricaturist, clever and callous, zeroing in on a character trait, an expressive tic, a social context, then planting the knife: Hazel—sexy, socially smooth, and evangelical: Nutbutter; Brain—learned and utterly square: The Box; etc. With Boo, known to the rest of the world as Bo, he had excelled himself— her name and her scowl, which did *very faintly* resemble a great ape's lowering brows, providing plenty to work with. Cruelty and hilarity.

Only, Eddy couldn't laugh; it was too much of a betrayal. "Boo" had been his own rechristening—she was so *sudden*—and Boo had responded with Mr. Kleinbein. German for Smallbone. A comical name in any language.

And now there she was again, at the vet. *Suddenly.* What's more, they'd exchanged phone numbers. Boo had offered hers—as a challenge, Eddy thought. He supposed they could have a beer. Did she still drink beer? She still read crap novels without apology.

Eddy had wound home slowly through Addington's poet streets, these thoughts thrashing about, and turned with relief onto Dickens. Mother, quiet all the way home—cowed by rectal inspection probably—perked up when he turned off the ignition.

"What's the story?"

"Christ, you tell me," said Eddy. He'd lain back against the headrest and closed his eyes, scoped the rest of the day. Debrief Sue Lombardo. Then a bus. Then walk to Paparoa Street. Hello, Delphine. So many people in his head these days. Plus pets. In just seven weeks. It was exhausting. But this was what he'd wanted . . . a menagerie to fill the Marley hole. Only now the pleasure in it was punctured by a Sudden Boo. He couldn't believe it.

A text appeared from Boo right then.

Mr. K. We could meet at Spigot. A week from today. 6 p.m. Should give you time to recover. Or back out.

19

He had been nervous, feeling about twelve—overly aware of himself, his gestures suddenly foreign, face gone spastic. Spigot was in Riccarton, the unlikely suburb where nightlife had migrated since the quakes. The bar had a makeshift feeling, cobbled together and unlovely. It was full of students newly released from exams, loud with bullish good humor. Eddy felt his usual distaste.

He dithered choosing a drink, remembering Boo's disdain for craft beer—or, more accurately, for craft beer fans. She was resolutely down-market about beer and food. It was contrary and kind of annoying, but here he was now, self-conscious about his selection. Defiantly, he chose a Three Boys Pils and sat outside to wait for her. She was sometimes late, he remembered. Also annoying.

Boo was a student herself now. Relocated from Auckland. She had missed the South Island. She had missed winter. More contrariness. She was back with her aunt Viv—The Earth Scientist, as Eddy had always thought of her. Four years ago, when Boo first sat beside him at school and they'd competed to make each other laugh, he'd believed briefly, blushingly, that an earth scientist studied the whole of The Earth. Every bit of it. A massive undertaking, he had thought, puzzled about how this could be done.

She was okay, Viv, only a decade older than Boo. Eddy had got on well with her—until, abruptly, he had not. He shut his eyes quickly, closing out that time, that other winter, concentrating on the raucous jollity around him.

When he opened them, there was Boo, considering him with a look that was surely the very definition of wry.

"Mr. Kleinbein. I honestly didn't think you'd come." She slid into the facing chair. The tables were very small; their knees brushed. It was a warm evening, and Boo wore a sleeveless tunic. A very nice soap smell came over the table to Eddy. Jesus.

"So, thanks," she said, looking him straight in the eye, and the long-ago moment of his original fall came rushing back to him. After weeks beside him in history, she'd passed him a gummy (she always had lollies; she called them lollies). He thought her smart and somehow lawless, but now the true arrangement of her face and self came startlingly into view—the combination of dark brows, hazel eyes, determined lips, ungroomed hair, and netballer's arms, all so good.

He was going to die of nostalgia.

"Still drinking Steinlager?" he said.

"*Natürlich,*" said Boo, and now he remembered the random German vocabulary that made him laugh. "Steinlager Pure."

20

In the Riccarton bar, Boo kept the conversation running. She popped a bag of chips and held it out to Eddy. Salt and vinegar. He hadn't had a salt and vinegar chip in two years.

"Shall we get the war stories out of the way?"

Yes, but where to begin? And also, how to avoid?

"The February quake. Where were you?"

"In a truck, on the Moorhouse overbridge," said Eddy, the memory immediately and heavily at hand, as he supposed it would be for the rest of his life. It was like that for most people, those ten ferocious seconds, the chaotic aftermath, ineradicable.

Eddy's truck had lurched and veered, then flung right, glancing off a taxi and then an SUV. Tools, bags, heavy cartons had pitched from the back of the truck to the front, bashing him about body and face. His head had rammed the truck's ceiling. He'd been badly bruised and dazed and thoroughly frightened. All around, car alarms were going off, great clouds of dust rising and spreading, seeping into the cab. He could think only of Brain, on the third floor of the library on Gloucester Street.

"But he was okay," said Eddy, the relief still there. "He was Civil Defense rep—"

"Of course," said Boo, and they smiled and Eddy thought how convenient it was that Boo needed no explanation of Brain. They'd done all that years ago.

"Plenty to keep him busy." This ridiculous understatement from Brain in the late evening of that day as he poured wine with an unsteady hand. They had both found their separate ways back home, apocalyptic journeys through the city and suburbs, connections severed, their minds and bodies simultaneously charged and stumbling, their eyes disbelieving.

"I was at school," said Boo. "Outside, with Philly and Ata and Adorna. Eating a ham roll. We saw the bell towers collapse. Holy fuck. Predictably, Philly had hysterics—my God, the torrent of water those eyes can produce. A *cataract.*"

A Brain word, if ever there was one. From a Brain-type poem and song. *And the wild cataract leaps in glory.*

"*Blow, bugle, blow,*" said Boo quietly, not looking at him. Eddy felt faint, as if he'd just heard bad news.

They'd had a bet in Year 13: memorize the Tennyson poem and recite faultlessly. Boo had said *snakes across the lakes* instead of *shakes*, so Eddy had won.

"But *snakes* is so much better!" she'd insisted, to Brain's amusement. "Tennyson got it wrong." After that she'd taken to quoting the lines when they were busy in bed. *The horns of Elfland . . . And grow for ever and for ever . . . Shall I blow your bugle, Mr. K?*

They were both silent, the same images chasing through their respective heads, Eddy supposed. He stared hard at the froth on his pilsner, the bubbles springing through the gold. Now his body remembered, too.

"Where's Philly these days?"

"Art school. Photography. Ethereal self-portraits. Very Philly."

Ethereal was a good word for Philly. Willowy Philly. Toss had, inevitably, christened her F-f-f-filly, because of her long legs, the fey-ness and high maintenance.

"And next?"

"Next?"

"On the twenty-second."

"Next, the Modern Priest came charging out of the presbytery and took over."

Of course. In fact, Eddy had heard the Modern Priest's own report from that day. He'd been crouched under the presbytery dining table with his lunch companions, had seen the bell tower domes sliced away, the stone towers folding in on themselves, his cathedral *dying, dying, dying.*

"To be *fair,*" said Boo, and Eddy laughed: it was the old parody of their history teacher who had tried always, madly, to be evenhanded about the good and bad actors of yesteryear (Boo word. Strictly satirical). Oh, he had *missed* Boo, but he hadn't known it, couldn't. He missed her right now, though she was there in front of him, gap-toothed and renegade.

"To be *fair,* he was pretty useful. Kids losing it. And teachers."

"He does like a crisis," said Eddy, unable to concede the Modern Priest the smallest virtue. "People falling apart works for him. Shame he can't minister to himself."

Boo pressed her fingers into the chip crumbs. Out in the middle of the road, students hung out car windows, yelling nonsense, bawling songs at their footpath audience.

"So, I read about all that," said Boo.

"Yes."

"Must have been terrible."

"Not really."

"Poor old Modern Priest, though."

"You feel *sorry* for him?" Boo? That most caustic of Modern Priest skeptics?

"Course. How could you not feel sorry for him—such a spectacular fall from grace. I felt a twinge."

He shouldn't be surprised. The most consistent thing about Boo had always been the unpredictability of her responses. She seldom toed a line.

"I mean, he's a disgraceful cock-a-doodle—not to mention a misogynist, despite all the altar girls. Plus, a hypocrite. But who isn't a hypocrite?"

"It was thousands of dollars!" His voice was laughably squeaky.

"Not arguing with you, Mr. Kleinbein. But you know, who *is* he now? No more shapely sermons and congregational love. What can he do? You have to feel sorry for him . . ."

Eddy thought of the Modern Priest, his fingers habitually drumming the kitchen table, always a restive air about him. He did not seem much humbled; he still dominated the room, only half listening to anyone else. But perversely now, he remembered the day of the Modern Priest's resignation, arrest imminent. He had arrived round at their house, shockingly abject and diminished, his face cheesy pale. He'd sat at the kitchen table, laid his head in his arms, and sobbed. Eddy slid away, not wanting to hear the gulping and crying, or to look at Brain, his hand on the Modern Priest's heaving shoulders, face unreadable. There would be no more pastoral appointments for Christopher Mangan, no more casually exercised authority or climbing the church ladder, no stirring homiletics, his resonant voice bouncing off church ceilings. He'd have to work for the Vinnies or something. New World perhaps.

"Hmmm" was his eloquent summary to Boo outside the Riccarton bar.

"Awful for Brain," said Boo.

"Clericalism built him up. Clericalism brought him down," said Eddy.

A Brain phrase, repeated regularly over the years as the parade of criminal priests and prelates fell, one after another, into scandal and opprobrium; said once again in resignation to the newspaper photo: the Modern Priest and his lawyer leaving court. He spoke it like a proverb, some kind of inevitable truth honed from the centuries' evidence of priestly error, and from Chris Mangan himself. Brain, Eddy realized, shocked, had always expected something like this. He knew the Modern Priest's deep self, had seen his fall from a long way off. So had Bridgie and Ginge. Eddy had stared at the Modern Priest on page three, vacant-faced, wholly different in a gray suit and tie, no clerical collar. He looked like someone's dad or a department of education officer.

In the days before his arrest, the Modern Priest had slept in their spare bedroom, so Eddy had holed up in Toss More's sleep-out. There had not been much sleep, Toss speculating into the small hours about the indignities awaiting a larcenous priest in both prison and the after-life. Eddy had packed out after three days, returned home to the stripped spare bed and Brain watching *The Castle*.

"Where did all the money go?" asked Boo.

"Who knows?"

"Not even Brain?"

"If he knows, he's not saying."

"Was there really a woman?"

"No idea. Maybe. Bridgie knows everything for sure, but she's not saying, either. His home detention's over. He's at some sheltering presbytery, waiting for life. It's like it never happened. Same as usual with the four of them."

"Yes," said Boo, finishing up her Steinlager Pure. "They're loyal."

Boo

That slipped out. The *loyal*. I didn't want to roast Eddy, taunt him with his complete failure to stay a friend. I don't think. But maybe my unconscious did. My unconscious was all over the place. My conscious self was mostly stuck on being across the table from him, batting words back and forth, looking at him and trying to work out the differences in his face and body. More defined jawline? Nose slightly more hawkish? Taller? I didn't know what I was doing. I didn't know why I was there. Maybe my unconscious did. It was like being in a recurring dream. Weird word-tennis, a bit defensive, a bit surreal. Funny how quickly we fell on the old safe subject—terminal annoyance with the Modern Priest. That slippery old trout—to coin a phrase of my grandmother's. Applied mostly to men.

I was never big for Chris Mangan. For a start, I was a latecomer; I hadn't been around his (alleged) charisma for five years, pulled into the romance (*myth*) of a Modern Priest, like the rest of my peers at College. I hadn't had him from birth, either, like Eddy, an honorary uncle dispensing baptism and bromides.

Also, though the O'Brien family has produced the occasional nun or brother (to wit: Uncle Bede, known to the rest of the world as The Venerable), the truth is we're constitutionally suspicious of priests—it's in the DNA. In the *terroir*, says Viv—aversion to any authority being a West Coast habit as old as the hills.

Plus, I was an agnostic. (To be clear: not an atheist. I don't deny; I doubt. "Seems reasonable," said Uncle Bede when I informed him. "Emphatic *denial* of the transcendent—now that'd be arrogance, surely?" He was separating tobacco strands, sprinkling them on his cigarette paper, practically a prayerful act. "Strictly between you and me," he said, rolling the paper back and forth, "doubt makes sense.")

And all that priestly performance, how could you take it seriously? The Modern Priest was a shocker, far too chuffed with his singing voice, with his personal stage set, the altar. Our family didn't go to Mass much. Eddy though, he'd had heavy doses of altar palaver all his life, in that cathedral, the works. Inevitably, the worm turned. I was there when his rebellion really got going.

It was Father Tom's funeral, half the College in the congregation—to pay respects and boost the hymn singing. Father Tom was a sweetheart, a scholar. No rococo altar displays from him. No grandiloquent pronouncements. No hiding behind the lectern. He came down from the altar to talk. "Too good to live," said Philly, big, globby Philly tears somehow clinging to her cheeks and shining briefly under the Cathedral lights, and her face still creamy white, unblotched and yearning, like St. Bernadette Soubirous in that crazy film we watched on YouTube.

Father Tom had a massive heart attack in the middle of the Year 11 religious education class; he died in slow motion, right in front of us. One steak-and-cheese pie too many. We were all sad and shaken up, some of us briefly believing in God again. We kept going over the way he'd pawed at his chest and grimaced horribly, had fallen down in front of the map of Israel at the Time of Jesus.

In the Cathedral the organ started "Lord of All Heaven," and up the aisle came twenty-five or thirty priests, I lost count, and three mitered bishops, everyone decked in their white wear: albs and stoles and chasubles. At the altar, they fanned out slowly into a large semicircle facing the congregation, most of them bent and frail. They crossed themselves in somber unison. I thought of the Knights Templar and the Knights of the Round Table and all those other wacko fraternities and was suitably disturbed. But Eddy was overcome. He leaned into me, aghast.

"Christ, we're a cult."

We got the giggles, which was unfortunate, and then worse, Eddy got the hiccups, and it was almost the Offertory before we could pull ourselves together, fastening on our hymn books, not looking at each other.

* * *

But the Modern Priest. I could almost like him better for his big fall. Proof he was no different from anyone else. Ontologically changed by ordination? Pull the other one. He was dead ordinary, and ordinary people fuck up all the time—check the evidence! Then they get back on their horse or their Bactrian camel. And he'd been an arrogant arse over *Murder in the Cathedral*; he deserved to be called out.

* * *

Unfortunate truth: the Modern Priest's not a complete arse. Behind that lapel crucifix beats a kind heart. Clumsy though. Bent out of shape.

* * *

Important fact: the reason Eddy's dark on the Modern Priest is only partly to do with his hypocrisy, that shameful theology. It's also to do with his bad-fairy number at Eddy's birth: a strenuous campaign against Brain adopting Eddy. His reason? Child-rearing was women's work.

* * *

Another thing: the Modern Priest was on the money about Toss More, and Eddy didn't want to know. But he refused to talk about Toss. I gingerly spoke his name across the footpath table on Riccarton Road, and up came the Kleinbein hand, that calloused palm, those lovely long fingers standing stiff.

"No," he said, very fierce. "Not going there."

21

This time they would drink beer in Opawa, another suburb that had sprung unexpected nightlife. Eddy picked Boo up from Viv's. Viv was away, scrutinizing The Earth somewhere, no doubt—the quakes had been good for her. No uncomfortable exchanges then, for which he was grateful.

Driving, he felt out of body. His hands on the steering wheel were another person's. This whole thing—Boo here, *here* in the passenger seat, it was so strange. He'd both earnestly wanted and not wanted to see her again, the irresolution making him feel like nothing so much as a befuddled old dog at the end of a leash, hostage to someone else's will. Boo was quiet beside him, perfectly at home with herself apparently. But perhaps she was just as unsettled by memory and curiosity and queasy doubt. Perhaps she was operating on instinct, too. After all, she'd been back in town for more than a month and—he assumed—would not have been in touch but for the fateful vet encounter. He couldn't help thinking in fateful terms. He knew nothing anymore.

The Opawa bar was all trestle tables and blackboards and, oddly, hay bales. Post-quake décor. And a heaving crowd. Eddy bought a Steinlager Pure plus a bag of salt and vinegar and, after sheepish deliberation, an Emerson's 1812. Boom. Crash. Ha. As he set down the beers at their table, a decent shake rumbled through the bar. Instantly, the din of voices dropped, everyone watchful.

"Four point one," said Eddy when it was done. "Quite shallow."

For months after the big quakes, Eddy and Brain had punted after-shock magnitudes: they both rated their internal seismographs. Your accuracy depended on where you were, of course—outside or in the car or in a wooden building, etc. And how dispassionately you could assess the turbulence. New World was Eddy's worst place: you stilled mid-gesture, alert as a rabbit to the immediate environment and your interior calculators, the adrenaline racing down your arms. The entire New World beast held its collective breath against the possibility of tins and bottles hurtling from the shelves. These days the rock-and-roll barely rated a mention.

"Viv does that," said Boo.

"A dearth of entertainment round here."

Eddy hadn't been to a movie in months, or a gig. Venues were slowly reappearing, but his habits seemed permanently altered. At the dag end of the dismal winter, Bridgie had treated him to a trip to Wellington to hear some music, catch up with Ollie. The trip was a blur now: rain and wind and Ollie's perishing flat, semi-memorable music, pad Thai and Japanese beer, and involuntary calculations as to the earthquake risk of every building he entered, especially on Cuba Street. Also Ivan, the garrulous international relations student, who'd droned on all night about joining the Security Intelligence Service. Eddy had contemplated punching him. He wanted to punch someone, maybe even himself.

On the last morning, he lay cold in his sleeping bag on the flat's half-sprung couch, reading a battered Georgette Heyer novel, which, incredibly, had fallen on his face in the night, dislodged when he reached for a glass. Some regressive flatmate, he supposed, needing quick comfort. Reading this had prompted a most melancholy spate of Boo memories: Boo and Brain, to Eddy's eternal puzzlement, had bonded over G. Heyer plot arcs and characters.

But *Arabella* proved strangely compelling.

"I accidentally read a Georgette Heyer," he said to Boo now.

"Were you sick?"

"Kinda."

"Which one?"

"*Arabella*. And then I read *The Grand Sophy* and then *Frederica*."

"Three! That's a terminal illness."

Kinda. Back home Eddy had gone to Brain's Georgette Heyer collection (complete) and found the other titles, each of which he read to the end, wondering all the while if he was perhaps having an unusual kind of nervous breakdown. The respective heroines flirted in curlicued sentences, wore Regency dress and chignons with winsome curls, but all of them somehow had Boo's busy face and boldness. It was like visiting Boo in action on the set of a costume drama, a would-be pleasure wreathed in gloom.

"Did you love Sophy?"

Kinda.

Of course he would not tell her that after nearly two years of a mental Boo-ban, having opened a door with the help of Georgette Heyer, he had then dived headfirst into a veritable wallow; half of his head read the heroines' romances and emphatically happy endings, while the other half gingerly revisited his own joyous and confusing romance with Boo and its sorry end. It was a strange kind of purgative therapy, dealing with the lurking nervous breakdown, Eddy believed. Georgette Heyer: Better than Prozac.

"It was when we knew Marley was on the way out," said Eddy. A plausible lie. But maybe it was half-true? Maybe a displacement activity for one loss sheltered another, and another, and another.

"How are the Rhode Island Reds?" said Boo in the Opawa bar.

"Fruitful. Egg-full. Big mothers. Brain's on a baking binge."

"Have you told him I'm back?"

"Not yet. The Modern Priest's there. Licking the beaters, like a child."

"Comfort eating. Biscuit Mix for the Soul."

"Yes. *Biscuit Mix for the Soul: The Road to Recovery* by Father Cristoforo Mangan."

"Straight to remainder," said Boo. "Five for a dollar."

Sometimes, for a few seconds, it was like the old days, egging each other to the next laugh. But then Eddy didn't know what to do when the laugh was finished. Get another beer? He was driving though.

"Any news on the job front?"

"Yes. But don't mock or I'll whack you."

But he wouldn't mind being whacked. They had not touched each other at all, no hugs or cheek glosses for old times' sake. A whack on the arm could be strangely nice. From the minute he'd seen Boo tonight, Eddy had felt not at all in charge of his physical self. He had to look away sometimes, her bright eyes and mad hair stirring him up. Also, the soap smell. Coconut.

"Knit World. Four days a week till uni goes back."

"*Knitting?* Who knits?"

"Not me, not since I was ten. I'll have to brush up—I exaggerated my skills. I did once knit a whole cardigan. For a baby, so not exactly big. Luckily there's YouTube School. You can learn anything there.

Bongos, the tuba. How to fix a garage door. How to knit into the back of a stitch."

"Doris knitted. Ugly jerseys for me when I was little. All prickly. But seriously, *who* knits these days?"

"Thousands. It's a thing again. Did Doris leave you her needles? I need some in a hurry."

"All to the Sallies and Vinnies. Except the Temuka pottery, which Brain is sentimentally attached to. Unfortunately."

"A bit ug?"

"Fully ug."

They were positively cozy, Eddy thought, chatting like old mates. And deftly avoiding sand traps. But knitting, really?

"So," said Boo, all concentration with the finger and the chip crumbs thing. "Hazel Malley?"

Boom. He'd thought too soon.

"My turn," she said. "Another 1812?"

Yes, and also a bullet through the head, thanks.

"Gives you time to dream up something credible."

But the thing with Hazel, *to be fair*, it had just happened. Spring fever? He'd stood in for a sick keyboardist in a band. Students. Hazel was back from uni, nestled with friends in one of her parents' houses. Party central. Sundry stimulants and vivid girls. Hazel, still evangelical but no longer saving herself for marriage.

"What, so your lips just went magnetically to hers, no actual Kleinbein volition," said Boo, exploding another chip bag.

"No. Or, not exactly. How do you know, anyway?"

"News travels. Bad news travels faster."

"Harsh," said Eddy.

"Those genuflecting virgins." Boo was sour. "All doing Law now. Lining up lawyer husbands."

"Yes," said Eddy. "Exactly right."

In Year 12, Hazel and her friends had begun prostrating themselves when they took Communion—until the Modern Priest had forbidden flagrant displays of piety. They had also declared themselves chaste for Jesus. Hazel's successive fervencies, Eddy discovered in time, were mostly whimsical and easily shed. She had thought him a good project, but he'd disappointed her. After their bloodless breakup, he'd missed only the family tennis court.

"She's got a good backhand."

"No more chips for you," said Boo. She placed a chip reverently on her tongue, like a Communion wafer, closed her eyes, and swallowed with a beatific face.

This was such a piercing reminder of their old games, that far-off time, Eddy felt he might cry. How was he to navigate these new barnacled Boo waters? He was light-headed now from one and a half beers, suddenly as panicky and undone as at other signal moments of bad luck or bewilderment in his life. That time he'd lost Brain in the supermarket—his first clear memory, age three: a great mountain of bunched bananas, long Brain-less rows of shelving, the dreadful rattling and rushing of trolleys. Or in the garden sleep-out the first time he had seen the welts on Toss's back and arms, the leather scourge belt. And that desolate moment in the choir loft, years back, in the middle of "The Lord Bless You and Keep You," when it had come over him definitively that he did not in fact have faith, did not believe in a God, that the whole thing was built on sand. He had stopped singing, transfixed instead by Brain—face serene with the music, hands gently marking the beat—and the wrenching feeling that he, Eddy, had emigrated to some distant place where he would never again truly know his uncle.

"Sorry," said Boo. "I was joking really. I can't talk anyway. I—"

"Don't," said Eddy. He did not want to hear what she might say. "It doesn't matter. Who cares?"

Boo looked at him, wary, then began carefully smoothing out the chip packet, folding it in half, and half again, and again. Eddy brought the beer bottle to his lips but put it down again without drinking.

"You fucking muppet!" roared someone drunk and ecstatic. "*Crazy!*" The noise of the bar surged around them.

Eddy studied the label on his bottle. Hoppy Pale Ale. The artichokey hophead comically coughed from the cannon's mouth. Joyful war. There was a recording of the *1812 Overture* somewhere among Brain's vinyl, for children, with grave narration: *Once, many years ago, there was a powerful emperor . . . too powerful . . .* Oh, fuck it. He drank the rest of the bottle. *If you must do it at all . . .*

"Viv's away," said Boo, very low. She held up the foil square, folded to the nth degree.

"I can drive," she said.

Eddy, dreamy, put his hand out across the table, and Boo dropped the plump little package into his open palm.

"I *missed* you, Mr. Kleinbein."

DE CEM BER

First Week of Advent

22

Eddy and Sue Lombardo drove west, toward the snowless Alps and the foothills, green and shrouded. Late afternoon and the softest light. Out Sheffield way there was a Christmas pine, felled especially for Sue by a friend of a friend of a friend. Some nun-loving lapsed Catholic.

"Christmas alms," said Sue. "From their shelter belt. Very kind."

The obliging woodsman was away; he had left the tree on his veranda. Eddy could have collected the tree himself, but Sue had a galloping case of cabin fever and wanted open space, the open road, what*ever*, she said, when he arrived that morning.

Mother was back at the house, in the proverbial dog box, having pecked an eight-year-old visitor the previous day. In Eddy's view, the eight-year-old, a nascent delinquent called Freeling Stormont, should rightly be the one in the dog box, if in fact his parents had ever used *any* disciplinary approach, which he doubted: Freeling had quite calculatedly wrapped his hands around Mother's abdomen and squeezed hard. He was apparently being friendly.

"He was bored," said Sue. "You know how it is for children—adults talking, nothing much doing except to patiently look on. As they used to say in books."

For Eddy, whose entire childhood had been about patience in the company of yakking adults, this was so much soft soap. He'd always found things to do, something to read or watch, some solitary game, daydreaming about his future career as a vet. It was hard to like children who behaved badly. He said so to Boo one hot afternoon as they walked Walter the cavoodle in Snorebins Park and observed a bunch of whining kids hassle their parents and provoke each other to small violences.

"They're just being kids," said Boo. "Nagging for an ice cream, that's normal kid behavior. So is pissing off your siblings." Not having siblings, Eddy was in no position to challenge this, but he was unconvinced.

"Fine, but what about the parents? They're not exactly on task. They just ignore the kids or feebly bat them away." Parents left a lot to be desired in his view. Or most of them. They were distracted, vague, and inconsistent. And often absent. This judgment was based on a narrow, though beady-eyed, study of Toss More's parents and Josie Mulholland.

"How to Parent: In Ten Easy Steps by Edmund Kleinbein. Orphan."

Boo had run off with Walter then, to lark about. Eddy watched them jibing and jumping, both yapping, Boo playing dead in the grass and Walter earnestly nudging her armpit.

Edmund Kleinbein. Some dusty old scholar, thought Eddy. A washed-up guy writing obscure books about forgettable figures: King Edmund, for example, his namesake along with Edmund Pevensie from the Narnia stories, the only one of the four children to have a character arc, according to Brain. Little was known about King Edmund's character arc, as far as Eddy could discover, except that he'd ruled the East Angles and been killed by a Dane called Ivar the Boneless, this last a detail fastened on by Toss More, who enjoyed excessive mirth at the thought of potential Eddy boners: if only *small* boners at least, not bone*less* boners. Christ, the legacy of a bestowed name.

"Freeling Stormont. What a burden!" said Eddy to Sue Lombardo.

He had taken against the unmet Freeling for his ridiculous moniker as much as his sadistic behavior. "What were his parents thinking? That he'd be president of the United States?"

"There's a thought," said Sue. "Nominative determinism. Could be in play. *Nomen est omen.*"

"Mr. Sales the auctioneer," said Eddy. "Dr. Limb the orthopedic surgeon. Cardinal Sin?"

"I believe, technically, that last one is an inaptronym."

Toss More, then. Named (accidentally) for a Catholic grandee and devoted to self-punishment.

They had a most interesting discussion then about Jungian dream analysis and archetypal symbols. Eddy was tempted to ask Sue for an interpretation of his recent dream involving an iron-banded wooden chest that arrived by courier for Eddy Small*bore*. It was too heavy to lift alone, and dream-Brain refused to help him bring it indoors.

But Sue Lombardo was not his therapist. She was an unexpected friend, and it was very nice driving westward with her and George Frideric Handel in the waning day. *Messiah* was their tune, ha. It was also now, as was customary in December, his dominant earworm. On the first day of December, Brain had begun his pre-Xmas *Messiah* orgy, and "Younger than Springtime" was temporarily drowned out by "The Trumpet Shall Sound," an improvement, all things considered. Eddy could whistle the trumpet part rather handsomely, if he said so himself.

Brain was devoted to Christmas. December was conducted to the soundtrack of G. F. Handel and Putumayo's *Best of World Christmas*. Also to a constant waft of nutmeg and toasted walnuts, brandy and rosewater, the unvarying flavors of Brain's homemade Xmas gifts. He hung an Advent calendar, too, on the living room wall beside the piano, where it reproached Eddy as he tinkered. Opening those dinky windows had been such an acute pleasure in his childhood, he had experienced actual saliva rushes, but no self-respecting nineteen-year-old male could indulge in such nursery nonsense. He tried to ignore the calendar, yet somehow every day he noted a new flap neatly turned back and squirmed at the thought of Brain's pudgy fingers, his delight at the scene within.

And now the old Advent wreath was back on the front door. Eddy and Brain had constructed it with twiggy maple branches when Eddy was seven. *Acer rubrum*, said Brain. He shaped the wood around the belly of the laundry bucket, and Eddy tucked in the springing ends. Wreath-making had doubled as a botany lesson. They'd wandered the Botanical Gardens assessing different branches for strength and pliability, Brain murmuring as they went, a secular litany of botanical names: *Salix matsudana*, *Quercus suber*, *Cordyline australis*, and Eddy's favorite, *Pseudopanax crassifolius*, which sounded like a spell and which he liked to say over and over before sleep. Blah, blah.

Pre-Christmas prep usually climaxed with a drive to the Snorebins kindergarten for a fundraiser tree, followed by the ritual decorating, with cake and bubbly and those willing Christmas elves, Ginge and Bridgie, plus any random strays. Eddy had ducked this for the last two years, finding the collective bonhomie enraging. Brain offered no rebuke. "Right you are," he said. "See you when we see you. Haveagoodtimedrivecarefully," and other such banalities from his bottomless supply of phatic communions. Last year, Eddy and Toss More had shut themselves in the sleep-out and written a scabrous punk carol skewering the myth of the Virgin.

The end of the Old West Coast Road loomed. How good it would be to carry on, swallow up the sere landscape and assorted conversational subjects, purr toward Castle Rock and the setting sun. There was something about facing forward into the open road that made any kind of discussion possible.

"Round yon Virgin Mother and Child, then," said Eddy. "What do you think?"

"Not much," said Sue Lombardo, apparently unsurprised by the question. "Mary's spotless womb? I don't think so. A cultural gloss to deflect from Jesus's illegitimacy. And the Hebrew word for virgin—*almah*—may merely mean young woman."

"So no nativity scenes?"

"Well . . . depends. In Peru, the *pesebres* have peasants in rough cloth, no whey-faced Mary in white-and-blue draperies. It's fleshy. Earthy. The properly human instincts."

"What about Christmas trees?"

"That's the evergreen, isn't it? As old as the ancients. Co-opted by Christianity, like much else. I'm good with Christmas trees."

"You're a puzzle," said Eddy.

"You, of course, are a model of transparency," said Sue Lombardo, which made them both laugh.

On the way back to the city, he played Sue his Odetta album, *Absolutely the Best*.

Waterboy, where are you hiding?

The pine tree's scent filled the Merc, minty and medicinal, pitching Eddy into a swamp of nostalgia. The unvarying Christmas living room. Midnight Mass and mincemeat pies. Presents beneath the tree. *A Christmas Carol* crackling on the turntable, Laurence Olivier crabby: "*Look to see me no more!*" The annual surprise of Pfeffernüsse biscuits.

Brain should have been the chatelaine of a grand establishment. Or a *House & Garden* editor.

Odetta's stark sounds cut the Christmas syrup nicely. You couldn't listen to your important music with just anyone, Eddy thought once again. It could carve you up, leave you defenseless. And if they didn't take it in just so, if they weren't brought to a halt by it, that was it for a friendship. Auf Wiedersehen.

"Glad I passed," said Boo, when he'd explained this to her years ago. After he'd played her Jeff Buckley singing "When I Am Laid in Earth," and she'd been properly stricken by Jeff's keening. Later, in the dark with Boo breathing into his back, he'd told her that over the years he'd imagined it might be his mother and father alternately singing to him in Jeff's eerie soprano, *"Remember me, remember me."* He'd stared again at their side-by-side photos on top of the piano, in an effort to feel something tender and wistful. There was nothing. Or just a vague disappointment, as with a muffed serve or a flat note in a tight harmony. And at failing to meet some unexpressed expectation of Brain's, he who had framed the photo of his brother in his unsullied youth and sought out the photo of Eddy's mother from her scattered family. Who'd made sure to tell Eddy every good thing about his parents— thin pickings, disconnected little stories that lived in Eddy's head with *The Tawny Scrawny Lion* and *The Party Pig*, and other titles in the fantasyland of Brain's Little Golden Books series (complete). His parents were hazy outlines, utterly remote, like the po-faced and overdressed Smallbones and Duncans in Doris's old photo albums.

"This is my favorite," said Eddy. He turned up the volume.

"I know this," said Sue. "Something, something Jerusalem. But not this version."

"The Weavers, probably," said Eddy. "This is way better. All nasal and desperate."

They were on Blenheim Road, the city skyline coming into view, the host of rearing cranes glinting in the late sun. They began to sing with Odetta, it was irresistible, and Eddy remembered the last time he'd sung it with Toss More, both of them transported, slamming their instruments, strained necks and great bellowings, *"My God, there were thirty-three souls on the water . . . swimming and praying to the good Lord, God, Run come see,"* thump thump *pah*, thump thump *pah*.

23

By the time Eddy had hauled the tree into Sue's living room and filled a bucket with water and two bricks, the sun was falling behind the trees on Sue's fence line. He tied string around the body of the pine and hitched it to the hook he'd previously screwed into the window frame.

"You could work for Hire-a-Hubby," said Sue. "Or some similar outfit whose name wasn't noxiously sexist." She was slicing ham; she could stand at the bench now, prepare food.

"Is your uncle a handyman?"

"Not so much," said Eddy. An understatement. Brain was puzzled by any tool not a garden trowel or a hand beater.

"I had a builder's apron when I was little, though. From my godmother. With miniature tools." The *pleasure* in that apron, its pockets, the hammer and wrench, their feel in his hands. The outfit was somewhere in the attic now, stored carefully, possibly even cataloged. Brain had preserved in metaphoric amber all the hardware of Eddy's childhood: his miniature cars, his miniature kitchen, the cardboard-carton washing machine with felt-pen dials and buttons, the puzzles, artwork, soft toys and dolls, his Superman cape and his tutus: Brain's parenting had been scrupulously nongendered.

"My father was good with his hands—could knock up shelving, build a fence." Wield a syringe. Dig a grave. "He had a job as a sexton for a while, started a carpentry apprenticeship, worked on building sites."

They ate at the small kitchen table. Mother, released from his exile in the garden shed and apparently contrite, sat sedately on the bench, taking a Nutri-Berry Bit in his claw at intervals, pecking the pieces apart.

"*Use a little wine for thy stomach's sake,*" said Eddy, watching Sue pour a glassful.

"Don't you quote St. Paul to me," she said. "It's for pleasure anyway, not stomach."

"Slipped out," said Eddy. It was the inevitable quote from Ginge, Bridgie, or the Modern Priest whenever they contemplated a fresh bottle of wine.

"Who fed you St. Paul?" said Sue, taking a little wine for pleasure's sake, looking at him over the rim of her glass. "Your uncle?"

"Nah. He was just *there*. RE class. Same Epistles every year at Mass. Eventually, they're all there inside you, storming and finger-wagging, raving about docile obedience to the spirit of God. Not that anyone takes any notice. Or hardly any."

"Those old patriarchs," said Sue. "Carbuncles on the Christian life. I kicked them out years ago."

"Lucky you. Ka pai," said Eddy. It sounded curt. He was thinking of Toss More and his yammering about the Spiritual Athlete: *I discipline my body and make it my slave.* The ham on his plate shone pink and sweaty. He put his fork down, no longer hungry.

Sue said nothing.

He could smell the damp, the human musk of Toss More's sleep-out, the lingering aroma of cooked oats, puréed porridge apparently the only food Toss could stomach. And the view out the window from Toss's bed. He sat there often, beside Toss, fiddling on the old chord harmonica they'd bought on Trade Me. They made their way through the *Fireside Book of Folk Songs*: "Wayfaring Stranger," "Nobody Knows," et al., Toss singing with such dolorous tremolo that things fell apart sometimes with their laughing.

Out the window was the Mores' Mediterranean garden, fig trees, and a tunnel house full of exotics. In winter, the figs' bare branches made creature-like sculptures against the gray skies. The garden was tended by a landscaping student, whom Toss, with his usual pitiless accuracy, had dubbed The Garden Gnome, on account of his short stature and unconvincing beard; they waved at the Gnome satirically whenever he plodded past the window. But how did you explain Toss to the uninitiated?

"An Advent wish?" said Sue. She clinked Eddy's glass.

The advent of what exactly? brooded Eddy. What *was* coming down the line? Additions or subtractions? Oodles more doodles? More pinching losses? More boos! The thought of a new year and its unknown quantity could sometimes make him nauseous.

"May she bless the house of David. And all the others, too." She smiled at him.

"She?"

"*So truly God is our mother:* Julian of Norwich."

"Hmmm," said Eddy.

"Just saying."

He laughed. *Our mother who art in heaven.* True in his case. Unless she was in the other place. Neither of which he believed in.

"So tell me about your tattoo," said Sue, coming at him in her slant way. "I've been longing to ask, and now my restraint has been loosened by using a little wine."

What the hell, thought Eddy. He used a lot of wine in one gulp.

"There's backstory," he said. He wanted to tell it. If you must do it . . .

"Once upon a time?" said Sue.

24

Delphine had asked him about the tattoo, of course. She grabbed his arm one day, held it tight, and stumbled through the quote, leaning over him, shifting slowly from shoulder to wrist. She challenged each word like some scholar poring over a Talmud tractate.

"*Wo-ey*—what is *wo-ey*?"

"It's *woe*," said Eddy, amazed at the strength of her grip, his willingness to allow it. "Heartache. Suffering. Great sorrow. Tribulation. You know, *Wednesday's child is full of woe.*"

"Who's Wednesday's child?"

"Someone who was fully miserable."

"*In*-to. Your tattooer can't spell."

"Tattooist. Yes, he can. It's *unto*—an old way of saying *to*. Like taketh instead of take, and goeth instead of go."

Delphine gave him one of her skeptical dowager looks.

"It's from the Bible—they say taketh and goeth and unto there all the time."

"The Bible's not a *place*, it's a book. A book for the balmy, Dad says."

Eddy had long since decided Simon the Dad was a rat and a tosspot. He thought of him as Slimon.

"What are *scribs*?" She breathed moistly into the crook of his elbow.

"*Scribes.* Writers. And the Pharisees were a Jewish sect in the time of Jesus.

"A sect is a group," he added, heading off the inevitable.

"*Hypocrites!* That's on our spelling list." And on and on.

"But what does it really *mean*?" she said finally. She looked at him in her oblique way, earnest and unblinking.

"Matthew twenty-three, eh?" said Rhys the tattooist, when Eddy had shown him the quote. "The old whited sepulchres. Turns my bowels to water."

Rhys had done his time in churches and Bible classes. He had a line from the Song of Songs circling his left nipple, *Let him kiss me with the kisses of his mouth . . .* But he was all for a fired-up Jesus, too, he said. Thundering in the Temple. Giving it to the man.

"*For ye are like unto whited sepul*cars," intoned Delphine now whenever she was annoyed with Eddy or Jasper or her mother.

Josie wasn't bothered. "Whatever floats your boat," she told Eddy. He was enlarging Delphine's vocabulary, at least.

"I went mad," Eddy told Sue Lombardo. "It was after the *Murder in the Cathedral* ding-dong."

He'd given her an edited version of the ding-dong one afternoon while she sat in the sun and he weeded the vegetable garden. Viewed from the distance of two years and the fragrant setting of a spring garden, sun on your back, soil warm under your fingers, the cancellation of *Murder in the Cathedral* seemed almost funny.

"How mad?" said Sue.

They were still at the table in the low-wattage light. Sue straight-backed, Puss in her lap.

"Moderately bonkers."

The Venerable had ruled the play impossible without adult direction, deaf to their arguments for a student-led production. And the Modern Priest would not be mollified. He could not work with such brats, he said, after his walkout. They were foul-mouthed and disrespectful. Disputatious. Unchristian. Full of bile. The Venerable had quoted him in full.

"So how about you get off your high horses and apologize?" suggested The Venerable. He was losing patience.

"Depends," said Boo.

"No chance," said Eddy, his eyes fixed on *How to Win Friends and Influence People*.

They'd had their own sharp disputation after that, Boo wanting an eye on the main goal, Eddy maddened beyond reason, seized now by a cold truculence toward the Modern Priest, The Venerable, religious schooling, a treacherous church, and everything else.

"Well," said Brain, when Eddy reported the impasse. Long silence. "Should you take an adamantine position, Ed?"

This had further enraged Eddy. "Go ask your pious pal!" he shouted. "Go on! Go on!" But Brain would not interpose himself between Eddy and the Modern Priest.

So the production was off, the Modern Priest disappeared from the Drama room, and Eddy seethed in Toss's sleep-out, not speaking to Boo and obsessing about the untenable hypocrisy of his private belief (no God) and his daily lived experience (religious school). Toss was briefly regretful about the play but largely uninterested in Eddy's crisis. He had moved on, he said, wanting only to decide a new name for their current band lineup. They had a list of possibilities, found-titles from the women's choruses in *Murder in the Cathedral*. Toss tolled through them like a demented cantor.

"*Does the Bird Sing?*" he warbled. Stage whisper: "*Does he what.*"

"The Death. Of. The. Old." He lolled against the bottom bed board, accompanying the dirge with dissonant guitar chords.

"Star-ved *Crow."*

"Give it a break, Toss."

"Bitter Spring. Empty Harvest." Here, some tuneless slap-strums.

"Shut up, you fuckwit. I'm dying here."

"The Death-Bringers."

"Very funny."

"Mouse. And Jerboa."

"For fuck's sake!"

"The Laugh of the Loon."

A silence while Toss gazed up appealingly at Eddy, who was perched on the end of the bed. Toss dropped his arm, apparently in resignation, and Eddy opened his mouth to speak.

"Incense in the Latrine!" screamed Toss in a piercing alto. *"The* Hor-*ror of the Ape."*

Eddy had left then, flinging the door behind him, cursing Toss for the selfish shit he was. He'd lain in his restless bed, hating everyone, even Boo.

"But that's a different story," he said at Sue Lombardo's kitchen table.

"Digressions are good," said Sue. "More wine? You can have the spare bed."

He wasn't ready for that digression. He might never be ready. Sue's spare room though, that could be nice. He could doss down fully in this little asylum, instead of just visiting: cool sheets, Puss on the other pillow, the circle of postcards on the white wall. He visited the room sometimes to stare at the postcards, ecclesiastical art from great cathedrals, gathered on Sue's travels. There was one of a bronze statue, the woman's flinty face and hooded eyes reminding Eddy of Sue; she strode purposefully, away from the cathedral, a bony knee kicking up her tunic . . .

"The madness was the next bit," said Eddy.

He had woken in the middle of the night, a perfectly formed idea arrived, a lifeline through his stormy feelings. Beside the bed, Marley shifted, whimpering softly. A dream. Chasing rabbits. Or Possum Meaty Bites. Eddy leaned down and stroked the top of her head, the bumpy topography soothing under his fingers.

The idea was a little grenade. He would lob it into the middle of school. Bang. It needed only the smallest amount of accompanying hardware. He had lain back on his pillow and consulted the plaster medallions and rosettes on his ceiling. Yes.

The next morning he found the two pink and purple row tally counters in the kitchen drawer, repository for string, tape, rubber bands, appliance instructions, and the occasional inexplicable item that defeated Brain's categorizing rigor. Brain had bought the tally counters for Doris after her *Woman's Weekly* knitting row counter—*free* in 1981!— had given up the ghost. But she hadn't liked them. How pleasing then that the counters could now be deployed in a research exercise that would surely get Doris frothing.

"It was ridiculous," said Eddy in Sue's kitchen, though his old idiot self walked the school grounds at lunchtime, tally counters in each hand, suborning (Brain word!) as many Year 10s, 11s, and 12s as possible for his ten-second survey. A sample of two hundred would do it, he reckoned. A third of the school. Simple yes/no, he told them all. Anonymity guaranteed. Not a single student demurred (BRAIN WORD). They didn't care. No one cared, he thought, fully aggrieved at the charade they were all cheerfully enacting. They just wanted to get on with stuffing food down their dinner holes or talking shit; they thought it was funny—Eddy Smallbone and his old lady tally counters, purple for yes, pink for no, *click, click, click, click* . . .

"One hundred and thirty noes, forty-five yeses, a bunch of don't knows that didn't count," said Eddy.

He pinged the side of the wineglass with his middle fingernail and it sang into the dimness.

"Allowing for a two percent margin of error—kids having an off day, lying for the fun of it, et cetera, still around seventy-five percent didn't believe in God. Bingo. Take that. Amen."

After a moment, Sue Lombardo said, "Are the knitting tally counters really true?"

"Affirmative." He sighed. "And worse, you know why purple was the yes counter? The ecclesiastical color. It felt ordained!" He remembered staring at the spools in each hand, his relish at the purple's aptness. Bonkers.

Mother had paused in his Nutri-Berry dissections, his head cocked. Sometimes it seemed as if he were genuinely absorbed by the adjacent conversation.

"What did you do with your findings?"

Eddy groaned. "Wrote them up in an 'open letter.' Sent it to the Modern Priest, cc'd The Venerable and the Board of Trustees. Posted it on the school intranet. Boom. Crash. Run for cover."

"Holy Mary," said Sue. "That'd do it."

Boo

Zirkus Berserkus. What a folly. There was an almighty furor: dismay, displeasure, disappointment. Scholarship student, promising future. Mocking the school's special character, bringing it into disrepute. Was he disturbed? Malicious? Acting out? "He's a goneburger," said Viv. And everyone else. Except Uncle Bede, who saw it for what it was: some weird fight to the death with the Modern Priest. A storm in an existential teacup. He stood Eddy down for two days to have a think. Eddy gave it two minutes and opted to leave. Auf Wiedersehen. To the school. And to me, as it turned out.

This was all mixed up with our terminal phase. It had all gone bad. We couldn't get back to our old selves, our old meshed self. I cried every morning and afternoon on my bike that month, winding through the wintry suburbs from Viv's to school and back again. No more easy time with that made-up family, uncle-father and nephew-son. Bold Bridgie and goofy Ginge. I even missed the slippery Chris Mangan who, *to be fair*, could be pretty funny sometimes. And no more time with Eddy, nights in his bed, in mine, in babysitting beds and party beds; sometimes, desperate, in the library storeroom after school. I cried every night in my room as well, sick about it all, wanting Eddy terribly. Wanting to set fire to him, too, for his stubbornness over the Modern Priest, for writing that stupid open letter. And all the rest.

A week after Eddy left school, I woke early. It was Saturday. I stood at the bedroom window, looking out on the bedraggled garden, and decided I must go round to Bishop Street, beard the lion, try to fix things.

I biked very fast so I wouldn't change my mind. Streets, people, trees, signs, cars, all streaking by. The swiftness made me almost hopeful. I raced up the drive, flung the bike down, and ran up the steps to the back door.

But Eddy was gone. He'd exiled himself yet again to Toss More's sleep-out, and Brain was comfort baking: Anzac biscuits. I stood at the bench with him and balled up the mix, flattened each ball on the baking tray with a knuckled fist and the sickest heart. Marley watched us from the corner of the dining room couch. I cried. After a while, Marley unfolded herself from the couch and padded over, leaned into my legs, giving doggy comfort with her big warm flank.

Later, I huddled beside the wood burner, brooding on the hearthrug pattern. Brain thought aloud. About Eddy's next move. Job possibilities. About Toss More: a demanding friend, but a bit thrilling.

"Familiar to me," said Brain, and neither of us mentioned Vincent Smallbone, fetching and doomed. I buried my nose in Marley's fur and she smelled like Eddy, so I cried all over again, and Brain pushed a big blue-and-white polka-dot hankie into my hand. Which I still have.

I left before it was dark. Bitter cold, the air dank and catching in the throat. Brain would tidy his CD collection and listen to Gregorian chants. Reliable panaceas.

"Stay in touch," he said. He meant it.

He stood with Marley at the bottom of the drive and watched me pedaling west and out of sight. But we knew it was over. It was like going into a grave, everyone else above earth, forever out of reach.

25

Eddy held his arm out across the kitchen table for Sue: two lines from shoulder to wrist. Bodoni 72.

"Like a headstone epitaph," said Boo when she first saw it at the vet's. Eddy, dazed, had rolled up his sleeve at her request. "A keeper," she pronounced. "It'll never date." Just as well. He'd never be able to afford removal.

Toss More had approved of the tattoo but was more interested in Eddy's pain levels during the procedure.

"Completely bearable," Eddy said.

"Imprecise," said Toss. "One-to-ten spectrum, ten: passing out."

But Eddy refused to play. Toss's love affair with pain, gathering steam all the while, made him sick to his stomach.

The tattoo session had lasted four hours, and by Eddy's measure was about as discomforting as a bandage being removed continuously from sensitive skin. Or a rubber band pinging against your flesh, a description he'd read somewhere. The weirdest thing was the body vibration from the coil machine.

"Mostly it was restful," he told Sue Lombardo. "Like being on a plane. Outside the space-time continuum."

He'd listened to Mary Gautier—*sinking in pain*, hmmm—and to Rhys's tales of tattoo parlors down the old High Street before it was gentrified. He was three weeks into his building job and had blown the bank balance built slowly from his old dishy job and summer work in Ginge's garden. It was worth it. A salve, a *vent* for his righteous indignation, the last words in the whole sorry episode. No doubt whatever.

"So interesting that you found biblical words to rail against religion," said Sue. She sounded genuinely intrigued. Eddy shrugged. Of course this exquisite irony had been pointed out by Toss, Ginge, and Bridgie. *Blah.*

"What did your uncle say?"

"He admired the craftsmanship. Worried about infection. Wanted to know why I used the King James version."

"I like the sound of your uncle," said Sue.

"Asked me not to be egregiously provocative with the Modern Priest. His very words, btw."

Six months later the Modern Priest had been charged with theft as a servant, and the tattoo had seemed prophetic: *Woe unto you, scribes and Pharisees, hypocrites! For ye are like unto whited sepulchres, which indeed appear beautiful outward, but are within full of dead men's bones, and of all uncleanness.*

Eddy had worn sleeves around the house all the same, to placate Brain. Plus, it was raw winter.

"I can think of worse quotes to go through life with," said Sue. "It's bracing. A stiff reminder about institutions. And the men who run them." She stood carefully and stacked the plates, carried them to the bench, and ran the tap.

"Fuck off!" said Mother, offended by pinging spray.

"And just when I thought you'd turned a corner," said Sue. The bird flew over to Eddy and settled on his shoulder.

"Making nice, eh?" said Eddy. Mother was so capricious in his affections, you could only feel flattered when he bestowed a shoulder visit. Like Delphine, Eddy thought. She played them all off, one against the other—Josie, Jasper, and himself. Slimon and breastless Claudia, no doubt. You had to be up for her at all times, no slouching around or quiet moments. She drove through your mental soundtrack like a big rig. He at least could go home at the end of the day. Who'd be a parent? Yet, there he was, daily more and more in loco parentis. What the hell? His life had splayed sideways like a spasming limb.

"Hey, Sue," he said, remembering. "Mother's new favorite song." He began to hum, and within seconds the bird started up his inner thrum, moving closer into Eddy's neck, nestling.

"*Swing low, sweet cha-ri-oh-ot,*" sang Eddy, and Mother accompanied him with rising squawks. "*Coming for to carry me hoooooooome.*" The bird's distinctive smell seemed to increase as his sounds crescendoed.

"He smells like the cupboard in Gran's hallway," Delphine had said. "Where the vacuum cleaner lives."

"Dust," said Jasper, his face in Mother's feathers, listening while Eddy taught Delphine "Swing Low," having her repeat the lines over and over after him. She had a quick ear and a startling, clear voice. She could hold a melody line when he harmonized with her. They sang three verses and a chorus to Jasper and Mother. Jasper laid his head back against the sofa and closed his eyes. Eddy, watching his stillness and transport, had felt a great and dangerous storm of sorrow rise up from somewhere. But Mother began cawing ecstatically in the second verse and saved him.

Now Sue clapped for Mother and Eddy's recital and offered Eddy the spare bed once again, but he had the Rhode Island Reds first thing in the morning. He packed Mother into his travel cage and strapped the cage into the back seat of the Merc. The bird spent more and more nights at Bishop Street now, a win-win-win, as it turned out: Sue was greatly relieved. Brain enjoyed Mother's ornery personality and the regular splendor of the flaring head feathers. Now Mother said "Stand by!" like Captain Flint in *Treasure Island*. And somehow, the gap Marley's absence had opened between Eddy and Brain became a little less cavernous. An animal, any animal, it seemed, was essential to their relationship.

Eddy knew what was likely now. Eventually, Mother would not return to Sue Lombardo's at all. He would be absorbed into Bishop Street life, like the stray or injured or abandoned creatures in the past: cats, birds, reptiles, insects—all named and all offering Brain the opportunity for a zoology lesson. Sophie, the seven-legged vagrant spider (*Uliodon frenatus*). John, the broken-winged song thrush (*Turdus philomelos*). Number 32's cat, Butcher, renamed Poti, who moved in unasked (*Felis catus*) . . . All gone to God, as Brain liked to say; he believed absolutely in an animal afterlife. And now, Mother might bind them together in pet devotion once again. On and on went the world, thought Eddy, swirling and determined, rearranging itself around his semi-baffled self.

"Today was a tonic," said Sue. "Thank you." She stood beside the car, holding Puss, contemplating Eddy in the driver's seat. The night air was warm; lemon scent from the tarata by the garage drifted into the car.

"Good times," said Eddy.

"Sleep well, my friend."

He drove to Viv O'Brien's and Boo was waiting for him in front of the bottlebrush, *Callistemon myrtaceae*. She'd texted him as he secured

Mother in the back seat, and he had made himself drive a sedate 45 km across the city, though his body went ahead of the car, fully woken and heated up, wholly careless of early morning Rhode Island Reds. The unexpected text as aphrodisiac? Argue for. One thousand words. No problem.

26

Eddy had been at a loss as to how he should explain Boo's sudden reappearance to Brain. Except parodically. As book titles, for instance. *Boo Returns! Comeback Boo!*

Bonobo Redux, he heard Toss More say, disgusted. *A Cautionary Tale.* Two years ago, Toss had been unblushingly gleeful at the end of Eddy and Boo's relationship.

"Good," he said. "Now I have your complete attention."

This was so outrageous that Eddy had felt the ghost of a laugh stir—a great relief since he'd believed he would never laugh again. He'd spent a week in Toss's sleep-out mostly lying on the spare mattress beside the terrapins' tank, his face stony. Body leaden, as they said in books. He studied the terrapins as never before, their brocaded feet and spiny claws, the red stripes of their outer ears, losing color now as they aged. He'd always thought the turtles had a look of Loretta Peatling—weary eyes and wide, downturned mouths—but this was no longer funny, just a depressing fact. He gazed at the whorls and hieroglyphs on their shells and wished earnestly that he, too, had a hard carapace into which he could retract for months, safe in the dark.

While Toss was at school—suddenly he was taking scholarship seriously—Eddy oversaw the terrapins' winter sun routine; he was capable only of this kind of undemanding task. He switched the lamp on at regular intervals and played ever more plangent songs on the harmonica, curious to see if the music would lure the pair onto the basking platform. He dozed, though this only brought on the fitful, disturbing dreams of daytime, so he read *The Day of the Bomb,* Toss's favorite childhood book. It was about destruction and death, very fitting.

Finally, dragging himself home, he announced a moratorium on the subject of Boo, but Brain came back at him with rare firmness. "You should talk about it," he said. "You must. It's important."

What would you know? thought Eddy. Brain had been single all his life.

"Yup," said Bridgie, during one of their many and fruitful post-piano-lesson confidences. "Brain skipped right over Eros, went straight to parenthood."

Bridgie, on the other hand, had favored the reverse. No children (*except you, of course, George*) but plenty of bedmates. Mostly female; the occasional collision with a breastless chest, preferably hairless.

"What about Ginge?" Eddy had inquired. He was thirteen at the time, greatly stirred, and puzzled now by Brain's and Ginge's apparently chaste histories. Ginge had once had a girlfriend, apparently, but she had shredded his tender heart, and after that, he'd channeled his affections toward *Felis catus* and the great collective of workers.

And the Modern Priest? Eddy did not ask. Once, years ago, on a hot Christmas evening, he'd seen Bridgie and the Modern Priest kissing drunkenly beneath the wattle tree. This had been confusing on a number of levels, so he had pushed it to the back of his mind. "Who will ever know about Cristoforo?" Bridgie had mused, as if Eddy had spoken aloud.

"How do you feel?" asked Brain in the living room, rain hammering the windows.

How *did* he feel in the new barren, Boo-less landscape? Nothing.

Or nothing profound. Nichts. Possibly he felt hungry, and definitely he felt irritable. With Brain. But Brain breathed kindliness and a patience that some detached morsel of Eddy knew he should be grateful for. He could not rebuff Brain. Or not immediately. They sat in the living room and stared into the wood burner. The flames stretched and fell. Marley settled herself over Eddy's shoeless feet. She could read a room. Brain cleared his throat, the Brain-invariable, four soft hacks: huh-huh-huh-*huh*. Beethoven's Fifth.

"Guilty," said Eddy quickly, wanting it done. "Fucked off. Lifeless."

"Yes," said Brain. Then looked at him sharply. "You don't—"

"*No*," said Eddy. "Not that. Just like a wet log. Weighed down."

"Yes," said Brain.

Perhaps they could talk about Boo without actually mentioning her.

"Is it partly about leaving school?" Brain asked.

"No," said Eddy. It really wasn't.

"A job might help."

"Yes." His feet were getting pins and needles from Marley's weight.

"Any ideas?" said Brain.

"Yes." They seemed to have swapped conversational positions.

More wood-burner staring. Eddy tried to slip his right foot out from under Marley, but she gave him a reproachful eye. He was stuck. A metaphor! Couldn't go back, nervous about going forward. He sneaked a look at Brain and felt an unexpected prickle of love, for his solid self, his never-nagging, the politeness of his Beethovenian throat-clearing.

"We'll all miss her very much," said Brain to the wood burner, and Eddy had begun to cry.

But now, an abrupt scene shift! Someone has pulled a new back-drop across the stage. Fast-forward. The years between dissolve. Winter is banished. It is late spring and the kōtukutuku and bleeding-heart flower along the fence line! Long faces give way to merry ones. Our lovers are reunited, locked once again in wordless passion. And Great Uncle Bulgaria, the oldest and wisest Womble of them all, will be—well-pleased? Jocose? Relieved?

In the end, Eddy came out with it suddenly over dinner one night. Asparagus risotto. Brain apologizing for Tetra Pak chicken stock. And was it too sweet with peas? Perhaps more lemon juice? Was the mint right?

Dinner autopsies made Eddy crazy, but six weeks into Boo's return, he felt almost affectionate toward Brain's dufferish tics.

"Call me childish," he said, "but I like a pea. Nice and mealy. The mint's okay. An echo of roast lamb. Two comfort foods in one!"

Brain looked startled, as if he should take Eddy's temperature. It was the jolliest thing Eddy had said in months. It sounded peculiar even to him.

"How are the *cuniculi*?" said Brain eventually. The most recent addi-tions to Eddy's portfolio were three Mini Lop rabbits. They were a handful in every sense.

"I should get danger money," Eddy said.

The bunnies were cute but also feckless home-wreckers. They had the run of an extensive living space while their owners were away for a month in northern Germany. Half of Eddy's work was vacuuming up their shit and spraying expensive room atomizer. The other half was locating the little beasts—they hid themselves most deviously—then giving them sufficient love for the next twenty-four hours.

"Hey," Eddy blurted to Brain. He scraped up the last of his risotto. On reflection, the mint was odd. "Something's happened."

Brain paused, fork stalled. "So long since I heard that."

Something's happened, Eddy had said when he was four and his sword flourishes in Doris's living room had knocked a ceramic jug from a side table. He'd hidden the broken pieces under bunched newspaper in the fire grate, but that night the deceit had nibbled at his sleep. He'd gone out to Brain, reading in the living room lamplight, and stood beside him, waiting for courage.

"Hello," said Brain, his eyes like blowflies behind his reading glasses. "Everything all right?"

Something's happened! Something's happened! An umbrella term for the dreadful and delightful, until he was eleven and the phrase was suddenly ludicrous. But here it was again, briefly helpful. Brain's face responded accordingly, a slight brow widening—anxiety, hopefulness—then a swift collecting of his features, ready for whatever was coming.

"Boo's back in town," said Eddy, and the wonder and uncertainty of it fell on him all over again. "She was at Friendly Vet. Crazy coincidence. I was waiting for the right time to tell you."

Brain wasn't taking it in. He put his fork down. Come again? said his face.

"Boo," said Eddy. "The redoubtable Roberta." A Brain phrase. Spoken with great approval. "We're—" But what were they? A thing? An item? Fuck buddies? He didn't know. "We've been hanging out."

"Boo," said Brain, like a sigh.

27

"Mr. K," said Boo into Eddy's back. They had settled quickly into their old spooning. The warmth of Boo's skin on his. The little tickling gusts on his back when she spoke. Her arm over his stomach, hand tucked under his waist. He was drifting off.

"Hmmm."

"You hear that?"

"Huh?"

"Morepork?"

"Mmmm."

"Is it the same one?"

"Prob'ly."

"Hear that?"

"Mmmm."

Ru-ru. One. Two. Three. *Ru-ru.*

"Nesting season," said Eddy, surfacing marginally. It would be the same one. Or two. In the big oak, two streets over. The owners cultivated the birds, left honeyed crumbs. But the birdcalls belonged to the whole neighborhood; they slipped through your open window on the night air.

"Old Ruru," he said. It was a plaintive call, stabbing at you.

"Ms. Ruru."

"She's on the eggs."

"Watchful guardian," said Boo.

Ru-ru.

Ru-ru.

He drifted off again.

Boo

I stayed awake, waiting for each wistful *ru-ru*, thinking about how those birds mated for life. Thinking how perfectly Eddy's naked bottom tucked into my lying-down lap. Thinking how good it was to be back in Eddy's bedroom, the smell of his pillows, Marley's old mat still beside the bed, the scent of night stock coming through the window with the *ru-ru*s. Ms. Ruru on her eggs. Only one of them would hatch. The others, apparently, were usually eaten.

DE
CEM
BER

Second Week of Advent

28

Eddy went down to a single New World shift. Sunday afternoon. Almost adieu. Judith was not happy. Her manager badge shouted at Eddy in block capitals.

"You can't just come and go for other part-time work," she said. She wouldn't look at him, stared determinedly at her screen, at the vexing roster app. "It's the worst time of year."

"I'm mostly just going," said Eddy. Reasonably, he thought. "And the other work's an actual entire job."

"Pet minding isn't a job," said Judith. Her earrings rattled.

Peevish and excitable, thought Eddy. A Mary Poppins line.

"A lot of pets out there," he said. "And people going away."

People like you, he wanted to say. Going to their seaside piles or skiing in Aspen and the Dolomites, wanting their moggies and chooks and dogs and guinea pigs fed and patted, their birds' cages cleaned, their aquarium water refreshed. Oh, and would you mind collecting the mail and putting out the trash bins on Wednesdays?

"What's wrong with kennels and catteries?" said Judith. "Where's your *loyalty*, Eddy? This is our busiest time, now till Christmas Eve."

"Yes, I'm sorry." He wasn't.

"Well," said Judith, "it's not convenient. And it's not fair."

Eddy boggled. Astonishingly, this was an exact quote from *A Christmas Carol*. Spoken uncannily like Laurence Olivier. *It's notttt convenient, and it's notttt fair.* What were the odds?

"It's not fair on me," continued Judith, blind to the boggling. "Training new people right now. Enough idiot students to deal with. I'm fed up. And what on earth are you doing with your life, Eddy? Wasting yourself feeding pets and babysitting? Aren't you supposed to have a big brain?"

"I like animals," said Eddy. "And it's not babysitting; it's nannying." This would annoy her.

"It's a dead end is what it is."

Judith did not deserve her New World family, thought Eddy, walking downstairs. She was awful. Bigoted and smug. He felt childishly like stealing something, something expensive. Mānuka honey. Or pine nuts. Or a French wine. At least he wouldn't see her anymore. She didn't work Sundays. She went to church and distributed Communion with a sanctimonious face. Then she dragooned her six grown kids and their several spouses around the table for a stupefying Sunday lunch. "Family time is so precious," she had told him—duffer-uncled Orphan Eddy— the one and only time he attended. It was summer and his tattoo had beamed at the gathered family as they all linked hands for grace.

But he did not swipe any comestibles (Brain word). The shame of once stealing a Perky Nana bar lingered down the years. "Could you *be* more snivelingly law-abiding?" Toss had asked. Well, no. Shoplifting was not for him. You needed to be actually in need, or get off on the danger, the cat-and-mouse with the cameras, the lurking security guard. He didn't have the bottle, as Ginge would say. He'd witnessed enough adrenaline junkies, though, at work in the New World aisles: Toss, of course, and kids after school, hungry and reckless; also west-side ladies in expensive leisure gear. They could vanish items with the fluency of a conjurer.

Instead, he bought a baguette and milk, and bacon so he could see Shamura. He retained some small love for her, despite Boo. This wasn't disloyal, surely? An exchange with Shamura was a passing pleasure, a shaft of sun in the sometimes dull daily round. Everyone needed those. Once, driving to Greymouth with Brain, the road opening out, and the old companionability there between them, Eddy had asked him about the sun shafts in his own days.

"*Morning Report* birdcall," said Brain immediately. "Port Hills in summer, tawny like the lion. Wednesday cheese scone and theological chat with Charlie. The theme to *Midsomer Murders*. The heliotrope perfume at the back gate. Home trousers after work."

A man of simple pleasures, thought Eddy. But his own list wasn't so wild: Shamura. The once-upon-a-time pork bun from the Arts Centre market, RIP. The opening beats of *The Sopranos!* Fresh bedsheets. Virginia creeper in autumn, all over Loretta's fence. The smell of new tennis balls. Toss singing "Annie Laurie" . . .

The baguette and bacon were for Delphine and Jasper's dinner. Also Rhode Island Red eggs. He had promised them French toast. Again. A kid's dinner. No vegetables this time, but what the hell. Josie was wining and dining investment clients. Eddy would pick up Boo from Knit World, which meant a complicated route around the entombed city center, by way of Arbuckle, whom he'd neglected for three days. So much going on. It was hot, so there would be a fly or two crawling up and down Justin's kitchen windows. There was a nifty bug catcher, and trapping the flies was *fun*. Ditto, releasing them live into the tank and watching the frog, suddenly alert, clocking his prey. Not at all like watching a cat play a mouse, that peaky mix of admiration and regret; Arbuckle's patience and deadly eye were fully enjoyable. Who could love a fly? *Musca domestica.* Other than a frog. Was he an animal bigot? A species-ist? Brain would not admit to animal preferences. They were all God's creatures, all wondrous, all necessary. Nonetheless, over the years Eddy had constructed a private hierarchy: mammals and birds, first equal; second, amphibians and reptiles; third, insects, except for spiders and butterflies, which, like a benevolent tyrant, he had scooped up and placed arbitrarily beside mammals and birds. Conversely, rats had been banished from mammal-dom to a Siberia beneath insects, along with cockroaches and flies. Brain's view of creation was too saintly by far.

At Justin's, Eddy lounged in the reading chair, watching Arbuckle, who watched his dinner dart and bump around the tank. He checked off his animal charges, the two-legged and four-legged, the cold- and warm-blooded. There was a more or less permanent rotation and health-status bulletin shuttling through his head.

Sue Lombardo now walked without crutches and, at this moment, was facilitating an Advent retreat: "Reflections on the Magnificat as a Feminist Text." Open to all. Even atheists? "Sure," said Sue. "The words are for everyone." Mother was at the Mulhollands'. He had stayed overnight in Jasper's room, and his behavior had been exemplary. The kid was a bird whisperer, though he seldom moved his lips.

Bunny the chipoo's folks had returned from their Australian jaunt. Adieu, Bunny, you joke of a dog. He'd walked Walter this morning after the Rhode Island Reds, and hung for thirty minutes with the Mini Lops, or Flopsy, Mopsy, and Cottonbud, as Boo had renamed them. He'd visited the vets Fat Bob and Thin Tim for supplies: more litter for the Lops; Iams Proactive Health and Hairball Care for the two Manx longhairs, petted princelings whose owner, Yvette, was rehabilitating in elder care following a stroke; and a bell collar for Agent Cooper, his favorite cat charge, a tabby who'd developed a taste for late-spring fledglings newly tipped from the nest. He had a separate bank account now for these kinds of expenses; he collected receipts. "Disbursements," said Brain.

"Whatever," said Eddy, but not unkindly.

Shame Boo's at work, he thought. She came with him sometimes to Phillipstown, to watch the Arbuckle show but also so they could make use of the bed in Justin's spare room. Eddy had drawn the line at Justin's own bed. He had also said no to Yvette's maidenly single with its candlewick bedspread, oddly reminiscent of Vincent's old room, which he had always avoided at Doris's, feeling it hung about with a jagged boyhood spirit.

In Justin's spare room, they threw back the covers and reconfigured themselves in the afternoon sun. Eddy shifted about trying to escape Boo's hair, which was always everywhere, over his face, in his mouth, up his nose.

"Christ almighty! There should be a law, some bed etiquette about hair. Mine's all tucked away."

"Whatever," said Boo sleepily. She turned into his back, and they made their question-mark cocoon.

No postcoital tristesse for him, Eddy had thought, heavy-lidded, complacent. Toss More had bewailed this affliction, every aspect of sex a disaster. But with Boo, Eddy felt only a blissed-out numbness, a good dream going on and on.

Lulled by this memory, he fell briefly asleep in the reading chair, then seconds later jerked awake, momentarily disoriented. Arbuckle was espaliered against the side of the tank, his throat pulsing mightily, the fly crashing around the top of the tank. It took a few misfires to land a froggy dinner.

Eddy sat at the piano and played "He Shall Feed His Flock." Only two more of his flock to feed today, ha. Three, counting Boo, though she wasn't part of his flock exactly. What was she again? What were *they*? He pictured the four of them together, another made-up family, at the expansive Mulholland dining table where dinner had almost never been eaten.

Time for Nut World.

29

At Knit World, Boo was deep in discussion with a customer. A tall guy wearing a suit, his cascade of hair held back by a scarlet knitted headband. He was absurdly handsome. "Tension squares *are* tedious," said Boo. "A must for a clothing project, though." Eddy loitered along the four-ply wall, puzzled. Tension squares? Something you sat in, hoping to calm yourself? He did recall that knitting *caused* tension: Doris, tetchy, pulling out needles, unspooling wool. A definition emerged from the brain-crypt: *the pulling force transmitted axially by the means of a string* . . . Of course. Wool had tension. Axial was a pleasing word. He took a ball of yarn from a cubbyhole and read the information on the band, understanding almost none of it, except for the yarn's color, which was pistachio. Also a pleasing word. Further investigation indicated a preponderance of food-related color terms: lemongrass, plum, tabasco. A couple of outliers: amethyst, petrol. Wtf? Petrol was colorless. But the dictionary app informed him that petrol was also *a shade of greenish or grayish blue*. Did Boo know this? Probably. There were whole subjects and lexicons that she knew and he did not. German. Sewing. Art history. Business (her folks were furniture retailers). Georgette Heyer. Also gaming, at which she was now accomplished, apparently. Some gaming boyfriend, Eddy had concluded.

From cotton yarns, Eddy watched Boo and her customer move balls of wool around the counter, debating color combinations. It was an odd feeling, observing Boo from a distance. Her familiar self blurred and ebbed, as if she were a small hologram, occupying a different time dimension, a brief visitor from a parallel universe. It was like that sometimes when they were together, too. The past and present nudged each other, meshing uneasily. Mid-conversation or a joke, things slid sideways and Eddy felt momentarily dislocated.

He shook himself and moved to the pattern table. *The Knitter's Handy Book of Sweater Patterns.* In his head, Toss More aped Brain: *A veritable cornucopia of color!* Could he, Eddy, wear an orange or purple jersey? Lime green? Almost certainly not. His wardrobe stayed determinedly in the narrow spectrum between black and gray, and no patterns please. Once, years ago, Bridgie had convinced him to buy a red shirt for a gig, but all night he had felt like someone else: a Beefeater or Garibaldi or raddled old Mick Jagger. Some*thing* else: a flag, a billboard. *Knitted Wild Animals. Projects have an adorable and humorous quality,* the back of the book assured him. *Will amuse children and adults alike.* He turned the pages, testing his amusement. Low. Knitting up wild animals instantly tamed them. They looked stupidly phlegmatic, like all soft toys. Beneath *Knitted Wild Animals* was *Knitted Fast Food.* Wtf?

And yet, a knitted slice of pizza with toasted crust, tomato base, mozzarella, and, incongruously, a gherkin was—how could this be?—compelling. Was it the ludicrousness of the mimicry? There was a book of knitted fruits and vegetables, too, and now he turned those pages with genuine interest. Strawberry: well-achieved, especially the stalk. Beetroot: clever enough, the red wool vein up the green leaf. Apple: pedestrian, though some marks for the dappled leaf. Garlic bulb: the unexpected winner! How *did* they get the voluptuous bulge of the individual cloves?

"Mr. K," said Boo, beside him. Suddenly. "You're smiling at knitted vegetables."

"Yes," said Eddy, closing the book. "But *to be fair*, that garlic bulb is freakishly accurate."

"Check this out," said Boo. She leafed through a Baby Knits folder. "We have to knit up samples—I'm doing this one. A classic. I had it as a baby, you probably did too. Cute, eh?"

Eddy considered the hooded jacket and the very plain baby. He could not look at Boo. "I did. Mine was brown, sort of flecked."

"Tweed," said Boo. "Super retro. Reappears every ten or so years."

The jacket had wooden Labrador buttons, he remembered. There were dozens of photos of him in it, hood up, hood down, on Brain's hip, on Bridgie's. Hoisted on Ginge's shoulders. Even on Doris's bony knee. He supposed it was wrapped up with mothballs in the attic now.

The jacket on the pattern was an unappealing yellow, the baby toothy and shiny-lipped, on the verge of a dribble. It looked eagerly at someone to the right, beyond the frame; it leaned forward, an arm half-raised, the tiny forefinger pointing crookedly.

30

At Josie's request, Eddy had moved in. A week or two or three, till Christmas if possible. Delphine's school finished early and her own work was amping up, she said; the market started to fly before Christmas.

"How come?" asked Eddy, being polite.

"No one really knows," said Josie. "Year-end bonuses increased consumer spending gain in stock performance general holiday spirit lighter volume due to holidays easier to move the market up . . ." It was another language.

"Whatever the reason," she said, in summary, "it's a real thing, globally: the Santa Rally. I'll be buried right up to Christmas Eve."

Santa, thought Eddy with distaste, then winced at this Brain-ish response. Father Christmas, please. No Americanisms. Brain did not look with favor on *cookies, candy, aluminum,* et al., and now apparently neither did Eddy. But Josie had lost him anyway at *gain in stock performance blah, blah lighter volume blah, blah, blah.* The words were recognizable, but the phrases detached themselves from meaning, floating off like dandelion particles. The one potent reality he could extract from Josie's world was that she made a shitload of coin. This enabled her to outsource most domestic obligations, including childcare. In three months, Eddy's presence in the Mulholland house had grown exponentially. He was staff, along with the cleaner and the gardener. With a plus-one. Boo stayed most nights, too. "No problem," said Josie. "Whatever you like. Whoever. Whenever." Perversely, Eddy found this airy unconcern slightly disturbing. For all Josie knew, he could be bringing Typhoid Mary.

"Just like the Bobbsey Twins," said Boo sleepily. "We're Dinah and Sam. Live-in help. Though not Black. Plus, you're the cook."

In Boo's grandmother's Hokitika spare bedroom, there were seventy-two Bobbsey Twins books, originally collected by *her* grand-mother, and Boo had read them all many times. For Year 13 English, she had written an essay titled "Race, Gender, and Class in the Bobbsey Twins" and argued, among much else, that Danny Rugg, the school bully, was the true embodiment of America in the stories, not the cherubic-faced, white-bread, mystery-solving double set of twins. Eddy had been mildly scandalized that Boo could write about crap children's books but impressed by her argument. His own essay had been on a short story—a *literary* story, he told himself—he'd first read when he was fourteen: "Batorsag and Szerelem." That story had slayed him, over and over. The Bobbsey Twins were junk and did not belong in the same enterprise.

"That essay," said Eddy, "it still burns."

They lay on the daybed in Yvette's sunroom. The Manx cats slept on their rag rug, oblivious to afternoon intimacies. Eddy leaned on his elbow and considered Boo, her face soft and blotched, hair spilled out around her head like a fragmenting pot mitt.

"A-plus, hmmm," said Boo. Eddy had gotten an A-minus, which somehow seemed like a C. Ms. Peck had written *A good effort*, and he had thought that the same could certainly not be said of Ms. Peck.

Boo studied the ceiling. Eddy lay down and studied it, too. There were cracks across the gib, earthquake souvenirs, and broken spiders' weavings, pendant and woolly, brown with dust. The Snorebins

Saturday afternoon carried on in the cul-de-sac. Kids shouting. The regular bounce of a football. A slow hand mower. Those inevitable suburban session musicians, the barking dogs.

The silence stretched out, and the ceiling began to seem sad, like Yvette's crumbling body and life. Eddy waited. He wanted Boo to speak, sure it must come. He had thoughtlessly opened the door on 2010, and now they were both thinking the same thing, he was certain, visiting the same time and place. First week of May. The far corner of the school library. Leaves rushing past the window. The smell of mince pies. Hockey sticks clacking outside. Boo's washed-out face, her steady voice and rational argument. His insides plummeting.

Through the glass doors, Yvette's mantel clock chimed 2 p.m. The nineteenth century speaking, Eddy thought, frock-coated and pontifical. It was a twin to Doris's mantel clock, Sunday afternoon's glum accompaniment in his childhood. The clock was an heirloom, Doris had often told him.

Beneath the sheet he found Boo's hand and curled his own around it. If only she would say something, finish off their old sad business.

But Boo shut her eyes, silent. Her hand inside his radiated heat.

He would say it, Eddy decided. He should. He must. But he said something else instead.

"You should be in charge of games."

You, said Toss More from far away, are a swingeing candy-ass.

Boo opened her eyes and looked at him. He couldn't read her expression.

"Games?"

The only games at the Mulhollands' had been The Game of Life and a pack of cards still inside their cellophane. Eddy had brought supplies from home and taught Delphine Last Card and Bananagrams. Jenga and Connect Four and Blokus were lined up and ready. Part of a proper education, he told Josie.

Boo looked at him still. Her hazel eyes seemed green today. A pulse banged at the back of Eddy's head.

"I look forward to rejoining the battle," she said finally. "I look forward to pulverizing you at Bananagrams." She clambered on top of him and nosed into his neck.

"I could surprise you," he said through all the hair, relieved and also disappointed. He had never beaten her at Bananagrams. He could not stop himself from fashioning Brain-type words—words like fashioning—and Boo whomped him every time with a barrage of three- and four-letter words.

"In your dreams."

"I have no respect for your victories," he said.

She bit his neck, and it was all on.

Boo

Well, fair enough. No respect? And talk about leading a horse to water. How much longer would he need, to find his big boy pants and pull them on?

Lucky for Eddy, I seemed to have discovered reservoirs of patience hitherto unplumbed.

Meanwhile, we were apparently going to play house.

31

By the end of Boo's first evening at the Mulhollands', Eddy had considerable respect for her victory over Delphine.

The child had been sitting on the front steps when they arrived, not welcome party so much as suspicious sentry. She said a toneless hello. Later, she sat at the kitchen island making loutish noises with a drink and a straw, occasionally giving a dead face to Boo, who sat over on the other side, casting stitches on metal needles. Eddy chopped broccoli and cauliflower, concerned about five-a-day. Thank you, Brain. A cruciferous entrée. With hummus.

"Wool is *horrible*," said Delphine. "It annoys my skin."

"With you there," said Eddy. "You need a cotton layer in between."

"It's actually cruel. To kids." She blew through the straw, not quite at Boo's ball of wool, a startling spot of color in the sea of gray marble and stainless steel.

"Kids wear layers," said Boo. "In winter."

"*Boo* to wool!" said Delphine. "*And* hummus. It looks like sick." She aimed her straw at the hummus bowl.

"No carrots in this though," said Eddy, moving the dish away. "Vomit always seems to have carrots, don't you reckon?" Delphine slid off the high stool and slouched from the kitchen, Rizzo skittering behind.

"Hmmm," said Eddy, offering Boo a piece of cauliflower and the hummus-sick.

"Was that the Kleinbein behavioral psychology in action?"

It was true his firm views seemed to have developed a lacuna when it came to Delphine. You had to be nimble and strategic, ignore stuff, hang out for what was important. "As with toddlers," said Boo. The O'Brien siblings were reproducing themselves at a speedy clip; she knew whereof she spoke.

At dinner, Delphine addressed herself ostentatiously to Eddy and Jasper. Jasper, on the other hand, had an actual conversation with Boo about the pros and cons of *Portal 2*. This pleased Eddy greatly but further maddened Delphine. She slumped in her chair, sullen, feeding Rizzo from a spoon, a practice Eddy had specifically forbidden. Cripes! The dynamics were a minefield. He felt prickly with parental anxiety, wanting both his charges to pass muster.

"Wanna help me?" he said to Delphine.

They stood, each in front of a pan, slotted spatulas in hand, watching the French toast bubble and spit. Delphine brooded. Eddy channeled Brain.

"How's it going?"

"Badly."

"Tough day?"

"Only since three fifteen p.m." When he and Boo had arrived. "Why does she have to stay?"

"It's nice! It'll be more fun."

"Fa-*lah*."

"Boo's great. Give her a chance."

"Her nose ring is weird."

"Not to me," said Eddy.

"She has weird toes." She did not.

"All toes are weird if you look at them long enough."

"Claudia's aren't."

Well, true, Claudia's toes were fetching specimens, no doubt whatever. Eddy had encountered them when Claudia and Slimon called unexpectedly one afternoon, to collect boxes from the garage. He'd been so busy not looking at Claudia's allegedly nonexistent breasts, he'd had plenty of time to appreciate the toes. They were long and elegant and tanned, with cherry-red nail varnish and several toe rings.

It had been an altogether uneasy visit. Delphine had regressed to near infancy and clung to her father like a koala cub. Claudia made a great fuss over Rizzo, carefully not looking at father and daughter. Eddy made cold drinks for everyone, all awkward about playing host to the co-owner of the house. Jasper had retreated to his room as soon as the couple came up the path, and Slimon did not ask after him. Instead, he asked Eddy what he was studying at university. "No uni," said Eddy. It was all pet minding and food retail for him right now. But he would be moving on to higher education, surely? "Probably not," said Eddy. He *might* do a religious studies paper, but only if it worked around New World shifts or a potential job at the tattoo parlor. None of this was true, but Eddy had been unable to stop himself from saying it.

"Interesting," said Sue Lombardo when he told her about it the next day. He'd called around with groceries, swept the kitchen floor, changed two lightbulbs, and now drank coffee at the kitchen table, Mother on his shoulder, gladsome and mellow. He felt the need to confess.

"Oppositional defiance," said Sue. "Most people have a trace."

Eddy thought of the time he'd said fucking Jesus, not softly, to a bank teller. The time he'd refused to surrender his backpack to a baby-faced library security guard.

"More or less standard for the young and hungry. Do you leave your dirty laundry on the floor to annoy Brian?"

"No," said Eddy. He was incapable of such layabout behavior. Besides, the laundry was his job.

"Do you consistently fail to comply with rules and laws? Leave parking fines unpaid?"

"No." He would never have a parking fine.

"Get angry with employers?"

"*To be fair*, sometimes." Well, Judith. What could you do?

"Always need to win an argument with a parent or spouse?"

"No."

"No diagnosable disorder, then," said Sue. "Why do you think the guy got up your nose?"

"He's a status snob. Also a terrible father. Also, he was wearing a striped shirt."

"To be fair," said Sue, "maybe he was just trying to make conversation."

"To be *fair*," said Eddy, "he's a king-size twat."

After her father's visit, Delphine had been downcast and querulous, picking fights with Eddy and Jasper. Eddy had tried to distract her with a game of checkers, but she'd upended the board when he crowned his third man. The sportsmanship of a four-year-old. The next day she'd greeted him at the front door, head down, holding out an envelope. Inside was a piece of paper elaborately decorated with puppy and skull stickers and SORRY repeated down the page in wobbly capitals.

Watching Delphine now, truculent, oppositional(!), and thoroughly incompetent with the spatula, Eddy felt mostly tenderness. She was like a rescue pet, needing steady attention and affection, and judicious firmness. He helped her slide the battered toast onto a plate and supervised as she oiled the pan, drained the bread before transferring it.

At the table, they each applied their preferred condiments to the French toast. Eddy was a purist: lemon juice and the merest sprinkle of brown sugar. Jasper favored Vegemite, which was certainly delinquent. Boo and Delphine slathered theirs with yogurt and maple syrup.

"*Delicious*, Mr. K," said Boo. Her enthusiasm for his cooking was very gratifying.

"Why do you call him Mr. K?" asked Delphine, an accusation disguised as a question.

And thus Mr. Kleinbein became Boo's gift to Delphine, a shared joke, a bridge she could walk over, ho, ho.

"Pass the maple syrup, Mr. Kleinbein."

"Can we have this for breakfast, too, Mr. Kleinbein?"

"I'm *full*, Mr. Kleinbein."

Boo raised her eyebrows at Eddy. Fine, fine. Whatever it took. It was worth it to hear Jasper give one of his *hrhurgahh* chuckles.

To finish, Delphine picked up her plate and lapped at the lake of syrup.

"Nah," said Eddy. "Nah! That's definitely not a go. No plate licking. Only wiping up with bread."

"I always lick," said Delphine.

Indecipherable muttering from Jasper.

"Respectfully, Herr Kleinbein," said Boo, "this is asking to be licked."

"Yeah, respectfully, Herr Kleinbein," said Delphine, licking vigorously and splattering her hair.

Boo had a blob of yogurty syrup on the end of her nose. She looked about five years old.

Two rounds of Last Card sealed the deal.

"I let her win the second one," said Boo later, when Delphine was asleep and Jasper played on into the night with Golub Bubanja and his merry band of global gamers.

"Knit one, knit two together, yarn forward." She read from the pattern with the drooling baby.

The baby was downright ugly. No doubt whatever. Eddy stroked Waffle's springy back. The dog was always nearby, usually standing, watchful and ready. Rizzo curled on the sofa beside Boo. They matched: a lot of coiled hair between them.

Couple with Dogs: a first-home mortgage advertisement. Or a knitting pattern from the 1960s.

32

Josie gave Eddy a credit card.

"Whatever you need," she said. "Food, petrol. Entertainment for Delphine, et cetera."

Eddy stared at the card. *Riches beyond the dreams of avarice.*

"How do you feel about Christmas shopping?" murmured Josie. She was painting her fingernails. Festive red. Christmas spirit.

"You could do it all online. Or check out the malls? Totally up to you. But an outing might be good."

In your dreams, thought Eddy. He hated shopping, Christmas or otherwise. And immediately, *adamantine* ideas about suitable children's presents appeared in his head. Improving, Brain-ish things: Craft projects. Puzzles. Wooden stuff. Good books.

Presents for others had mostly been homemade. Festive biscuits shaped like stars and pine trees. Miniature Christmas cakes, Eddy measuring and weighing, Brain turning the stolid mixture with a wooden spoon. Fudge that must be stirred forever, steaming up your face. As a child he had made FIMO clay ornaments and paper tree decorations for Bridgie and Ginge, even the Modern Priest if he wasn't swanning round the Vatican. And for Brain, every Christmas since his seventh, he had created indigenous animal pairings from modeling clay, for an as-yet-imaginary Ark, which would memorialize in miniature the fauna of Aotearoa when the ice caps melted and the seas rose. Or so he had conceived it after Brain had explained global warming to him. This year, he planned a pair of chevron skinks, rare and secretive. He had brought the old Making Box from the back of his wardrobe to the Mulhollands'. Delphine could help.

As for actual Christmas shopping, Eddy had experienced it only once: with Hazel, who went about it like a deranged field marshal plotting a military assault—a limitless credit card, a lengthy list of recipients, an actual map of the shops. In fact, he'd only half experienced it. Or a quarter. He had walked out of Riccarton Mall after two gruesomely tedious hours and a fight with Hazel in front of Muffin Break. She had insisted there was no time for food.

"I was thinking homemade presents," Eddy told Josie. "Doubling as holiday activities."

Josie looked blank. Then, to his dismay, her eyes welled and she covered her face with her hands. It was late and they sat now at the kitchen island, Eddy drinking tea, Josie hugging a glass of wine. Eddy had saved a plate of chicken and lentils for her, but she had only picked at it. Delphine was asleep. Boo, her new best friend, had read her two chapters of the Baby-Sitters Club in bed. "Genius series," Boo assured Eddy, though the cover suggested otherwise. Right now, Boo was in front of Jasper's console playing the latest installment in a brutal game of *Assassin's Creed III*.

"Sorry," said Josie. She seemed to dig the tears from her eyes with her red-tipped fingers. "I'm a useless mother."

Eddy opened his mouth to protest but couldn't summon the right words.

"Don't," said Josie, waving her hand at him. "What can you say?"

This was uncomfortable. If only Boo would emerge victorious from the crepuscular cave and rescue them with some ironic comment. He wasn't bothered by crying, he'd been around it often enough:

Ginge wept readily—at funerals, at injured animals in films, during his annual read of *Anne of Green Gables*. And Eddy was always putting a comforting arm around someone's shoulder at New World. Blessica in bakery was especially blubbery, ill-suited to the head baker's fanatical rule. Hazel's emotional barometer had been labile; she could cry and laugh in the same breath. But despite the hours spent in Josie's house, he didn't really know her; they were like garrison defenders, connecting briefly as one stepped down from the watch and the other signed on, snatched functional exchanges. A visible emotion was unnerving.

"I used to be better," said Josie, not at all unnerved. "More *present*. And patient. I used to do the mum things. This damn job, it eats you up."

She looked eaten up, her face thinner than when he'd first come, panda patches beneath her eyes despite the makeup.

"I couldn't manage without you, Eddy," said Josie. "I *didn't* manage without you." She grimaced, raised her glass. "Here's to you. Don't go anywhere! I know I should encourage you to go to uni or something. Get a qualification." She drained the glass. "But I'm too self-interested. Don't get ambitious, okay? Or not yet."

"Tough for her," said Boo when they were curled in bed. "The usual story—old Slimon's washed his hands. You shouldn't judge."

"I'm not." He was. But he judged Slimon, too. He was an equal-opportunity judger.

"Viv's never having kids," said Boo. "It'd shaft her work. She reckons she'd just be resentful."

This statement fluttered between them momentarily, like an invading moth.

"Academic, surely?" he said. "She's never had a partner." Viv cleaved to the Earth, as far as Eddy could tell, was concerned only with its history and secrets. He'd seen her again recently, knowing he must front up sometime. She had welcomed him back cautiously.

"Mr. K," she'd said, "you're taller. And broader." She assessed him as she would a piece of the lithosphere, he thought, checking radioactive levels, the shifting plates. Likely instability. "Wiser, I hope." She wasn't quite smirking.

"Positively burdened by wisdom," said Eddy, deciding not to be intimidated. It was true anyway.

She gave him a brisk hug then, and that was it. All good, more or less. The last time he'd seen Viv O'Brien was the winter of 2010, at the hospital. She'd smacked his face and been bawled out by a nurse.

33

Delphine came with Eddy now on his morning rounds; he was wooing Jasper, too, determined to show him a wider world, but that was a longer game. They left the house early, fed the Rhode Island Reds, collected eggs, and cleaned out the coop. More accurately, Eddy cleaned the coop and Delphine sat on the grass watching the hens grub about, filling him in on the friendship wars in her class. No one was actually her friend it seemed, but she watched with forensic attention the different clusters—gangs, thought Eddy—and their shifting alliances.

They took the eggs to Bishop Street for Brain's Christmas baking, and Eddy indulged Delphine's lengthy inspection of the house: she combed his bedroom, Brain's bedroom, the photographs of Eddy through the years, the curios and pictures and books.

He introduced her to Eddy's Ark, the twenty-four animals spread across the living room bookshelves: his first clumsy effort, the tuatara pair (*Sphenodon punctatus*), through to last year's moa (*Dinornis robustus*), of whom he was rather proud. It had taken a long time to achieve the correct weighting and balance of the birds' peculiar construction, minute adjustments and readjustments to ensure they would finally stand upright.

"Excellent *embonpoint!*" said Brain when he'd unwrapped the pair and examined them lengthily. He was very attached to his Christmas surprise. They all were. Bridgie and Ginge offered species suggestions; the Modern Priest liked to check in on new additions. And, whatever his emotional weather, Eddy was committed. It was a kind of annual corrective. Somehow, at work on the gift, whatever knot of complex Brain feelings he was harboring eased a little. Even last Christmas, when his irritation had reached a new pitch, molding the clay, mixing the paint, attending to the smallest details of claw, beak, feather—all this had gradually rinsed and soothed him, so that by the time he wrapped the birds in tissue and brown paper and wrote a card, he could with sincerity scrawl *Love, Ed.*

Delphine lingered over the photos on top of the piano. She knelt on the stool, still and silent, studying each of them one by one. Eddy stood there, too, wondering what she made of it all: The wedding photo of Doris and his grandfather, Doris unrecognizable to Eddy, this open-faced young woman with a cap of dark hair, her neat form tucked into the side of the unknown Dr. Kevin. Brain, in academic dress at his graduation, slim and grinning—before the trials of unexpected parenthood, which had perhaps sobered him and for sure had plumped him up. Infant Eddy, toddler Eddy, adolescent Eddy. Vincent in his singlet, leaning on some farm gate, his long hair lifted in the wind. His mother, fair and slight, caught by the camera just as she turned away, so that she was eternally in the process of not being there.

Later, Eddy gave Delphine a tour of the depleted Snorebins streets, then headed up Cranford and Innes toward Mairehau, where he had two new charges: schnauzers. The website had described the breed as "hardy and merry," quaint language but curiously apt since all schnauzers looked to Eddy like old Uncle Howard, Doris's deceased brother, a rugged fellow with a goatee and out-of-control eyebrows and a disposition as cheery as his sister's was curdled.

The schnauzers waited in their sunken bungalow. Their owners, fed up with taped windows and sloping floors and a bully insurer, had spat at fate and bought themselves a pair of pure breeds. Goodbye, five thousand dollars. Better than freezing your nuts off up a ginkgo followed by a stay at Hillmorton, Eddy supposed. In the passenger seat, Delphine was unusually quiet; she stole occasional sidelong looks at him.

"What are you thinking?" he said.

Incredible really, what you could say to a kid, the demands you made. He'd never ask an adult what they were thinking. Not even Boo. It seemed presumptuous, practically an invasion. And the only person who'd ever asked him, though often enough, was Hazel. He couldn't answer, or not truthfully. Not in those raw, frangible moments after sex with the wrong person when a clot of feelings seized you up.

"What's your mother's name?" said Delphine.

Funny that. He'd noticed lately that he always thought of his father as Vincent and his mother as my mother. In his head and his talk, she was mostly nameless.

"It *was* Jehann."

"What?"

"A version of Jean." He spelled it out. "Pronounced Jarn."

The road was crap, all humps and troughs. You needed to pay attention. The rate of blown tires had surely surged. On the other hand, the orange cones kept traffic at a crawl, thereby reducing other risks. Loss and gain. Sort of. Delphine seemed to be considering the name Jehann.

"It's really a boy's name," he told her. "I looked it up."

There was a birth certificate, too. Jehann Marie Walsh. Female. Born: 1970. Mother: housewife. Father: railway clerk. But these were adoptive parents. There had been another family once, or another mother at least. Like me, Eddy had thought when Brain explained it all, fastening on this connection with his mother. Jehann. "That mother, your grandmother," said Brain, "died, too." A dying kind of family, then. Father unknown. "An awful term," said Brain, his face puckered, as if the words actually tasted bad. *Father unknown*. His own father was known, thought Eddy. Though not really. Vincent. A name, a face, tanned arms, and Byronic hair. A story. But there was an aunt, the grandmother's sister. "Your *great*-aunt!" said Brain, so pleased to have this breathing, biological relative from the other family. The great-aunt lived in London and had visited when Eddy was small. He didn't remember this, but she had left him the Kaiapoi Pure Wool rug that now fed the peaty Snorebins soil beneath the wattle tree.

"Why did she have a boy's name?" said Delphine.

"Mistake probably. It's French . . . maybe they didn't know. Way before the internet, all those baby name sites."

Eddy had scrolled those sites years ago, a little shifty, feeling it was not something a boy would do. An unavailing search for more substance on his parents. Vincent, he read, meant Victorious. Jehann, God Is Gracious. Edmund, Riches. Total bollocks, then. He searched further anyway, checking out Brigid (powerstrengthvigorvirtue) and Raymond—Ginge's actual name—(counselprotection) and finally Brian (highnoble): okay, jury out.

"Delphine means delphiniumdolphinwomanfromDelphi," said Delphine. "And Jasper means Bringer of Treasure."

"Let's all stay close to Jasper, then."

"Gran gave me a delphinium for the garden once, but I forgot to water it, so it died."

The traffic flow went to hell at the intersection of Westminster and Hills. Road works. Sewage pipes, no doubt. A stop-start situation. The road worker with the STOP/GO sign appeared to be asleep standing up. Sick of responding to all the motorists' thank-you waves, probably. They were a nation of thank-you wavers. Polite, but annoying. He'd read it somewhere.

"Then Mum quickly went to the garden shop to get another delphinium before Gran came round, but I forgot that, too, and *it* died."

This was a depressingly Mulhollandish sort of story, Eddy thought. Inattention. Things lapsing. No parental guidance. Wtf? He *was* turning into some censorious patriarch (Boo accusation).

"You've got Wallace now, I guess," said Eddy, trying to seem less judgmental, if only to himself.

Wallace was the gardener, a Scottish arborist biding his time in suburban front yards while he looked for serious work with actual trees. He'd arrived in the city a month before the quakes, work only now beginning to pick up. Meanwhile, he said, he was having a *pritty gurd* time with Josie's credit card at garden nurseries.

The road worker came to life and turned the sign to GO. Eddy did not salute, to save her the effort of return, then felt oddly churlish. So many tricky little social rituals to navigate each day. Why Toss had opted for bed, no doubt. Delphine was looking at him again.

"You're the only teenager I know whose parents are dead."

The specificity of this statement made him laugh. He could see her thought process, wanting a way to express the gravity of his situation, as she judged it: lots of people's parents were dead, but mostly they were old, so that was normal, but Eddy was young, though not a child.

"It's not *funny* having dead parents."

"No, but I never knew them, so it's not exactly sad, either."

"Don't you miss them?"

"Not really." He sometimes missed the idea of parents, but not their flesh and blood.

"Jasper doesn't know his dad, but he misses him."

"Did he tell you that?"

"No. Mum did."

Jasper's father had blown through. Josie had met Slimon when Jasper was three. It had always been difficult between them, and finally Slimon had given up. He was uncomfortable with anything that strayed from the norm, said Josie. She didn't know why she married him. She had begun confiding all sorts to Eddy now, and sometimes Boo, over the kitchen island and late-night glasses of pinot noir.

"There's a sign etched on your forehead," Boo told him. "*Please Tell Me All About Yourself.* Invisible to everyone except Boomer and Gen X women."

"On your head, too, then."

"Nah," said Boo. "I'm just there, adjacent to you. It's because you look like the Loving Jesus, they mistake you for their confessor. And because you're motherless."

"Did they die in a car accident?" asked Delphine.

"Yes," said Eddy. "Going too fast." The latter was true at least, in a different way. He couldn't tell her that his father had died of an overdose before Eddy was born, and his mother had died figuratively, of shame, and run off to Australia, where later she'd died again, by her own hand (Brain term). It was all too X-rated.

Delphine reached over and patted his arm. This was so unexpected, it made Eddy's throat ache, and he could say nothing for some moments.

On the corner of the schnauzers' street was a collection of shops, a gathering of the halt and the lame, a number of the buildings sagging or boarded up. A couple had been demolished, and now dandelion, clover, oxalis, et al. flowered in the empty sections, yellow and white and specks of purple. New urban residents; preferable, at least, to the cockroach parking company that colonized the empty lots nearer the city center. The quake-god had struck arbitrarily here as everywhere. Just the hairdresser, the horse-tack shop, and the dairy plodding on. These were the saddest sights, Eddy thought, the corner shops. Wounded little retail families, their dead still among them.

"Ice creams before or after the schnauzers?" he asked Delphine.

"During?"

"Nah, you'll need both hands for the leash. They're hardy and merry."

"Okay, after."

Can do deferred gratification, thought Eddy. Promising.

34

That night, Eddy, corpsed on the plant room sofa, watched Boo teach Delphine to knit. It was painful viewing, but he was too whacked to do anything else. Three dog walks that day. He must start combining his charges. Watching Delphine labor over purl and plain, he saw that she could stick at something determinedly, too, if she wanted it enough. In this instance, sadly, a turtleneck coat for Rizzo. Boo had brought home *Stylish Knits for Dogs*, a revolting book, full of demeaning pooch-wear worn by dog models: pink sweaters, rainbow-striped hoodies, eyesores made of glitter wool.

"They're funny," said Boo. "Also easy to achieve."

"Yeah, Mr. K," said Delphine. "And Rizzo chose the pattern."

"No, she didn't," said Eddy. "She accidentally put her paw on it."

"Good work!" said Boo now, assessing Delphine's progress. "Five rows, only two mistakes, which no one will notice. And no dropped stitches. Wanna keep going?"

"Canine abuse," said Eddy softly.

"My arms are tired," said Delphine, flopping. Her face was red with effort. She breathed only occasionally as she doggedly(!) completed the rows.

"After the band, it's just stocking stitch," said Boo. "You should get it done by the winter. Nifty how the neck rolls over, eh."

"I will *never* walk a turtled-up Rizzo," said Eddy. "Also, Waffle would be humiliated."

Would he still be walking the Mulholland dogs next winter?

Boo brought out the Bananagrams bag then, and they lured Jasper from the crepuscular cave. Eddy roused himself to help Delphine.

The games were mostly Boo saying *PeelPeelPeelPeelPeelPeel*, quick and low and ruthless. She aimed to humble her opponents, no matter their age. Delphine countered this by cheating. Midway through the first round, Eddy quietly scooped up the tiles she'd secreted beneath the coffee table and returned them to the pile. Delphine glared at him, even more red-faced, manic.

"You already have an advantage," Eddy whispered. "Me."

Boo and Jasper were oblivious, eyes only for their grids and tiles, their hands in constant motion.

"You are a whited sepul*car*," said Delphine.

"I'm teaching you sportsmanship."

"Sports*person*ship."

Jasper came a creditable second. His grid was full of gaming words. Nerf. Hitscan. Cooldown. Aimbot. Eddy had got Delphine stuck on congre_ation, waiting for a *g*. Boo had the usual array of two- and three-letter words: ki and se and tui and koi.

"Less is more," she said. "But look, plenty of fours and fives, including purl!"

Delphine scowled at the table, wrestling no doubt with the urge to wipe out Boo's grid or throw some tiles.

"Congratulations," she said at last, barely audible.

Better, thought Eddy. He had given her a little lecture about graciousness in both defeat and victory. She'd thrown her hand at him when he'd beaten her three-nil at Last Card and crowed most unattractively on winning Snap. He considered showing her YouTube footage of Rafa, humble winner, gracious loser. But Boo had laughed so hard at this idea, he ditched it.

"Mini-Brain," she said, "you're *such* a dag."

"No one says dag anymore" had been his only comeback.

"*To be fair*," Boo said now, "Bananagrams is my best game. Mr. K always used to beat me at Jenga. And Blokus."

"Used to?" said Jasper. "Always?" They turned to him, lying on the floor, hands clasped over his chest. He said so little, seemed to dissolve within a room, it was easy to forget he was there.

"Yes," said Delphine. "I thought you just moved here."

Eddy and Boo each waited for the other to reply, then spoke at the same time.

"Same school," said Eddy.

"Old friends," said Boo.

Not counting the two years we didn't speak to each other, Eddy did not say.

Jasper turned over, balancing on his side.

"But you're a thing, right? A couple?"

This seemed oddly intimate and also a little confrontational. Eddy could only stare at Boo's Bananagrams grid. Axiom: a very nice word. Ant: feeble.

"Kinda," said Boo.

"Are you practicing?" said Delphine. "Like engaged people?"

"Practice makes perfect," said Jasper. It wasn't ironic.

"You got it," said Eddy, to put an end to this awkwardness. "Ten thousand hours and we'll make the Aussie Open."

They all looked at him as if he was insane.

"Bedtime," he said to Delphine, and began sweeping the tiles into the banana bag.

Tomorrow was Saturday, and they had a date with Christmas trees at the Snorebins kindergarten. The Mulhollands had only a fake tree, a tinsel job on a metal spine that rustled in a way Eddy found sinister. He'd set it between the sofas in the plant room, but it was pitiful in the company of bounteous greenery. The silvery strips smelled only of dust and shed liberally. Wtf, he thought, why *shouldn't* Jasper and Delphine have a decent Christmas tree? With decorations (home)made from organic materials, no tinsel shit.

"Will you read them *The Polar Express*, too?" Boo had asked.

"What if I do?" said Eddy, offended. "It is a classic. For all ages."

He pulled Delphine to her feet now. "Early start. There's stiff competition for good trees."

"Fah-la," said Delphine, dragging her feet to the door. Jasper grunted something and stood, a protracted process, like a beached log come to life. Boo studied Delphine's five-row turtleneck sweater. Keeping her counsel.

35

In bed, a silence lay between them. Like a sodden thing, Eddy thought. He tried to dream up some droll anecdote. Something about Delphine, there was always something. Someone at New World? Brain? Or Mother, who was surely on his last legs at Sue's after having shitted all over the bed in the spare room, where Sue had hastily housed him when two cops knocked at the front door; they were doing a house-to-house, questions about a runaway. His heart was thumping.

Boo had turned on her side, away from him. She was on the left side of the bed. In his own bed Eddy, too, lay on the left side, but shifted over when Boo stayed. Had he and Boo discussed this in the past? He couldn't remember. And now, they had simply gone back to their old arrangement. Incidentally, the same arrangement he'd had with Toss during his long Bed-In. Toss on the left, Eddy on the right. Did this mean he was docile and supine, yielding always to the other? He'd slept on top of Toss's bedcovers, in his own sleeping bag—except in Toss's uber-fragile times when the smallest movement irritated him and Eddy was banished to the floor mattress. And in the middle of last winter when Toss had been so cold he'd worn pajamas, leggings, a jersey, a knitted beanie, and two duvets, but still could not get warm.

"You'll have to warm me," he'd commanded. "I'm hypothermic. I need body heat."

Eddy, pleasantly warm with his lower body in the sleeping bag, the *Fireside Book of Folk Songs* propped on his knees, was practicing the accompaniment for "Careless Love" on the chord harp.

"Not on your nelly."

"I'm serious. And that jaunty fucking accompaniment isn't helping. C'mon!"

"No thanks."

"Why not? I'm in extremis."

"I prefer this."

"Don't go all androphobic on me, you heartless twat." His voice was muffled beneath the duvets. Eddy could see only the beanie's possum-fur pom-pom, resting on the pillow like the back end of a bunny.

"I'm not scared of touching you," said Eddy. "I'd just prefer not to."

"You don't have to fucking touch me. You can just lie there and emit heat."

"I'm not wearing my underdaks."

Toss had pushed back the covers and glared at Eddy. He looked like Rumpelstiltskin in Brain's old Ladybird book, pinched and furious, his face sallow.

"Christ!" said Eddy, throwing down the chord harp and shuffling out of the sleeping bag. "We're just not the hugging kind." He pulled on his boxers and got under the duvet.

"I don't want you to hug me. Just lean your back into me."

Eddy did so, wondering why on earth he was conceding. He'd be boiling in two minutes.

"Good," said Toss. "And keep your head under, otherwise there's a draft."

Under the covers had a particular smell. Frowsty? (Bridgie word.) Toss's unwashed clothes, no doubt. Vegetabley? Not *quite* unpleasant.

"Stop sniffing," said Toss.

"You're such a grubby fucker."

"It's too cold to shower."

They lay with their backs hard against each other, and Toss stopped complaining.

Eddy visualized the chords of "Careless Love" on the five-line stave of his front brain. He'd memorized the lyrics without really examining them. When he did think about them, they seemed silly . . . *Once I wore my apron low* . . . and later, *Now I wear my apron high* . . . Puzzling, until he'd looked properly at the picture at the bottom of the page and seen that the weeping figure was *big with child*, an archaism Ginge rolled out if ever he mentioned a pregnant woman. *You see what careless love has done.* PS: Use condoms.

"Thanks," said Toss, pushing on Eddy's back.

"Happy to oblige," said Eddy, returning a gentle lunge. He listened to Toss fall asleep.

Play-Doh, he thought. That's what the under-the-covers Toss world smelled like. That old, salty wheat smell. He thought of Brain, an enthusiastic dispenser of Play-Doh. They'd made plenty of pretend biscuits and cakes together, houses, too, with small Play-Doh inhabitants, squashy and limbless. On the dresser in Brain's bedroom sat a desiccated Play-Doh ménage made by four-year-old Eddy: Brain, Marley, and Baby Eddy, an all-year, cross-species nativity, slowly fading.

He'd fallen asleep himself that night beside Toss, then woken a few hours later, drenched in sweat.

No sleep right now though. Boo wasn't asleep, either. He could feel her body across the silence, taut, hovering above the sheet. He should say something.

"Boo," he said.

She didn't answer. He said it again, louder. He turned into her back and put his arm across her not-quite-welcoming body.

"What are we exactly?" he asked. It was a cowardly question, he knew it. But he wanted her to tell him. Less risk.

"What do you think we are?" said Boo.

Damn. Turned the question round. He tried to read her voice. Annoyed? Fond? Effortfully patient?

"What do you want us to be?" she said.

"What do *you*?" he said, and it was so abject and feeble, they both sniggered. Boo's body softened a little. It was nice lying this way with her, her bottom tucked into his lap. Why did they always lie the other way? The hair thing, that's why. Already his face was itching. He pushed away the great thatch and leaned into her smell, at which Boo straightened like a planker and turned over to face him.

"*Arschgeige,*" she said.

It meant arsehole. He knew this because Boo had shouted it at him in great rage two years ago. Actually, it meant arse *violin,* which Eddy had chosen to take comfort in at the time, though this had done him no good at all.

"I know," he said. He did know. He was definitionally pathetic.

"Am I more of a *geige* than an *arsch* though?"

"Why can't *you* say?" said Boo. She sounded disappointed rather than mad. But was that worse?

"Okay," said Eddy quickly, "okay. I know what I want, I *do*."

He pulled Boo tighter, spoke into her shoulder blade.

"I want to be . . . us to be a . . . thing. A—" He wouldn't say couple, horrible word. "A thing." A thing? A *thing*? He wanted to gouge out an eye. Had he ever been less coherent? He was seven years old. No, three. He sat up, to feel fractionally more manly and collected.

"Eddy," said Boo, sitting up beside him. She never called him Eddy.

A silhouette show appeared then on the bedroom wall—some cat activating an outside light. The light threw tree shadows, trembling lace patterns.

"I do, too," said Boo.

Eddy went cold. Then hot, an actual rush of blood, he supposed, right through his body. He groped about for Boo's hand, but her arms came around his neck. So, it was okay? They were okay? He felt tearful with relief. He kissed her coconutty neck. Her skin was warm and salty.

"But," said Boo seconds later, pulling back.

No buts please, thought Eddy, trying to hold on. Not now.

He knew though. Amidst the relief, he knew what was coming. He lay down, imagined shoving his face in the pillow and howling.

"We've never talked," said Boo. "Not properly."

The outside light went off, and the shadow show disappeared. Eddy breathed in and out. Boo looked down at him; he tried not to be distracted by her nakedness.

"Okay," he said. "I get it."

"Yes," said Boo.

"The baby et cetera."

Boo

It wasn't a baby. It was a clump of cells and then a zygote and then an embryo. Then it was nothing. Nichts. But Eddy kept calling it *the baby*. Which was the reason for our terrible fight. "Don't say baby," I said. "Don't call it that," and out of nowhere he was furious, said he could call it what he liked, it was half his and he felt like it was a baby. And I said it was scientifically inaccurate to call it a baby and it was inside me because of some fucking contraceptive failure, probably *his* fault, and that's what counted and I didn't want it there. And he said we should talk about it, and I said we *were* talking about it but he was being weird and unreasonable and it was me that it made a difference to and that's what counted, I don't know why I kept saying *counted*, and he went silent and I asked him if he wanted to be a father, and he said not *now*, and I said, well, there's your answer, and he said of course he felt really bad for me but he felt worse about getting rid of it, and I said yes it wasn't great but what else could we do, and then I had to race to the dunny to vomit and when I came back he was all stricken, his head in his hands, and he said he couldn't stop thinking about *himself* as a baby and what if—and I cut him off and said that *sucked*, the worst kind of emotional blackmail and it wasn't about him, and he said he didn't mean it like that, he was trying to be honest about his feelings, and I said what about *my* feelings, and he said he was trying to think about me but he couldn't stop thinking about it being a *baby* and somehow, he didn't mean to, it had just happened but now he had a name for it in his head, and that's when I screamed at him if he said that name I would never ever speak to him again—

Back then I had to think about it my way. I didn't want a baby. And I didn't want Eddy's emotional crisis. I could see all the ways it might be awful for him, but I couldn't care about that. I left Eddy to Brain. He pulled himself together, sort of, but he was prickly and distant, and then he came with me to the hospital and cried all over Viv, who lost it spectacularly. Luckily, I was elsewhere.

We never talked about it again. The Kleinbein specialty: not going there. He just wanted to get back to what we were. Only we weren't it anymore. The undiscussed not-baby hung between us, held aloft like some kind of ectoplasm by Eddy's feelings, seething beneath the silence. We dragged along, getting our parts wrong, not having a script for this. And then it was the *Murder in the Cathedral* fandango, and Eddy did his full Vesuvius and blew the mission. Or to really pile on the metaphors, he pinged about, a headless chicken spraying gore over everything until he fell over. The not-baby triggered something, I guess.

It was unreal, getting back together and neither of us saying anything. But Eddy sure can exert a powerful not-going-there force field. And, *to be fair*, I was loving the back-together, so I let it ride. Too difficult. Don't rock the boat, etc. Then there we were playing fake mum and dad at the Mulhollands' and me knitting baby jackets and Eddy's face when he looked at the baby on the knitting pattern, and Jasper and Delphine curious, and *someone* had to say something . . .

I did think about the not-baby, off and on. Months afterward, Eddy out of the picture, me back home and then at uni, new city, new people, everything a bit weird, I had a reaction. The not-baby had gone from my body, but it grew in my head; it turned into something: a near-baby, an outline, a half thought that would never complete itself. I didn't regret my decision, but now I wanted the near-baby to have a place. In my head, in the universe. I thought of it as a fleck, weightless and calm, floating in its own corner of the cosmos. I almost wanted to give it a name.

DE
CEM
BER

Third Week of Advent

36

Brain had broken his wrist. Possibly. Probably. An unlikely injury while making walnut and parsley pesto. "Careless," said Brain, wheezy over the phone, the pain apparent in his voice. "Oil on the floor. Turned too quickly and skidded, hand out, et cetera."

Eddy, wondering what *too quickly* might look like in Brain's adagio universe, drove immediately to Bishop Street with Delphine. It was Saturday, Josie and Boo both at work and Jasper asleep after a late-night session, a new game, global excitement, rah-rah, though his excitement was discernible only to the initiated: a smidge more eye contact, random *hrhurgahh*s.

It was 7:30 a.m. Brain had started early. Eddy pictured it: the alarm set for six, no luxuriating between the sheets. Off with the striped pajamas (summer version), on with his weekend duds and inside shoes. Tea and marmalade toast. A puddle of sun on the kitchen bench. Studying the list, assembling the ingredients.

"What is pesto?" said Delphine.

The least important aspect of this crisis. But she knew nothing about food. Until his arrival, Delphine and Jasper's diet appeared to have consisted almost entirely of crackers, cheese, and Tegel chicken tenders: pale food. An occasional carrot.

"A kind of sauce. A paste. Herbs and nuts and stuff, pounded to a mush. Brain makes it for Christmas presents and puts it in pretty jars. Labels them and ties a ribbon round."

Months in the preparation, he might have added. Walnuts harvested late autumn, laid out to dry on newspaper in the sunroom, stored in baskets, and shelled late November in time for the Advent kitchen adventures. Biscuits of the World mostly, subcategory walnut: walnut shortbread (Doris recipe); hup toh soh (Xiuying, colleague at work); Vanillekipferl (German Eva at church); and—new last year!—brunkager (Danish Aksel at the SPCA).

"*What?* He bails up every foreign national he meets for a walnut biscuit recipe?" Toss was incredulous, the brunkager addition apparently a bridge too far. Brain had sent him a ClickClack boxful via Eddy—something to tempt the deadened palate.

"Not always," said Eddy. He watched Toss check out the biscuit. Like a mouse, sniff, sniff, twitch, an experimental nibble. "It might be hazelnuts. Or nutmeg. You know he's obsessed with flavorings. He reads up on the history of spices, how they traveled."

Brunkager merely meant brown biscuit, which might have been disappointing, but Eddy's interest was limited anyway. He was allergic to walnuts. His tongue swelled dramatically; it cracked and stung like hell. A metaphor probably.

"Brain for the *whole* day now," said Delphine. She lay back against the headrest, stretching luxuriously. Her day was improving by the minute, as Eddy's angled south. Brain had invited both Delphine and Jasper to the annual tree-decorating palaver. Also Sue Lombardo. This sudden conflation of his working and family life (Brain, Bridgie, Ginge, Boo, a nun, a cranky kid, and a silent one) made Eddy nervous. But some fifth-column part of his psyche had ordered a surrender to the unknown.

Brain would be benched now, Eddy supposed. Observer status

rather than genial host. If they didn't spend all day in Emergency. He warned Delphine of a long wait.

"I don't mind," she said. "I'll keep Brain cheerful."

Eddy laughed. Her certainty. He had thought precisely this himself, in fact, as he hurried her from the house. The previous Saturday when they'd turned up with the pine tree, Brain had been ready with pancakes. Pale food. He'd always known the direct route to a child's heart. Delphine had surveyed the laid table with dropped jaw. "A *lot* of pancake condiments," she said. Brain chortled his way through breakfast, delighted by Delphine, her inquisitiveness, her artless disclosures. Eddy saw suddenly that childhood would not be when Delphine made friends. Maybe not even her teenage years. She was the wrong side of wacko, and with no nose for adaptation. It might be better when she was older, released from the tyrannies of childhood normcore. She slurped up the oxygen, too, unappealing to her peers no doubt. On the other hand, it was ideal for Jasper. Delphine was his advance party, scoping the situation, distracting the peeps so their heat-seeking telescopes did not turn toward him. He was three times her size, yet she cast the greater shadow, and he took comfort in that.

Brain knew to address Jasper with just a smile and a general air of goodwill, no questions, no painful efforts to draw him into conversation. Meanwhile, God's Icebreaker was helpfully in attendance. Mother had been with Brain since the spare-bed shitting routine. From the dining room mantel, the bird assessed the pancake gathering and flew straight to Jasper's shoulder, from whence he gave racy commentary throughout breakfast.

Later, it was "God bless! God bless!" when Eddy and Jasper placed the tree in its bucket, and Brain fastened it to the brass hook that sat all year in the wall waiting for its Advent moment. Mother flew to the top of the tree and the feathery branch plunged beneath his weight, but the bird dodged a face-plant with some impressive acrobatics and a great racket of wings.

"GOD BLESS US @%& @$%&!" he screeched, recovering on the couch. Eddy knew what Brain had been doing: playing *A Christmas Carol* while he baked, shouting "God bless us, everyone!" with Tiny Tim and Ebenezer Scrooge.

"Yes," said Brain, meeting his eye. "I confess. Declaiming to myself."

"But the *biscuits!*" said Delphine in the car, all concern now. "What if he hasn't made them yet?"

Brain had assured her of sundry sugary comestibles to accompany the tree decorating. He had described the tree tradition in loving detail, and Delphine had been brought to new summits of rapture in anticipation. Eddy thought of his own childhood salivations over food, in life and in books, and then of the feast Brain had produced for Ginge on his fiftieth birthday, a replica of the high tea for the minister and his wife in *Anne of Green Gables*. He found the book in Brain's bedroom and read the passage to Delphine and Jasper: *"jellied chicken and cold tongue . . . two kinds of jelly, red and yellow, and whipped cream and lemon pie, and cherry pie, and three kinds of cookies, and fruit-cake, and Marilla's famous yellow plum preserves that she keeps especially for ministers, and pound cake and layer cake, and biscuits as aforesaid; and new bread and old both, in case the minister is dyspeptic and can't eat new . . ."*

"What are ministers?" Delphine asked.

"Church-type people," said Eddy, which seemed the simplest explanation. "Same ballpark as nuns."

Delphine had been rendered briefly mute by the concept of nuns and then by Sue herself when they'd gone round to Dickens Street for a gardening session. Considering Sue through Delphine's eyes, Eddy saw she might be formidable: her bearing, the crisp consonants and unfaltering gaze. Delphine had hugged his side, watchful and unsmiling until the subject of Mother came up. "What do you think I should do?" Sue asked her.

"Give him to my brother," the child said immediately.

"*There's* a thought," said Sue, and after that Delphine relaxed.

These new people—their places, their pets, their things, their habits—all were minor astonishments for Delphine. Her world was shrunken. No school friends came to the house, and she went to no one's. Aunts, uncles, cousins, grandparents, all were varying degrees of aloof. And Josie didn't have friends. She'd *had* them, she told Eddy, plenty once, but they'd dropped away because she was hopeless at maintaining them. Work took over, *life* took over. Also, people were weird about Jasper.

This had caused Eddy to think hard about his own friends, his neglect of them over the winter, his continued remoteness, what with pets and owners and childcare and The Return of Boo. Was it possible to wind your way back after being so conspicuously unavailable? What if everyone had moved on?

Walking the petted princelings after the Saturday pancakes, he passed the Snorebins Tennis Club and smelled the newly mown grass, heard grunts and the *ponk* of balls. He felt the tug of the court, dormant for more than a year, and texted Harry at once, before he could talk himself out of it. He was both relieved and a little ashamed by Harry's prompt response: *mate! so good to hear from u. the court calls.* On Sunday Eddy hauled his tennis gear from the Bishop Street laundry and drove to Fendalton, to Harry and his freshly painted, newly netted tennis court, where he suffered a humbling defeat. His game had gone to hell.

"You'll pick up," said Harry. They sat on the bench at the side of the court, puce-faced, sweat drying tight and salty. "A few hits'll do it. Not bad really, for what, a year?" He turned and looked at Eddy, appraising. "But you're looking healthy. All the dog walking?"

Eddy filled Harry in on the menagerie, and Harry talked about uni. Engineering. Structural. He would have a secure future, earthquake-strengthening the country's building stock. His own future, Eddy thought, resembled an empty lot: dust, gravel, and spindly weeds. Untilled. Or lying fallow?

"Ed," said Harry as he walked with him to the car. Eddy, enjoying his all-body weariness and the great canopy of elms (*Ulmus minor*) lining the driveway, caught a tone in Harry's voice and knew suddenly where he was about to go.

"I'm sorry about—"

"Thanks," said Eddy swiftly, very firm. "Thanks, Haz." His all-tired body prickled, overalert.

Harry said nothing more. Door closed. Eddy felt bad at cutting him off. They'd almost never talked about personal stuff.

Cars lined the street, snaking around the bend, bumper-to-bumper and fractious. "The usual," said Harry, shrugging. Drainage. The leafier suburbs had dodged most of the quake ravages, except for the big residences on the banks of streams, though the toll was as random here as anywhere—Harry's family's property largely untouched, the two either side destined for rebuilds. And here, as any number of other places, hidden streams had been thrown up, slumping houses, playing havoc with the water and sewage pipe networks. The collective memory had been occluded; the city had forgotten it was built on a swamp. Now, *there* was a metaphor.

Eddy climbed into the car. His mood dipped: the thought of a traffic queue and tumbling blood sugar, needing food. He lowered the window.

"Nice wheels!" said Harry. "Get *me* a nun." He stood, waited two beats. "You okay, mate? Really?" Door not quite closed then.

"All good," said Eddy, hands on the wheel, quick grin. He felt chastened. Harry, whom he'd always thought undemanding, cruisy life, bit of a jock, not overly sensitive.

He was the insensitive one, Eddy thought, fully glum now. The Modern Priest had once told him he was too swift to judgment. But the Modern Priest had the judgment of a ragworm, so Eddy had ignored him.

"Really good to see you, Haz," said Eddy. He meant it, which cheered him slightly.

"Next week," said Harry. He slapped the car roof, signing off. Eddy flicked the indicator and waited for a generous motorist.

37

True to her word, Delphine entertained Brain in Emergency: a wide-ranging monologue that required only nods and smiles, occasional yeses and noes. Eddy, wishing for his earphones, wondered if Brain, too, might have preferred to be left alone, to look vacantly into the peopled space, *Messiah* blasting on his iPod Classic 2G. That old thing. The device irked Eddy every time he looked at it, a quite irrational response he knew. But his uncle's long and fastidious maintenance of the thing, despite the abundance of superseding models, seemed to Eddy the quintessence of Brain-ishness. Cautious. Fussy. Contentedly out of step with the zeitgeist, wherever it was. Quintessence: Brain word.

Brain sat, pale and stoical, his arm in a temporary sling tied by Eddy (thank you, New World first-aid course), the swollen wrist, oddly angled, resting on a folded hand towel. It was broken for sure. Delphine, very solicitous, inquired if Brain could manage a game of Last Card (thank you, Eddy-foresight-about-cards). "Let's give it a go," said Brain, trying for heartiness, fake-it-till-you blah, blah. He fanned his cards with supreme awkwardness and was occasionally driven to use his teeth. Delphine, not obviously cheating, nevertheless lied blithely about her comprehension of Last Card rules, to score second chances. "Of course, of course," said Brain, not at all gulled.

Eddy refrained from comment. Not the occasion for moral instruction. Plus, he was distracted, assailed by sensory memories: rubber soles on linoed floors, murmuring nurses, the antiseptic odor, magazines older than Moses, and the oppressive fluorescent lighting, elevating the surreal. He'd been at Emergency twice in the last two years—the broken metatarsals and, months later, a long hot Saturday night squiring Toss, who'd gashed his hand on a broken beer bottle. Eddy had sat bare-chested, his white T-shirt, blotched with blood, wrapped around Toss's hand. But mostly the hospital brought back the chilly morning in 2010 when he'd come with Boo for her termination. The heartless heavens had apparently determined that now was the long moment he must square up to that which he had chosen not to remember.

Last Friday: the Mulholland spare bed. Having agreed they must talk, he and Boo had then fallen into a gluey silence, watching the on-off shadow play across the bedroom wall, listening to each other's breathing, locating their old, overwrought selves. Eddy's brain-dial swiveled to near-dead. He tried to form meaningful thoughts and coherent sentences but could summon only the *winter* of all those dramas—the biting cold, Boo's frigid hands, Toss's foggy breath in the sleep-out—and the great swerves of mood, elation to violent despair in seconds. He got as far as "I think that—" but Boo spoke first.

"So. I'm sorry."

But wasn't this his line? He shut his eyes and saw in technicolor his seized and obdurate self of two years ago, that fevered boy, driven by primitive impulses he still couldn't adequately explain. He had lived in a red haze. He had been deaf and blind to Boo's harsh choice, consumed by the belief that it was *he* who would somehow be obliterated.

"*I'm* sorry," he said.

"Okay, you win," said Boo. Half laughed. "Not for the thing," she said. "I'm not sorry about that. It's more . . ." She paused, trawling her brain box, no doubt. "I'm sorry about how you felt."

"I was—" Eddy began. Crazy? He wanted to say he was *crazy*. It was true in one way. Now, behind his eyes, he saw Brain, too, the soft landscape of that dependable face suddenly inflexible, replaced by an unyielding Brain who—astonishingly—had only limited sympathy for Eddy's position. After the hospital incident, duly reported by the traitorous Viv, Brain had fully lost his temper and accused Eddy of *infantile and unforgivable self-absorption*. Eddy, until that moment unaware Brain had a temper to lose, had been shocked cold. But it was all too late. Damage done. Other storms gathering. He had been shoved forward helplessly to new dramas, a different future.

"Oh, pull the *pud*," said Toss More, faux weeping beneath his pom-pommed hat, unmoved and mean, whenever Eddy peddled his Ineluctable Fate explanation of that time. To his eternal surprise, Toss had been on Boo's side. But then, Toss detested babies and children. Messy. Leaking orifices. Clawing at you. Psychologically and actually. After *The Day of the Bomb*, his favorite childhood books were *The Beastly Baby* and *The Gashlycrumb Tinies* by Edward Gorey. "Thank God you didn't come trailing grabby siblings," he said once to Eddy.

"I was self-absorbed," said Eddy to Boo, in the Mulhollands' spare bedroom. The brain-dial had creaked minutely clockwise, enabling borrowed words at least.

"It was infantile," he said.

"I'm sorry I kept saying *baby*," he said. "Sorry I said it just now." His own words. He meant them.

"It doesn't matter," said Boo. "Not now."

More silence. Did it matter? Eddy didn't know.

"It wasn't nothing," said Boo. "It was something. Ontologically."

They laughed for real, thinking of the Modern Priest, who never missed a chance to bat that word about.

A possibility, thought Eddy. A wish. A dread. He had not known how to sort his feelings about it all. So he'd done what he usually did with the unwelcome: he shoveled it all into the brain-crypt, where it had obediently stayed put. Until these last few months when his emotional state had fluctuated wildly, when both the past and the future had come calling with inconvenient regularity.

"It's better to talk about stuff," said Boo, as if she were listening to his thoughts.

"Not really my style," said Eddy, trying for another laugh.

"True," said Boo. "For someone with a truckful of words, you're utter shit at it."

Or, thought Eddy, feeling the need to be kind to himself, you could put it the other way: he was absolutely *excellent* at not talking about the stuff he didn't want to.

38

The wrist was broken. "A distal radius fracture," Brain explained to Delphine, after the X-ray and being fitted with a splint and plied with painkillers and antibiotics and coming for them in the hospital café. Delphine was gagging on scrambled egg like a defiant baby, a morsel at a time, face contorted, on the promise of an ice cream if she ate half a plateful. It was bad juju to bribe children with sugary treats, but Eddy had suspended high-minded caregiving for the day. The day had been lost to the distal radius.

It was 2:30 p.m. now and stiflingly hot. Eddy and Brain sat in the shade of a giant ash in the Harman Grove at the Botanical Gardens, concentrating on their ice cream. Delphine stood before them in the sun, dancing from foot to foot, making a dog's breakfast of hers. Eddy could barely look at her, ice-creamed face and the eye on walkabout, sticky rivulets down her arm, the cone softening by the second. Brain supplied one of his immaculate handkerchiefs, polka-dotted, ever at hand.

"Back for a cast when the swelling is reduced," said Brain, between licks. "A simple fracture, no bone realignment necessary. Hallelujah. Six weeks with the cast, alas. No bicycle."

"The good news is it's your right wrist," said Delphine. Eddy and Brain looked up from their ice cream dispatch.

"How'd you know he's left-handed?" said Eddy.

"Because I *notice* things. I noticed that he held the tongs in his left hand, and I noticed that he keeps his handkerchief in his left-hand pocket." She gave a small bow: the cat that swallowed the ice cream.

Eddy felt a great judder of fondness for Delphine. These little seizures visited him about as frequently as the equally strong desire to shut her in her bedroom without food or water. Roughly the same jolting seesaw between affection and exasperation he had with Brain. And Toss.

"Ice cream alert," said Brain, pointing. Eddy's ice cream was shiny and sinking, his finger felt a drip. They giggled at his furious licking.

Pass the gelignite, said Toss in his head, encased in duvets despite the soaring temperatures.

39

Back at Bishop Street, Eddy made Brain a cup of restorative Earl Grey and listened to him agonize about the evening ahead, then suddenly conclude all would be well after all. "Nothing to worry about," he said, almost surprised. The decorations suitcase was down from the attic. Tree was in place. Food ready in fridge. Ginge and Bridgie were bringing wine. Of course they were.

"Christmas tree and sugary tea," said Eddy. He texted Boo an update.

"And fruit of the vine," said Brain. "And carols." He looked exhausted, his face sunk like the ice cream.

"You should lie down," said Eddy. "We'll manage. We'll wake you up when everyone's here. We're picking up Jasper, then Boo, then Sue."

"You rhymed twice," said Delphine. She sat at the table arranging the passengers from Eddy's Ark in different formations, explaining the moves, her preferences. Mother perched on a chair beside her, watching.

"Break those and you're dead," said Eddy.

"That's actually abusive," said Delphine. "To a child."

"It is a trifle violent," said Brain absently. He stood with some effort. "I think I will lie down for a minute or two."

"Fah-*lah*," said Delphine, right up in Mother's face. "*Fah-la-LAH! Say* it!"

No luck. The bird was unaccountably mulish, despite her frequent bawled instructions.

"You'll get pecked," said Eddy.

"But why *won't* he?"

"Too hard to pronounce? Could be your teaching style."

"What do you mean?"

"You're bellicose."

"You're bellicose, too."

"Oh, really? What does bellicose mean, then?"

"You shouldn't use it if you don't know."

"I do know."

"Why did you ask, then?"

They went on like this sometimes. Eddy enjoyed it. It was a junior version of his and Toss's saw-toothed, cul-de-sac exchanges when they had nothing better to do. He supposed this was how siblings talked to each other, half-cantankerous, half-gleeful.

"God bless us!" said Mother seconds later. And then, as if he knew Delphine would be aggrieved, hopped one chair away and out of reach.

"See!"

"He prefers Laurence Olivier's voice to yours. As do I. Less squeaky."

"Who on *earth* is Laurence Bing Bong?" said Delphine.

"Someone with a most emollient voice."

"I'm not listening to you."

"Ditto."

Eddy suddenly wanted a lie-down, too. His thoughts were running away, calculating how Brain would cope over the next few weeks. Shower and dress and cook one-handed? Bus to work. Or walk. Was one-handed work even possible? Three-finger typing? It seemed unlikely. Eddy would have to come back and help. But he couldn't desert Josie; she'd implode. Unless he transported Delphine and Jasper, plus dogs, to Bishop Street. Though Jasper would have to relocate his entire desktop caboodle. And share a room with Delphine. Unless he slept in the living room . . .

And now the coming weeks crowded in: one more New World Sunday before Xmas, finishing touches to the chevrons, and Boo's present; Justin and the Rhode Island Red owners were back this week, so adieu to hens and frog—a pity, he'd miss them, but there was a slew of fresh pets coming at him as people piled their lives into cars and drove as fast as possible away from the unlovely city for solace at lakes and rivers and sea. Brain and Ginge's plans for day treks in the Kaikōuras would be off now; Sue was going, Motherless, to a cousin in Tākaka for a week, leaving Eddy her car, really his car these days. He could visit Boo in Hokitika, meet her family.

Things were good with Boo, weren't they? He thought they were. He was pretty sure. It was good they'd talked, however desultorily; things seemed clearer, *lighter*. Though it was true, too, that Eddy had several times caught Boo's concentrated gaze on him, her brow crimped, as if he were a particularly brain-tickling rebus she must decode.

"What is our *plan*?" said Delphine. Our plan. She said this daily. Often very early. She had no compunction about coming into the bedroom, despite the firmly shut door. One morning he'd woken in fright to find her standing beside the bed looking down at him, eyes at odds, willing him to wake up.

"Go away," he'd hissed, turning over toward the slumberous Boo, all warm and fragrant. But Delphine had stuck an insistent finger into his bare shoulder and hissed right back. "*Arbuckle?* What time will we see him?" She was his permanent shadow now, dogging him like a conscience.

"Our plan is simple," said Eddy. "Get in the car, get everyone, get straight back here." Straight back? Laughably imprecise. Road cone battalions and Xmas traffic, who knew how long it would take?

"By the time we're back, Ginge and Bridgie will be here and we'll be ready to roll. Or possible alternative: you stay here and listen to the emollient Sir Bing Bong?" He was desperate for some quiet.

Delphine rearranged the Ark animals once more, placing the albatrosses in the lead.

"These are my second favorites," she said.

"Toroa ingoingo," said Eddy. *"Diomedea epomophora."*

"Whatever."

If you say *one* more botanical name, Toss More had snarled as they wandered royally stoned around the Botanical Gardens, I'm going to punch you.

"Don't you want me to come with you?" said Delphine, fake pathetic.

"Of course I do, but what about no talking? Just for a change."

"Why?"

"Because silence is golden." Doris's favorite cliché.

"I was going to ask you all about *them*," she said, sweeping an arm over the animals. Transparently untrue.

He went to the CD player and pressed open. There was Brain's CD of Sir Laurence Olivier's *A Christmas Carol*. Recorded at the Theatre Royal, Drury Lane, London, in the Bronze Age and transferred to CD by someone at the library. Eddy had explained the evolving listening platforms, to no avail. "I'm happy," said Brain. This was clearly true, though somehow more annoying.

"C'mon," said Eddy. "I'll introduce you to Sir Laurence."

"Sir Bing Bong," said Delphine. She held up the Maud Island frogs. "These are my actual favorites."

"*Leiopelma pakeka*," said Eddy, defying the Toss earworm. "Also known as pepeketua. Maybe my faves, too."

"Their eyes are sad though," said Delphine. She brought a frog's eye up close to her own vagrant one. Eddy had labored over those eyes. Their pooling blackness and dappled pupils, the tiny shaft of light.

"All frogs look sad," he said. "But really they're not. We just assume they're like us: anthropomorphism."

"Professor Kleinbein," said Delphine wearily.

"C'mon!" he ordered.

They left Mother on the kitchen sill with Christmas cake offcuts. Dried fruit for bowel health. And how would Brain deal one-handed with Mother? Should the bird be given over to Jasper, perhaps permanently? Or would he be a cheering companion for the period Brain was *discommoded*? The logistics mushroomed in his head. One evening, over the kitchen island, Josie, well pinot-noired, had declared him a born project manager. He should check out CERA vacancies, she said. Thank you, no, thought Eddy: a fast route to social ostracism. CERA was reviled. CERA was down there in hell with insurance claims adjusters and the abdominous (Ginge word) Minister for Earthquake Recovery.

In the car, Eddy shared more Maud Island frog data with Delphine. *If you must do it . . .*

"Fun fact," he said as they belted up. "*L. pakeka* don't have a tadpole stage. They hatch fully formed from eggs."

"Whatever," said Delphine.

"Also, they don't croak. Barely frogs, if you think about it."

"Can I play this?" She waved the CD at him.

He scanned the navigational options in the Google Maps of his front brain. Should he risk Papanui Road? Or take the back roads? Six of one.

"Nevertheless, they're the longest-living wild frog in the world."

"Fa-*lah*." She shoved the CD in the player.

The familiar static. A recording of a live performance, transferred to vinyl, played to death for fifty years by Brain. But the static was a vital part of the soundtrack, Eddy thought—as if it were being reported directly from the Victorian Age, down the long funnel of history.

"This is weird," said Delphine. A choir, not so much singing as swooping: spectral wails and portentous string accompaniment.

"*Thisss is Laurence Olivier*," said Eddy with Laurence Olivier, syncing perfectly with his precise enunciations, his lavish sibilance. "*Over a hundred yearsss ago in December 1843, Charlesss Dickensss wrote thisss story.*"

"You said no talking."

"I did?"

Brain had also read the book to Eddy, and the ghost of Sir Laurence Bing Bong had hung over the reading, the pulse and cadence of Brain's narration echoing the actor's. Eddy had followed the print as Brain read, caught in the sprawling sentences, the thickets of adjectives, which, by the time he was ten, were written inside him along with all the other inscriptions of childhood.

Papanui Road proved an epic mistake: gummed-up traffic reduced to one lane and potential side-street escapes unaccountably blocked off. Eddy cursed Christmas shoppers and global consumer culture, leading them all to perdition. Fuckwits buying purposeless crap destined for the Great Pacific Garbage Patch.

"*If they would rather die,*" said Sir Laurence Scrooge, "*they had better do ittt,*" *and decrease the surplusss population.*" Delphine listened closely, her mouth slightly open, as always when she concentrated. She was adenoidal, a mouth breather. There'd been talk of surgery, said Josie, but then the earthquakes and, you know . . .

They inched past the All Seasons, slated for demolition, though still no sign of the wrecking ball; the hotel had been fenced off for months, the faux-Georgian façade weathered now, a tasty challenge to squatters and taggers. Also, the godly and godless alike: a graffitied banner tied to the fence proclaimed JESUS IS LARD.

"Bah, humbug!" said Delphine experimentally. *"Bah!"*

"Do you get it?" Eddy asked.

The story was ruthlessly abbreviated and the sound engineering third rate, atmospheric static notwithstanding. He'd misheard a good deal himself when young. The Ghost of Marley, for instance, did not say *You have* laid but *on it, ever since,* when talking about Scrooge's heavy chain. He said *labored.* There were a sackful of these misunderstandings in his song- and story-listening history.

"I'm not dumb," said Delphine. "Some ghosts are coming."

Eddy stuck his head out the window to see beyond the curving cones, divine traffic prospects up ahead. For all they knew, the queue stretched to Kaikōura. Cars and cones from arsehole to breakfast.

Papanui Road was old. The original route north. Papanui: great plain. Thank you, Brain, who knew the city backward and upside down, its surfaces and layered history. He knew its pre-city self, the boggy truth, its indigenous mappings and names. The earthquakes' eruptions and cleavages had brought no surprises for Brain.

"It was a strange figure that led him out into the night," said Sir Laurence as narrator. The first spirit had arrived.

"Like a child: yettt. nottt. so. likkke. a. child. aslikeanoldman." Spit, spit. Eddy felt his customary queasiness at the Ghost of Christmas Past, a shriveled and wispy-voiced being, bowed down by everyone's disappointments, but chilly and remorseless. His legs were working up to a titanic attack of restlessness. But his phone pinged, distracting him. Boo. She would walk home; she wanted the exercise.

One less thing to do, he thought. And Boo would organize things in the kitchen.

"What a *super-duper* wife you'll make someone," said Toss, duvet-swaddled and crotchety when Eddy, sick of disorder, the dubious odors, had set about tidying the sleep-out. "You're an old lady domestic fusspot," said Toss. "As bad as Brain. Possibly worse."

"Whatever," said Eddy, determined not to bite. In the end, he'd just stuffed things into the old blanket chests they'd bought on Trade Me, dragged the spare mattress out into the thin winter sun, and flung open the doors and windows to banish the funky smell. Then, to mollify Toss, he'd lain on the bed with him, and they'd harmonized a few numbers from what Eddy thought of as the Treacly Sickbed Songbook: "Sometimes I Feel Like a Motherless Child" and "Kevin Barry" and "Amazing Grace," Toss doing the full Judy Collins and Eddy being the choir. The anthemic and the doomed: Toss's preferred currency.

The queue crawled forward now, spaces lengthening. Some idiot tooted his relief—it was always a guy—and every car followed suit. Festive spirits, spirits lifting, blah, blah. Fools. His own shaky Xmas spirits were flagging once more.

Delphine leaned into the speaker, trying to hear amidst the din.

"Who's Fizzywink?"

"Fezziwig. A capitalist. A generous one. Likes a party."

"What's a capitalist?"

Your mother, Eddy did not say. "We'll get to that."

They approached Merivale at 30 km, practically reckless, then were slowed once again along the shopping center strip. Jolly, bag-laden buyers clogged the footpaths and spilled out onto the road, defying buses. More irascible tooting. Eddy tooted himself now, seeing Harry just feet away at the crossing, bags in each hand. He rolled down the window and shouted him over, paused Sir Laurence.

"Feliz Navidad, hombres!" said Harry, grinning into the car.

"Spontaneous combustion seems more likely," said Eddy.

"Gidday," said Harry to Delphine, who stared at him with her usual boss-eyed curiosity.

"Harry, Delphine; Delphine, Harry," said Eddy.

"I need ideas," said Harry. "Something for the folks."

The Life of Mammals," said Eddy. "Can't go wrong."

"Or a Chores-for-a-Day voucher!" said Delphine, which was her present for Jasper. "With your best writing and stickers."

"*And* you're moving," said Harry as the lights changed. He banged the roof of the car. "Voucher sounds good! Don't combust. Peace and love, hombres!" He was gone, round the back of the car and swallowed by the footpath crowd.

Peace and love? Harry must be stoned. Probably the only way to commit Christmas shopping without self-immolating.

"Tennis Hazza," said Delphine, very smug. She knew about all his friends—she had ferreted out most details of his biography—and he had characterized them thus: Tennis Hazza, New World Sylvester, Wellington Ollie, etc.

"Is he your best friend?"

She was a friend anthropologist, digging around in other people's inventories, trying to piece the phenomenon together. She had quizzed Boo as well, who had obliged with quite the list; this had disheartened Delphine until Boo assured her they'd all come after she was thirteen.

"Best friends aren't really an adult thing," said Eddy. Was this true? No idea.

"You're not an adult," said Delphine. You're a teenager. Nine*teen.*"

She pressed Sir Laurence back into life, the orange cones dribbled out, and a second line of traffic opened up. Eddy's legs relaxed.

Scrooge, though, had become upset with the Ghost, with the sight of himself in his own past, solitary and unloved, and with guilty thoughts of Bob CraTchittttt, wretched workhorse, toiling away at the countinghouse.

"*Rrrre*move *me from this place!*" said Eddy and Laurence Scrooge.

They passed the gracious stretch of Papanui Road: big sections and serious fences, the remains of English gardens and once-grand houses enshrouded by oaks and alders and elms, their leaves limp in the heat.

"Look," said Eddy. "Some capitalists' houses!"

But Delphine was riveted to Sir Bing Bong.

"*These are the shadows of things that have been,*" whined the Ghost. "*If they are what they are, don't blame me!*"

"One down," said Eddy as Paparoa Street loomed. He flicked the indicator.

"*Leave me!*" said Sir Laurence Scrooge. "*Take me back!*"

Haunt me no longer! mouthed Eddy with Scrooge.

40

It was 6:10 p.m. when Eddy ushered his pickups through the back door at Bishop Street and into the evening's business. Someone had hung the battered glitter Christmas bell. Its hook, too, waited hopefully all year in the entranceway architrave.

"Be my guest," said Eddy to Delphine. But it was just out of her reach, so he lifted her up by the twiggy legs. She pulled the gilt clapper with ceremonial slowness, and out came the ludicrously speedy version of "Silent Night." Sue burst out laughing.

"It's from Brain's childhood," said Eddy. He felt oddly protective. "He loves it."

"Mi-i-graine Night, Fa-amily fight, All are crazy, all in flight," Toss More had sung, pulling the bell over and over, the Christmas they were eleven and had finished off the dregs in the adults' wineglasses. The galloping tempo made them laugh so much, Eddy's stomach had rebelled, sending him urgently to the laundry sink. Later, Bridgie at the piano and the rest of them gathered round, Toss had hissed in his ear, *"Round yon Virgin BrainBox and Child, Oily Eddy, with vomitous smile,"* and they had been hopeless for the rest of the carols. Everything had been hilarious that year, especially adults—randoms passed in the street, teachers, Toss's mother clutching at the steering wheel, her jutting jaw, even Brain asking, "May I have the Vegemite?" Why that year, that age? Eddy wondered, staring at the dented bell as the plink of "Silent Night" slowed and stopped, *"Sle-eep in heav—"*

But Delphine pulled him into the living room, and there they beheld the table, groaning with comestibles, savory and sweet. Brain had surpassed himself.

Delphine stood before it, dumb with pleasure, checking off the promised treats . . . *three kinds of cookies, and fruit-cake, and . . . and . . .* Jasper made straight for Mother, the most reliable sentient in the room, despite his fitful love. Boo, propped against the unlit wood burner, was folding crepe paper into chains, fingers working fast.

"At last!" she said, hugging Sue, then Eddy, draping a chain around his neck and an arm around Delphine. "Help me," she said, thrusting red and green paper strips at her. "This is purgatory."

"What's purgatory?" said Delphine.

"An imaginary place for needless suffering," said Sue promptly.

Eddy felt briefly giddy at the thought of all the personalities that would soon be in the room, relationships old and new, the latent combustion.

Brain was parked on the couch, folding napkins one-handed into Christmas trees.

"In easy state upon this couch, there sat a jolly Giant!" said Eddy, having only half an hour earlier heard Sir Laurence as narrator exclaim thus about the Ghost of Christmas Present.

"Not altogether easy by the look of it," said Sue. Brain smiled up at them, almost shy.

"How very good to meet you, Brian," said Sue. She sat down beside him and gently touched the splint above his right hand, puffy and red.

"Yes, yes, indeed," said Brain. He patted her hand with his free one.

Watching this, Eddy felt an odd knot of things. Satisfaction, curiosity, and a flicker of disquiet for what might unfold. It was like seeing two historic figures, or book characters, uprooted and fetched across time, brought together for some necessary summit. Hildegard of Bingen and Albus Dumbledore. Matthew Cuthbert and Kate Sheppard.

There was knocking at the kitchen door.

"Excuse me," said Brain to Sue. "That's Loretta, our neighbor." He signaled to Eddy, stalled in front of them contemplating friendships across a fifth dimension. "Ed, I forgot to say—she came last year. Would you?"

Eddy went to the door, rapidly recalculating the evening's relationship equations. And then—a first—he was sideways hugging Loretta, who smelled of roses and smiled hectically. She held a plate covered by another plate.

"Lovely to see you, Ed. You've been away, I know." Eddy took the plates. "Just some deviled prunes. Brian said I mustn't, but you know?"

"Lovely to see you, too," said Eddy, more or less meaning it. Loretta looked different, younger somehow. Her eyes were bright. She wore a cream-colored dress with a flouncy tulle skirt.

"Great dress!"

"My festive dress," said Loretta. "I'm doubly festive, Ed! Wonderful news: the insurance nightmare is over. It's all settled. I'm *crazy* with relief! I've brought two bottles to celebrate twice over!"

"Great news!" said Eddy. The petition could rest in peace.

"I *know!*" said Loretta, suddenly hugging him again, so that the plates and the great puff of skirt nearly collided.

"You'll be in good company," said Eddy. Bridgie and Ginge were coming through the French doors as he spoke, each carrying a box of wine.

"*Bridgie!*" said Loretta. "I love that woman!" She left Eddy and made her way to Bridgie, who greeted her with equal fervor. Who knew? Eddy supposed they'd met last year when, as the previous year, he had absented himself and conducted an anti-tree-decorating protest (characterized principally by inertia) in the sleep-out with Toss More.

It was all introductions then, the flurry of hugs and hearty voices, blah, blah. Eddy looked for Jasper, who might be quietly dying. But he was with Boo beside the wood burner, folding crepe paper ribbons very deliberately, Mother on his shoulder, both bird and boy apparently coping.

Bridgie wore a peacock-blue velvet cloak trimmed with fur. Her hair was piled on her head and studded with sparkling hair clips.

"You look like a magician's assistant," said Eddy.

"My Queen of the Night rip-off," she said, kissing him with her customary enthusiasm. "Merry what-have-yous, George. And don't panic, one of these boxes is for Christmas Day." She surveyed the room. "This is festive!"

Eddy surveyed it, too. More unlikely interfaces: Ginge was pouring a glass of Asti Spumante (Brain festive tipple) for Loretta. Delphine stood beside them, looking expectant. Before the evening was over, she would have invited herself to Ginge's house, Eddy was sure. She had interviewed him thoroughly about Ginge and Bridgie. She could recite the names of Ginge's cats.

He looked across to Brain and Sue, and back to Jasper and Boo, and now Bridgie, clasping Boo in a reunion hug. There were only nine people, but the room felt thronged and highly colored—like Fezziwig's Christmas party!—effervescent clusters, perky and primed, ready for *a very good time* of comestibles, carols, and general God-bless-us-everyone.

But then, from nowhere, came one of those odd dimming-hologram moments where everyone shrunk, as if they were being sucked out of view, and Eddy's connection to them seemed to fray dangerously.

Connection? said Toss, out of sight, too, his voice dwindling in the enveloping dark, his hand cold in Eddy's warm one. I don't feel connected. Don't *feel*. Only when we sing. Or when I'm, you know. Eddy had held his breath in the dark, sweat breaking, Toss's arid inner landscape oppressing him.

"Mr. Kleinbein," said Boo, beside him, sliding her hand into his. "What's the order of service?"

"Get everyone a drink," said Eddy a little too loudly. Pushing away rogue thoughts. "Then get going, I guess. I'm out of practice."

Nothing forgotten, though. Just submerged, during his two-year tantrum. He was overwritten with it all, inside and out, the years and years of rituals, events good and terrible, people present and absent, and now, suddenly, stuff rearing up from the brain-crypt and making him feel incredibly weird. He squeezed Boo's hand, and gradually the room and its inhabitants assumed their normal proportions. Ginge was passing him a glass of spewmante (Toss), Delphine exclaiming at the contents of the decorations suitcase, and Bridgie handing out Loretta's deviled prunes.

Brain was up from the couch greeting Loretta, Bridgie taking his place with the plate of prunes, making the acquaintance of Sue Lombardo. Another unlikely pairing. Joan of Arc and Madonna: the queen of pop, not the queen of heaven. But that was off to a good start, they were clinking glasses and both taking good slugs for stomachs and unbridled pleasure.

Eddy drank some spewmante. It was like fizzy raisins. Not unpleasant. He tried a few steadying breaths, squeezed Boo's hand again. She looked at him, quizzical. He waggled his eyebrows. Wtf?

Brain was beside them now, looking purposeful. "Time to get things underway, I think, Ed."

Delphine was laying out the decorations in rows on the floor, something Eddy had done himself many times, fond of them all over again each year, the odd little family of snowmen, soldiers, birds, dolls, and their attendant signifiers—reindeer, gingerbread men, pine cones, bells, stockings, et al. He had his favorites of course; they all did. The paper snowflake. The peg doll in lavalava. The beaded kōtare. Brain had been adding a new ornament every year since the Bronze Age, selected after lengthy deliberation in Ballantynes' Christmas shop, a ceremonial visit that Eddy had always enjoyed, until abruptly, at age eleven, he absolutely had not.

"Nothing new this year," said Brain, apparently privy to Eddy's thoughts. "Or last year."

"No?" He hadn't noticed.

"The quakes, somehow. Thoughts of upcycling. I had plans to repurpose Doris's china."

China pieces, in fact, gathered from beneath Doris's china cabinet, another deathless heirloom (*with cabriole legs!*), which had been emptied out in the September quake and flung down on top of its shattered contents. They had cleared out Doris's house together, and Brain had been commendably ruthless with Doris's possessions, except for the Temuka pottery and the bone china fragments, which he had swept into a cardboard box and taken home to the garage.

"Tea-set recycling," said Boo. "It's a thing. Post-quake craft zeitgeist. Kicking the colonial legacy to touch." Or not. Every second Knit World customer wore a piece of recycled teacup jewelry.

"Really?" said Brain. "Tell me more about this."

"Later, B," said Eddy. He took the kitchen scissors from the top of the wood burner and rapped the metal gently against his glass. "Comrades!" he called. This made him feel more normal.

"The peo-ple's flag is dee-pest red!" sang Ginge, predictably. He raised his spewmante in salute.

"Not yet, Ginge!" said Eddy, going harder with the scissors.

"What's that?" Boo asked Brain.

"Old joke," he said. "'The Red Flag.' Same tune as 'O Christmas Tree.'"

Eddy pointed the scissors at Brain. "Take it away, B."

Brain did a mini throat clear, then seemed to lift himself up, shed his tired face. "Season's Greetings, everyone, and welcome. So good to see you all here. Welcome back to Loretta, and welcome to Boo, away these last two years. And a most warm welcome to our new *Tannenbaum*-decorating friends—"

"It shrouded oft our martyred dead," continued Ginge, sotto voce.

"Thank you, Raymond," growled Bridgie.

"—Sue, Jasper, and Delphine," said Brain, laughing. "May this be the first of many."

"Hear, hear!" said Bridgie and Loretta, together on the couch now, their glasses already refilled.

Eddy watched Delphine. She knelt at the base of the tree, a bundle of decorations ready in her lap. She was utterly still, her eyes glued to Brain, her face splotched red, heated by mysterious emotions. Who knew what she was thinking? Sue stood close by, framed by the tree, her silver hair blooming against the green. She raised her glass across the room to Eddy.

"So, we'll festoon the tree," said Brain.

Jesus. *Festoon.* Eddy blushed on his uncle's behalf. Boo's finger pressed into his side, and he had to stare ahead at the wattle tree out the window, picture Marley two feet under so he wouldn't laugh.

"Then some food, then I hope you're all in good voice. So!" Brain inclined his head to Ginge.

"*Clear away, my lads,*" said Ginge in a stage voice. "*Let's have lots of room here!*"

Ginge's Fezziwig moment, ushering in the proceedings.

"*Hilli-ho, Dick! Chirrup, Ebenezer!*"

Thank you, Sir Laurence Bing Bong.

"I've chosen all the decorations!" said Delphine. This was her privilege, Brain had told her, as the youngest at the gathering.

"O Holy Fuck," said Boo, under her breath. "Look who's coming up the path."

Eddy turned his head and, having seen, swiveled involuntarily as if stung, so that he suddenly faced Jasper, directly behind him, still folding.

"Stand by! Stand by!" said Mother, taking fright at this sudden change. He fled from Jasper's shoulder to the top of the wood burner and anxiously ate some crepe paper scraps.

"No show without fucking Punch," muttered Eddy.

"What's the story? Fuck off!" Mother added.

"Punch?" said Jasper.

Fuck off, all right, thought Eddy, turning back around. He felt both furious and infinitely weary. The Modern Priest had pulled open the French doors and paused, so the company could behold him, the eternal leading man making his entrance.

"Buon Natale, amici miei! Meri Kirihimete! Tēnā koutou!" He held out a gigantic frozen turkey. "From a grateful parishioner!"

Some supermarket plutocrat, thought Eddy. Possibly even Judith.

"Enough for a feast, scores of diners," said Cristoforo Mangan. "You up for it, Brain?"

"Who's that?" asked Jasper.

"Beelzebub," said Eddy.

"Weird name."

"A fallen angel," said Eddy.

"What?"

41

Eddy leaned against the piano, listening to Bridgie's medley of Christmas tunes and old musical chestnuts. All part of the ritual. This had once also been a game: as each melody elided another, Ginge, Brain, and the Modern Priest competed to name the new tune. Boomer Bingo, Toss called it, though he joined in whenever he attended, keen to outshout and outshine the Modern Priest, who was handicapped by his scorn for all music since 1954 (except "Climb Every Mountain," which Bridgie loyally inserted every year). The game had been retired in Eddy's absence; this year the music was simply the accompaniment to everyone's postprandial digestive processes (Brain phrase).

Sue was deep in conversation with Boo; Ginge sat with Jasper and Mother, trying in vain to tempt the bird onto his balled fist; Loretta stood at Bridgie's shoulder, mesmerized by her hands on the keys. Brain sat on the couch with the Modern Priest, who knocked back red wine and nursed his food baby, a wobbly little lodger spilling over his trouser belt. What a greedy old gobbler he was, hungry for sugary comestibles and Christmas meats. The ravenous adolescent to Brain's maternal feeder.

Eddy had thought the evening safe from the Modern Priest, but he had arrived back unexpectedly early from the mountains—some retreat, "ECT for his moral compass," whispered Boo in the kitchen as they rinsed plates and utensils—and decided he must join the festivities. Typical, thought Eddy, he never waits for an invitation. Their house was somehow also his whenever he wished. Eddy had managed not to address him all evening, but he could not stop himself keeping an eye out, watching him work the room, the chameleon cleric readjusting his persona for each encounter: respectful with Sue Lombardo, a little frisky with Loretta, boisterously fraternal with Bridgie and Ginge, solicitous with Boo. Jasper and Delphine got a big fat swerve because the Modern Priest had no idea how to talk to children—once upon a time he'd patted heads and caressed little cheeks, but Bridgie had put a stop to this, declaring it patronizing and inappropriate at best. Over the groaning Christmas tea table, Brain had looked at Eddy, his face beseeching and apologetic at once. Oh, what the hell, Eddy thought, and had begun to drink the spewmante with real intent.

His head was muzzy now, but he didn't care. He was soothed by Bridgie's playing, semi-inoculated against the Modern Priest and the other importunate visitor who was trying to take over his brain box. At the other end of the piano was Delphine, propped on a stool, chin resting in hands. She watched the circling angels on the Swedish candle chimes, in its Advent position on top of the piano. Her face was rapt, her happiness complete. Like Anne Shirley with her puffed sleeves. It did something to Eddy's heart. He thought it was his heart.

The candle chimes had come from a long-ago Swedish lover of Bridgie's, Pernilla the double bassist. Bridgie had left her abruptly after a year in Stockholm. She'd missed them all too much apparently. At the time this had seemed only proper to Eddy, who believed their family immutable. Now, thinking of Pernilla, ditched in favor of the Whack family's wine-soaked bosom, it seemed downright perverse. He knew better—he was a nine*teen*-year-old adult. Nothing was immutable: *Im Gegenteil.* On the contrary.

Except for the candle-chime angels, he amended, a minute later.

They *were* unvarying—fixed in place, driven round and round in help-less circles, propelled by the turbine and the heat from the candles. They blew their silent trumpets; their little gold rods tickled the bells: luckless Christmas slaves. Trapped by myth! And physics! Science and theology unexpectedly in lockstep. His stomach gurgled and roiled. Bridgie was modulating her way out of gloomy old "Let All Mortal Flesh Keep Silence." The king of carols, said Toss. Whatever, said Eddy in his head, waiting for the new tune to reveal itself. There it was, "Tin Angel." Bridgie claimed this an Xmas carol in its true heart, too bad what Joni Mitchell thought when she wrote it. She always played this last because, though it was in a minor key and as mournful as an elegy, the song finished on a major chord. A tierce de Picardie, Bridgie had told Eddy. Minor to major! The unquenchable human inclina-tion to the joyous! She had wheeled out examples from Bach to Bob Dylan, mad for this bonny worldview: the creed of tierce de Picardie. Oh, jolly, jolly, said Toss, unimpressed. Oompah-pah. Let's all smile ourselves to death. That year at the tree decorating, he repudiated Bridgie's optimism by singing "Joy to the World" in a minor key, quite the high-wire act. Bridgie, filled with spewmante and seasonal love, had been only amused and admiring. But the Modern Priest, home from Italy for the summer, tanned and well-tailored and smug with confidentialities about the new pope, had taken Eddy aside to warn him against the cheapness of cynicism, the cold comforts of nihilism, the corroding—

"George," said Bridgie. She was done. The tierce de Picardie had passed, and he hadn't even noticed. His stomach definitely felt iffy. He might need another cooling beer.

"Time for carols."

42

They made a semicircle around the piano, each with a copy of the booklets Brain had printed years ago and stapled together: the words for each carol, and each carol part of an unvarying order. The booklets were crumpled and stained but hanging together. A serviceable description for some of the assembled singers, Eddy thought. The children were an excellent development. There'd been no children for years. Delphine, standing between Boo and Jasper, looked ready to detonate with glee. Exploded child: unfortunate Navidad side effect. But he was looking forward to the carols himself—these elemental artifacts, as Brain had once described them, worn smooth by numberless voices. And truthfully, he missed the choir, missed the relief of being lost to self in ensemble, your voice subsumed and transformed in one great chorus. Bring on the angels and shepherds, the men from the East. The cold stubby had dealt with his old lady stomach. With luck it would also hush the Toss aperçus that kept escaping the brain-crypt.

"O Come, O Come, Emmanuel." "O Come, All Ye." "O Little Town of." Oh! Oh! Oh! said Toss, not at all hushed. Eddy sang louder. Jasper turned and grinned at him. It was definitely a grin. While singing! Eddy was so surprised he stumbled over *thy deep and dreamless sleep.* Wow. Jasper's singing was more accurately described as a drone, though it was tolerably tuneful. Eddy had checked out the children's carol literacy and found it barely adequate, so he'd taught them "The Poverty Carol" (*his* favorite) and "Gabriel's Message" while they knelt with him beside the coffee table in the plant room, assisting with the chevron skinks. *"All poor men and humble,"* sang Eddy, and brother and sister dutifully sang it after him. *"All lame men who stumble"*: ditto, and so on, as Delphine daubed the gold base on the claws, and Eddy drew in the V markings along the dorsal surface of the female skink, and Jasper painted with exquisite precision the black-edged teardrops beneath the male skink's eyes. Having done this, Jasper rinsed his paintbrush and said he could not sing and paint at the same time, and he chose singing. He lay on the floor with Mother in his hood and focused on answering Eddy the cantor in his bass buzz. Delphine, on the other hand, proved a multitasking natural, in these two enterprises at least. She painted the pale spots on the throat of the male chevron then began on its undercarriage, all the while effortlessly nailing the tune and words of "Gabriel's Message." They ran through this several times, Eddy singing the alto part beneath the children's melody line. Mother cawed at intervals—he was a major key fan. It had been a good afternoon. New skills. Tasks dispatched, tick, tick. Endorphins released. And afterward, Jasper volunteered to come on the dog walk.

Now Delphine's voice gleamed through their aging chorus. Her sound was quite something. "Dulcet?" said Boo, when Eddy struggled for apt descriptors. "Bell-like? Silvery? Crystalline?" She read from the online thesaurus.

"Like an Irish folk singer," he said. "Or a boy chorister." Now Bridgie looked sideways at him as she played. Goodness *me*, said her face. Deputy choirmaster Smallbone, beside the piano, widened his eyes at Eddy. *"While mortals sleep, the angels keep."* More to come, B, more to come.

But first there was Ginge, Brain, and the Modern Priest singing

"We Three Kings." Eddy went to the loo, unable to stomach Cristoforo Caruso bellowing *"Frankincense to offer have I."* His bladder was bursting. Spewmante plus beers. He was well over the limit. Boo would have to drive. He stood in front of the toilet bowl and gazed at the map of the Earthsea archipelago that Brain had given him for his twelfth birthday. Years involuntarily reciting the names of the islands meant that now, whenever he stood in front of *any* toilet bowl ready to piss, the litany instantly bloomed in his head: *Eppaln, Seppish, Torning, Low Torning, Pendor* . . . More proof for Pavlov. Toss had wanted to see if it worked in the reverse, if saying the names would bring on the urge to micturate (actual quote). He experimented with this at various unsuitable moments. *Hosk, Nesh, Pody, Serd* . . . Please fuck off, Toss, thought Eddy, so sick of it. Get out of my Inmost Sea.

43

The final song in Brain's booklet was "The Wexford Carol," the first and last verses traditionally sung by Eddy. Brain's favorite. Also Doris's: her great-grandparents had come from that Irish county. "Mixolydian mode," Professor Brain had said years ago, and Eddy had been enchanted by the word. "A medieval sound," said Brain, "but right through jazz and blues. Celtic, too."

"Good people all, this Christmas time," sang Eddy, his voice strange to him. Years since he'd sung this, but the words were instantly there. A somber carol, or bittersweet. Doris squeezed out a tear every year. Eddy might have squeezed one, too, if his mouth hadn't been moving—a tricky piece of multitasking, singing and crying.

All the singing had stirred him up. Everyone else's voices, earnest and eager. Jasper grinning while droning, multitasking after all. Ginge and Brain singing "Good King Wenceslas" with perfect seriousness. Boo and Sue alternating verses for "The Holly and the Ivy." Even Loretta, about as melodious as a buzz saw, but her face straining and wholehearted. His nerve ends were charred and sensitive.

"Bravo, Edmundo!" said the Modern Priest when it was done. "Still got the magic."

Eddy rolled his eyes at Boo, but only halfheartedly; the will to war was leaking away. What was the point? His hostility just slid off the Modern Priest. He'd taken some noncombative vow. It was like flinging toothpicks at corrugated iron.

Brain patted Eddy's back, a tacit thank-you, and Ginge refilled everyone's glasses as the party rearranged itself. Bridgie dropped onto the couch with Jasper, who looked briefly alarmed; Brain perched on the arm of Loretta's chair. Ginge and the Modern Priest leaned against the wood burner, the Modern Priest with arms folded, sermonizing no doubt, Ginge swaying a little, a faraway look on his face.

"Time for 'The Parting Glass,' I suppose," said Ginge half to himself. He hated parties ending.

"Good night and joy be to you all," sang Bridgie.

"Not yet," said Eddy. Not at all, he hoped. It went on forever, and the feckless four became revoltingly sentimental.

"There's one last carol," he said. "Late entry. A Christmas present for B." Delphine pulled at his T-shirt, taut with excitement. Eddy put his hand to Ginge's back and gave him a little shove. "Take a seat, comrade, you're on our stage."

Delphine had fretted about a present for Brain. What could she *make*? Would Eddy help? They had discussed vouchers and stories and drawings, reciting something.

"Sing a song," said Eddy, finally. "A carol." The homemade and traditional in one, right up Brain's alley.

"Yes!" said Delphine, instantly keen.

"Performance gene," Eddy told Boo. "Promising."

"You're like a Tennis Dad," she said. "Or a Stage Mum. You're a Stage *Nanny*."

Jasper, green at the thought of something similar coming his way, said he was roasting cashews for Brain because they were his favorite nut. Brain had told him so at their pancake breakfast. He'd downloaded instructions. All sorted.

236

"The children are coming along very nicely," said Eddy to Boo later, not quite satirical, and she had given him a most enigmatic look.

Eddy and Delphine trawled YouTube for likely carols: "The Coventry Carol," "A La Nanita," "Balulalow"—

"What's 'yon-gee'?" said Delphine, pointing at the screen. A picture of a boy in chorister's robes. "Yon-gee child?"

"It's an archaism," said Eddy. "Obsolete."

Her nomad eye rolled to its corner, as usual when she was tired and losing patience. "I don't know what you're *saying*?"

"It means young—pronounced youn-*ger*. 'That Yongë Child.' It's too hard though."

But she insisted, so they had watched it—a kid from Catalonia singing in a stone abbey. The melody moved through Eddy as of old, unvarnished, plaintive, speaking of emptiness.

"You need a harp, see that thumping big harp," said Eddy. "We *got* no harp." But he knew already that she would not be deterred.

So Boo accompanied Delphine on the ukulele. She sat on the arm of a chair, and Delphine stood on the raised hearth of the wood burner, the color drained from her face now that everyone was looking at her. They'd rehearsed well; Eddy had a taste now for the raw *plunk* of the opening notes. How forbidding was that first repeated motif. "Some lullaby," said Toss at choir practice in the past. "A dirge more like." Eddy stood in front of the festooned and lit-up tree so Delphine could look toward him, as they'd practiced. He sang every note with her silently. *"That yongë child when it gan weep, With song she lull-ed him asleep."* Modal and bare and aching. *"That was so sweet a melody."*

Pretty good, said Toss. For a Gashlycrumb. Okay diction. Good skills, Maestro. *"It passed alle minstrelsy."* Pass-ED, Ed. Middle English.

Nice little lecture from The Box. *"Alle."* That's from the Saxon, remember? *"The nightingale sang also:"* Colon! said Toss. Can't get away from them. Here lies young Smallbone: haunted by colons. *"Her song is hoarse and nought thereto:"* Christ, another colon! And now the tricky bit . . . high C, can she nail it? *"Who-so attend-eth,"* sang Delphine straight at Eddy, *"to her song."* Good girl, he thought before Toss could interrupt. Beaut. Perfectly pitched. *"And leaveth the first."* Buggery intervals, said Toss. Oops. Squiffy on the D, but I'm feeling generous, no marks lost. *"Then doth he wrong."* But who the hell ends a lullaby on *wrong*, for Christ's sake? Remember, said Eddy silently to Delphine, stand still while Boo plays the last notes. Yes, indeed, said Toss, grace and presence. Like uncle, like nephew, like Gashlycrumb. But, a word from the wise, Ed. Ditch the uke.

And, a resounding *hush*, said Toss, when no one spoke for several seconds. But here it comes: yes, yes, big sighs, everyone suitably moved. Some damp eyes? Clap, clap. Possibly a standing ovation. Awkward bow from the kid. Bonobo's grinning. And here comes the kid for a hug . . .

"Was that good?" said Delphine. She squeezed Eddy around the waist, like a cub, like a limpet.

"Good," said Eddy. "Very good." His voice was wispy, like the Ghost of Christmas Past.

Ewww, a Gashlycrumb embrace, said Toss. *G is for George smothered under a rug rat.*

Eddy patted Delphine's back mechanically. The rest of his body somehow would not move. She let go finally to hug Brain and receive a glass of spritzed apple juice and all-round approval. I will move now, Eddy thought, get a drink, too, say something nice to Boo. But he couldn't. He was stuck to the Christmas tree, an outsize decoration: Tattooed Elf. Inert.

Boo came over.

"That was so good! What about *Delphine*—a natural! Are you a proud Stage Nanny?"

"Good," said Eddy. He couldn't think of other words. A feeling of great doom crawled over him. "Good," he said again, not looking at her.

"Did you enjoy it?" said Boo. She moved close in to him. "Are you okay?"

"No," said the Ghost of Christmas Past.

"These are the shadows of things that have been," whined the Ghost. *"If they are what they are, don't blame me!"*

"Eddy," whispered Boo. "What's up?"

"Toss ruined it," said the Ghost.

Boo

It was Sue who finally got Eddy to move away from the Christmas tree, to walk a few paces to the French doors, then down the steps and out into the night. I held his clammy hand, and Sue hooked an arm around his, steering him gently across the grass to the bench beneath the walnut tree. We sat there together in the warm dark while Sue told him quietly to breathe with her, one, two, three, four, five in . . . one, two, three, four, five out. And again, one, two, three . . .

Delphine stood at the French doors, her nose against the glass. Watchful guardian. Little Ruru.

JAN U ARY

Fa-la-lah

44

Eddy lay on the bench under the walnut tree. The bench was in fact an old pew, retired from some deconsecrated chapel, the varnish weathered and blistered. On hot days it smelled churchy. He'd come outside to read, but within fifteen minutes his eyes closed and the book had fallen on his chest. He'd taken it from Brain's bedroom bookcase because the blurb said it was a story *for people who care about children, or hate them* . . . So far, so diverting. It was the heat and sleep deficit that had made his eyes heavy. Awake now, he stared up through the body of the tree, at the chocolate-colored branches and pinnate leaves, the clusters of speckled walnut husks, the summer sky beyond. It was a good old tree, 140 years plus. Brain had told him about the guy who'd planted the sapling, some nuggety colonial, but the details had gone in one ear and out the other. Shame. The guy deserved respect for his efforts, this offering to the future. Not only did the tree bring forth copious nutty comestibles, but here, now, nearly a century and a half later, the tree was both sun umbrella and peaceful harbor for Edmund V. J. Smallbone.

It was Sunday. A day of rest. Bless you, my son. He'd swapped shifts with Jia-Li in checkout and henceforth would do Friday afternoons. He'd subbed out a dog walk in Papanui to Jasper. He had reorganized his pet and human portfolio so that for the foreseeable future Sunday was free of any obligation.

"The way it used to be," said Brain.

"In the Bronze Age," said Eddy.

"In my lifetime," said Brain. Everything closed.

"Except churches," they said together, and smiled wryly.

Brain had been to Mass today. Feast of the Magi. He was inside now, making one-handed raspberry jam with berries that he, one-handed, and Loretta, two-handed, had picked very early this morning out at Marshlands. Eddy had offered to help, but picking was work, said Brain, and he must adhere to this new day-of-rest prescription. So Eddy slept till midmorning, waking when the room was bright with sun. He'd reached down for Marley, then remembered, felt the old clutch in his chest. He lay there for a while, eyes closed, working to quell the curl of panic in his bowel: the prospect of an empty day. Remember to breathe, Sue had instructed.

It was 1:15 p.m. now and he needed food. A ham sandwich? Lunch for the last ten days. Too much meat? But there was still half a ton of flesh to get through. Waste not, want not. Would Brain ever be able to cater for just himself rather than a horde? More to the point, would Brain ever actually be sole resident at 136 Bishop Street?

The house was filled with the cloying sweetness of hot jam, a smell that made Eddy irritable and wistful at the same time. A scone would be good, though. With butter and warm jam. But was he eating too much butter?

"I was thinking of scones," said Brain. "You fancy one?"

"Sure," said Eddy, sighing inwardly. But he was resigned to this now, the mystifying ability of those in his private orbit to divine his random, banal thoughts. "Afternoon tea? Thought I'd go for a walk." He had also offered to help with the jam making, but Brain assured him one-handed jam making was surprisingly straightforward.

He made a ham sandwich, *sans* butter, *mit* mustard, and set out.

45

He walked north through Edgeware, tattered and dingy, its old contours rearranged by the quakes. He listened to Odetta. "I've Been 'Buked and Scorned, Children." Odd walking without dogs; he'd done so little of that over the last four months. His hands felt idle and too large, flapping at his sides. He stuck one in his pocket. His head, on the other hand, was busy enough for his entire body, scrolling through the constituent parts of his life, the persistent timetables, ticking things off. It had been like that since Marley died, he'd told Sue, since the onset of the pet portfolio and its human adjuncts. Keeping track of everybody, everything. There was nothing he could do about it.

"I'm not sure that's true," said Sue.

"What a demulcent way of disagreeing you have," said Eddy. She pointedly did not ask him what demulcent meant, so he told her anyway. Honey was a demulcent, thank you, Brain. There was an enormous glossary of Brain words banging about in his head, too, he told Sue. Nothing he could do about that, either.

"If you say so," said Sue, impatient with him.

At Snorebins Park, Eddy sat on a swing, for old times' sake. He ate his sandwich and stared out over the green. So many parks in his life these days. Oases in the glum city. He automatically graded them all, according to tree quotient and genus, park equipment, lushness of the green, litter issues. Snorebins Park was exempted from assessment, scoring ten out of ten simply for nostalgia value. Odetta sang "Devilish Mary." An energetic number, which made him suddenly want to run a circuit of the park. Work off all the ham. He hadn't run since Marley died; it had felt wrong.

How good it was talking to Sue, he thought, the grass warm and spongy under his bare feet. Saying the things that had so long been unsaid. She got cross with him sometimes: for derailing lines of inquiry with jokes or taking refuge in recherché vocabulary. They had both laughed when she said recherché.

"It wasn't therapy," Eddy told Boo. "Just talking."

"Therapeutic talking though," said Boo, not looking at him. She was hurt that he could not talk to *her* about it all. Or not immediately. Boo was on the coast now. She'd been with her strangely normal family over Christmas, amusing her nieces and nephews. Right now, she was tramping in the Paparoa National Park with her new friend, Carys, from Knit World. She hadn't said when she'd be back.

Delphine was in Bluff with her father, visiting the paternal grand-parents, who had an aviary in their back garden and a half-built boat. When she was little, she'd played house in the half-boat. Now she just sat in it. Claudia and her tasty toes were at exactly the other end of the country on a beach with white sand, sipping drinks with umbrellas. "She always goes there," Delphine told him. "Since she was ten years old. It's an immovable feast. Dad said." Jasper's inert facial muscles had practically twitched at this—Eddy was fluent now in the microscopics of Jasper comms. Later, as they walked three new summer charges—a schnoodle called Noodle; Frances, a lovely beagle; and a quite bananas shihpoo called Selwyn—Jasper told Eddy that Claudia was a wicked-stepmother-in-waiting who Delphine needed to be saved from.

"So ordered," said Eddy, wondering exactly how this would be done. Kidnapping, after all?

Since Christmas, Jasper had accompanied Eddy on many of his rounds. It wasn't the same at home without Eddy or Delphine, he said, and Josie was back at work. He was a genius with the Mini Lops and the new hens—Black Orpingtons who laid pretty pink-tinged eggs but were nervous types. He'd helped clean out a large aquarium and several birdcages. He enjoyed the dog walking. "Being outside is a whole different thing," he said, "when you have a dog to hold on to." A very promising subcontractor, Eddy thought. He could leave the business to Jasper when he went away. If he ever went away. Meanwhile, he paid Jasper a good rate. He also gently suggested that he get a new hoodie and tie his hair back.

"Important not to frighten the pet owners."

Jasper did some rapid blinking. "Okay," he said.

Jasper would never be garrulous, but he was sufficiently comfortable with Eddy these days to chat about this and that. Eddy enjoyed it. He supposed they were friends. Jasper had surprising areas of knowledge: Old American TV comedies. Indie rock. YouTubing. Weird corners of the occult. He asked questions, too. As they walked the north end of Walter Park one afternoon with Waffle, Rizzo, and the merry schnauzers, Jasper, eyes steadfastly forward, asked Eddy, "What really happened, the night of the tree decorating?"

46

"What is happening to me?" the Ghost of Christmas Past had whispered, very frightened, on the bench pew in the warm night with Sue Lombardo and Boo. "Am I having a stroke? Am I going crazy? I'm having a psychotic break, aren't I?"

"No," said Sue, very calm, very sure. He would always remember her certainty. He had stared through the dark to the wattle tree's solid trunk, holding on to her voice.

"You're having a panic attack," said Sue. "The key is to keep breathing, focus on your breathing. One, two, three, four . . ."

He did as she said, in and out, in and out, counting, and Boo held on to his sweaty hand, and Sue kept hold of his arm and talked softly, steadily. Very slowly, the horror of the Ghost had receded, and Eddy had returned to himself and the night, the solid fact of the bench, this little grotto beneath the walnut tree, the lit-up living room across the grass, a whisper of wind shifting the walnut branches—and to the queasy knowledge of his spewmante- and beer-sodden system, which now staged its overdue revolt. He'd pitched forward and vomited a *cataract* of sugary comestibles and alcohol onto the grass and Boo's right foot.

"Thanks," said Boo, and her deadpan voice had almost raised a smile in Eddy. "Better out than in, I suppose."

She unbuckled her sandal and wiped it on the grass. "No offense, but I'm keen to wash this off."

"Sorry," said Eddy. He sat up and shakily wiped his mouth with his T-shirt. "Terribly sorry."

"Are you a bit better?" said Boo. She touched him briefly on the shoulder.

"I think so," he said. He had no idea. He watched her cross the grass and disappear around the front of the house. In the living room, the Christmas tree lights strobed. Loretta was preparing to leave, empty plates in hand. Delphine stood pressed against the French doors. Trying to see into his soul.

It was utterly quiet under the walnut tree in the warm dark, Sue Lombardo silent beside him, unconcerned apparently by the puddle of vomit at their feet, its sour stink. The quiet was so complete it seemed almost loud. He realized that his mind was quiet, too. Void. He had vomited out his thoughts!

Eddy closed his eyes and waited for Toss to make fun of his old lady constitution. But no voice came. He leaned his head against the back of the pew and caught the welcome perfume of the tobacco plant over the fence. *Nicotiana sylvestris.* He sat up quickly, ready for the rebuke. Nothing. It was an incredible relief. But his face went hot and tears rushed to his eyes.

"Who is Toss?" asked Sue.

"A revenant," said Eddy.

"I see."

"No, you *don't*," he said, suddenly annoyed with her serene tone. He felt another upwelling from his pathetic stomach.

"He was my friend," he said, in a hurry. "He died. And then he came back."

47

What a foul winter it had been. Lowering skies and endless rain. Southerlies straight from Antarctica. The city looked utterly forlorn. Butt ugly. The arsehole of the world, in fact, which seemed a terrible thing to feel about your hometown. Brain told it differently. It was a winter of two halves, he said later, don't you remember? Very cold and wet, then unseasonably dry and warm. Eddy remembered only that he seemed permanently to be drying off and changing clothes after a *bicycle* ride—to work, to home, to the sleep-out where Toss lounged, waiting for him.

In the summer months, Toss's parents had decamped to Central Otago, to their crib—a laughable misnomer: it was a mansion at the edge of a lake. Toss refused to go there anymore. "Too hot," he said. "Boring as batshit, and too many Americans." Eddy had stayed at the mansion. It was boring. There were a lot of Americans, all rich and well-mannered, like the Mores.

Instead, when Eddy wasn't at work, they went driving in the Mores' "old" car, an Audi—north, south, and west, to rural towns, to beaches, back and forth along the Waimakariri Gorge, browned and beautiful. Toss seldom wanted to *do* anything when they arrived anywhere, except eat an ice cream. His preferred place was the passenger seat, the landscape passing, music blasting. His was a long convalescence, he said. Salmonella could indispose people for a year or more. Eddy had no idea if this was true. But it was true that in the ten months since he'd fallen ill and the terrapins had been banished, both Toss's flesh and energy had fallen away. Also his friends—though there were not many of those. A few old bandmates, the ones who'd forgiven him. Guys from the university fencing club. Oriana Townsend, trying to stay friendly despite the disastrous episode in Toss's mother's car. Toss ignored them all. His mother rang him from her cushioned sun chair, and his father texted every few days, asking questions that precluded any response other than the one he wanted. "All good? Feeling stronger?" Meg, laid low in Melbourne by morning sickness, FaceTimed him with nutritional advice. Toss was terse with them all.

"I can't be *bothered*," he said grandly, a boy king tired of his dull subjects. "I can't be bothered talking to anyone. Except you."

Eddy, temporarily retired as Hazel's boyfriend on account of her family holiday in Mexico, had enjoyed keeping Toss entertained. If they were not driving into the shimmering Canterbury heat, they walked in various parts of the Botanical Gardens, or they bought things for the sleep-out on Trade Me, or, when the Gnome wasn't around doggedly weeding, they lay about in the fig tree grove, while Toss tried out their old songs in a new burning countertenor and Eddy extemporized accompaniments on the chord harmonica.

In the middle of autumn, Toss dropped out of uni. He could read classics in his bedroom, he said. Also English literature. Also religious studies. He would conduct a private education, tailored to his own specific needs and interests. He ordered books online and read hungrily. His parents, suddenly concerned by this development, offered to take him to Bali for a tropical convalescence, a pick-me-up, full bells and whistles. He could do yoga there. "Yoga?" Toss yelled, outraged. *"Yoga?"*

One afternoon in May, after an excellent Steal Away session—singing still provoked a hectic exuberance in Toss—Leoni More waylaid

Eddy as he was about to climb on his bike and head home. Would *he* go on holiday somewhere with Toss: Rarotonga? Fiji? Byron Bay? Cairns? Wherever they liked. Of course they would pay for everything, no problem with money. Toss needed a tonic, a jump-start; they worried he could be depressed.

"I need to check some stuff," Eddy said, knowing time off was impossible; he was only three months into the New World job and due precisely zero holidays. Also, he was Brain-washed about luxury holidays and could only think of lying round with pineapple drinks at an international hotel on a tropical island as a louche and dissipated undertaking. But Toss would never go anyway. And was Toss depressed? Eddy didn't think so. He was just thin and lethargic.

To compensate for not escorting Toss on a sybaritic getaway, Eddy agreed instead to go with him to the doctor. An excruciating undertaking. The doctor was young, tall, and slightly stooped, with a face as lugubrious as a basset hound's. He was very thorough, but quite without humor, and this somehow made Toss inarticulate with giggles. Eddy, mortified, was obliged to translate Toss's incoherent answers to Dr. Dog's increasingly probing inquiries, which included, among much else, the repulsive details of his bowel movements. Eddy had no idea if Toss was telling the truth about any of it. Dr. Dog's diagnosis: Toss was underweight and dehydrated, and his blood pressure was on the low side. They came away with a dietary advice sheet and a script for blood tests. For two weeks Toss drank electrolytes, ate fish and leafy greens and ever more ice cream. He gained 1,500 grams and a slightly better color. The Mores judged him vastly improved, enabling them to leave for their biennial European holiday. Eddy would stay with Toss, keep an eye on him.

"A responsibility," said Sue.

"It didn't feel like that," said Eddy. It really hadn't. "It was good times."

Now, describing those good times, he heard and saw them anew: they had been a sequestered, ardent little world of two. Early dark and long nights. Eddy arriving home from Nuevo Mundo (Toss). Song sessions until they fell over with tiredness. Movies on Toss's laptop. Backgammon, the only board game Toss would play. Sometimes they just lay on the bed and batted back and forth facts and opinions and preferences: the point of recycling, the worst Star Wars film (I), totalitarianism or democracy, kōwhai or pōhutukawa, Pompey's jealousy of Caesar, the ludicrousness of ballet, institutional religion, kererū or tūī, a taxonomy of folk music, parents or uncles, blindness or deafness, leglessness or armlessness . . . Every few days Eddy checked in on Brain and Marley, and Brain sent him away with soups and casseroles and winter puddings, to feed Toss up. Eddy couldn't bring himself to tell Brain that Toss ate only porridge. He gobbled up all the food himself and gained a kilo.

"It was two lives," said Eddy. The light and color and industry of the supermarket, and the loafing, shuttered intensity of the sleep-out. "And Toss—he did his usual thing during the day—reading, listening to music, dozing . . . the penance shit." Eddy had only a shadowy sense of what this entailed and refused to acknowledge it, though Toss dropped unsavory morsels all the same.

"Self-harm," said Sue.

"Yes," said Eddy after a pause. Strangely, he'd not thought of Toss's habits in those terms. He'd thought *penance shit*, and tried not to think further, and had certainly never told anyone else, knowing in some uninvestigated part of his mind that it was distorted behavior, a personality warp, but feebly hoping that it would wane over time and one day disappear.

"It *was* good times," he said again. The only fight they'd had was when Toss, disagreeable after a day of stomach cramps and nausea and wanting a distraction, began reading aloud passages from *The Life of St. Gemma Galgani*, one of his more batshit online purchases. Gemma Galgani was a crazed Italian ecstatic who'd (allegedly) manifested stigmata and been harassed by the devil. And that was only part of the book's rabid nonsense. Eddy, tired after a double shift, wanted only to zone out and listen to music. When Toss refused to stop, reading louder and louder, Eddy had grabbed the book, opened the door of the sleep-out, and thrown it far out into the black night where it belonged.

Toss laughed like a loon, and Eddy made his bed on the floor mattress. It was June by then, and the Mores were lying in the sun with friends on a day cruiser in the Aegean before heading home leisurely via California. Toss, on the other hand, complained constantly of the cold, though he was togged up like the Michelin man and lived inside two duvets, and the heat pump was set permanently at 80 degrees. The sleep-out wasn't really a sleep-out in the same way the Mores' crib wasn't really a crib: it was a fully self-contained bedsit with bathroom and kitchen facilities, a granny flat that would never house a granny. Sometimes, to get away from the overcooked bedroom, Eddy sat on the toilet with the bathroom windows wide open, the moist winter air glorious on his bare arms.

"It was nuts," he told Sue. "But I didn't think so at the time."

"Boiling frog syndrome," said Sue. "Though that is apparently a myth."

"One thing," said Eddy. "Sylvester brought me home to the sleep-out one night; my bike chain snapped. He came in for a beer."

Eddy had figured Sylvester was big and ugly enough to deal with whatever Toss mood greeted them. He was in his twenties and worldly; few things surprised him. Toss, fully dressed and sitting on his bed, had been cordial, even genial. He had quizzed Sylvester on the supermarket economy—"Creaming it, mate," said Sylvester—and had even sipped a beer. But it was strange having a visitor. Or more precisely, their visitor made the sleep-out world seem strange to Eddy's eyes: the cloistering perverse, their fervency peculiar. And possibly malodorous.

"How long's he been sick?" Sylvester asked Eddy the next day, and Eddy had been shocked to realize it was nearly a year. "Seems odd," said Sylvester. "And his folks on the other side of the world."

It *was* odd, Eddy saw. But why hadn't he thought that before? He'd become accustomed to it somehow, the warped standard of an invalid Toss, his parents only peripheral.

"Very common," said Sue. "You adjust little by little to the changing norm. You accept the rising temperature." She made a face. "I need a new analogy."

The frog analogy was no longer a norm. It had been made redundant by the actual facts. The facts are always changing, Eddy thought. Or was that simply your beliefs? When you were young, your beliefs were facts. Family. Friends. The permanence of your surroundings. The stability of your feelings. God's in His heaven, all's right with the world. Thank you, Anne of Green Gables.

He had walked his bike from Fendalton to the nearest bike shop, which was 8 km away in Hornby and into the teeth of another southerly. Toss was like a southerly. Battering. He left you feeling exhausted. Head down against the wind, and rain coming almost horizontally, Eddy had a sharp longing for home. For the living room, and the blazing wood burner, for Brain in the kitchen and Marley nearby, even for the theme of *Midsomer Murders*, which usually made him want to set fire to the house.

The southerly blew him back to the sleep-out, at least. He picked up fish and a scoop along the way in the faint hope that Toss would eat a chip or two. But Toss was in bed, swathed in layers of clothing and huddling beneath the duvets. The bedroom was like a sauna. Eddy snarfed the dinner, lukewarm and sad without tomato sauce. He asked Toss about his day, but Toss was too miserable to talk. Eddy had a cold shower and climbed into his sleeping bag with the *Fireside Book of Folk Songs* and the harmonica, and a determination to learn the tricky accompaniment to "Careless Love." But ten minutes later, Toss was demanding he get under the covers and do his duty to stave off what was for sure galloping hypothermia.

48

In the Play-Doh-scented dark, Toss's back softened against Eddy's now, his breathing even as he slept. Eddy quietly made an air pocket so he could breathe—if not fresh air exactly, at least something less composty. He kept still: don't poke the bear. What an absurd situation. He was like a child bride, scared to rouse a ravening spouse. A child bride in cotton boxers. If only he had his earphones. He could listen to Ray Charles singing "Careless Love." Or Lead Belly, with his long murmuring intro, another kind of music. But his earphones were in his backpack, which was drying out in the kitchen. He listened to the storm instead, lashing the trees and the window. He regretted the fish and chips. When didn't you regret fish and chips? He could feel them, a lardy wodge trying to move from his stomach to his small intestine. The first couple of chips were the best. It was always downhill after that. Toss gave a little sleepy groan and pressed his back once more against Eddy's. It was fucking steaming under these duvets. If only he could turn off the heat pump. Eddy gingerly stuck his head above the covers, slowly pushed one of the duvets aside, and slid the other down his body so his skin was briefly exposed. Slight relief. He thought of Marley, sleeping at the bottom of B's bed in Eddy's absence, of Brain, missing him probably, but pleased he was here with Toss . . .

He woke in a fright two hours later, slick with sweat, the sheet damp and clinging. The storm was over, the only sound now the hum of the heat pump. The room was stifling. He waited to see if he'd disturbed Toss, then slid quietly from the bed and searched for the heater's remote with his phone torch. It was on Toss's bedside table. Toss was hunched down in the bed, under the covers, only the ridiculous pom-pom visible. Eddy switched off the heater, drank a long glass of cold water, and lay his bare back against the cold kitchen window. He got his earphones from his backpack and crept back to bed, easing carefully under the duvet until his back was once more against Toss's. Which meant only one earphone uncomfortably on. What an obliging friend he was. He should get a medal. He scrolled through his song lists and selected the Cheesy Song compilation they'd made in the summer. He fell asleep in the middle of Al Martino singing "Blue Spanish Eyes."

49

Eddy woke to the muffled alarm, the phone under his pillow: 6:45 a.m. He had an 8 a.m. start. Enough time for porridge, then on his bike. He was ambivalent about the porridge, feeling somehow complicit in Toss's grim diet, something he was beginning to think was willed, rather than the consequence of a delicate system. He should talk to B, tell him about Toss's intake, ask his advice.

The sky was blue out the window. Rivulets of moisture ran down the pane. He had woken on his back, the earphones gone, discarded in his sleep no doubt. He should turn on the heat pump before Toss woke. Toss was on his back, too, head outside the covers, and bare; he must have overheated, too, pulled off that stupid hat. The duvet was pushed back, a hand across his chest. His hair had grown back slowly after the number one malarkey, a few thin curls starting. His chin was stubbly; he couldn't be bothered shaving. Pale lips. Thin and unforgiving even as he slept. He looked like an elderly baby, his face free of lines but pinched somehow, his skin dry and oddly tinged.

It was absolutely quiet in the sleep-out now—no heat pump clicks and gusts, no wind or rain outside, no music, no Toss monologue. "It was the quiet," Eddy told Sue. He was listening for breathing and couldn't hear it. He had leaned right into Toss, to make sure, touched the hand on his chest, his forehead, his neck. He had cupped his hand to Toss's dry cheek and pushed gently and then less gently. But it was no good.

Boo

I knew about Thomas More, of course. Not from Eddy because he'd *forbidden* it. But, you know, news travels, and bad news, etc. No one knew the details, or not accurately, but everyone knew that Eddy Smallbone had been there and that Toss had been sick, though nobody knew how sick. And that his parents were overseas and his sister eight months pregnant in Australia and that the police came and there had to be an autopsy and it was a week before they could have a funeral. And after the funeral no one saw Eddy. He went to ground, worked all hours at New World and avoided everyone we knew. But things leaked out, someone's mother's cousin's wife had talked to someone at church or knew the undertaker or the doctor or a cop or a priest, and somehow people knew that Eddy Smallbone had been in bed with Toss More when he died. You can be sure people speculated the hind legs off *that*, but no one really knew anything, me included.

It was shocking to hear about Toss. Of course it was. I wanted to call Eddy. It was the right thing to do, but I thought he might not answer. I didn't want to text because texting sympathy is just wrong. So I wrote him a letter, and then another, and then another. I didn't send a single one—they were all wrong, too. They seemed glib, full of clichés, sappy or mealy-mouthed. And I knew why. I *did* feel terrible for Eddy. His best friend had died and he would be suffering. The problem was, I hated Toss More. I thought he was a malicious, black-hearted little goblin, a selfish, self-absorbed toad. A pretentious gobshite, too, raving on about capitalism while swimming in privilege.

There. I've said it. Plus, he didn't like me, and who's saintly enough to make nice when waves of odium are coming their way? Toss More didn't like Eddy having a girlfriend; he would never like it. Eddy was *his*, apparently. I suppose it was as simple as that: a case of galloping possessiveness. I intruded on some long-harbored Toss fantasy about soul brothers-in-musical-arms.

In the end I left it. I didn't get in touch with Eddy. I didn't *reach out*. And then, when we met up again, he absolutely refused to talk about it. Not that we *had* ever really talked about Toss. Or only tentatively, toe-dipping conversations quickly backed away from. Eddy talked to no one about Toss. Not even Brain.

But Toss More wasn't having that. *He* wasn't shutting up. He might have died of heart failure as the result of malnutrition, but he wasn't leaving the stage. Not his style. He barged his way into Eddy's head and demanded to be heard. Or so Eddy described it to me, when he finally got round to explanations.

He offered to drive me to the coast. Christmas Eve and the open road, both of us looking ahead at the big sky, the car swallowing one heat shimmer after another. Eddy's head well-rinsed from talking to Sue. I was jealous of that, I admit it. Eddy pouring it all out to Sue before me. Of course, I got it. He needed a neutral ear. Still.

50

At Springfield they had stopped for an ice cream.

"Traditional," said Eddy. "Brain always stops here."

But the last time he'd bought an ice cream here had been with Toss the summer before.

Ice cream and porridge. Foods that slipped down without effort. No chewing involved, a swallow so easeful you weren't really eating. The salmonella had depleted Toss, but after its worst, he had begun deliberately to deny himself food. Another kind of mortification, with mysterious attendant thrills.

"But *why*?" asked Boo. "Why was he into that?"

"A control thing?" said Eddy. "Sue has theories. A desire to *feel*. A message to his parents. An exploration that got out of hand. Or a way of suppressing things. But you can't interview a corpse."

He could say things like this quite calmly now. He had cried a good deal while talking to Sue, but he hadn't minded. She had passed him tissues and waited. They'd sat outside beside the vegetable garden, Puss alternating between their laps, and Eddy had told it all, over several days, a choppy narrative, remembering things later, backfilling, much sighing and sometimes almost shouting.

"Sue had theories," he told Boo. "But mostly she asked me what I thought."

"Like what?"

"Like, why did I think Toss came back. I mean he didn't come *back*, but that's how it felt."

"So why?"

He told Boo about the brain-crypt, where he'd stuffed everything and sealed it up. It was too horrible to think about Toss. The circumstances. The aftermath.

"Interesting word, crypt," Sue had said. "From *crypta*, Latin for vault."

He knew that.

"But also, the female form of hidden, from the Greek: to conceal."

Eddy had stared at the sweet peas, pink, purple, blue, smothering the trellis along Sue's east-facing fence. He hadn't known the Greek meaning.

"Even more interesting," said Sue. "Do you know the word for placing a body in a crypt?"

"No," said Eddy, taking Puss from Sue's lap. He felt the need to hold something.

"Immurement," she said. "Meaning confined, incarcerated."

"What?" said Boo. "So Toss was trying to make a break for it?"

They were climbing now, toward Porters Pass, tussock and matagouri all around. It sounded mad, Eddy thought: Toss, inside his head, trying to bully-talk his way out of confinement. He'd thought it was mad in Sue's garden, kneading Puss's neck and staring at the sweet peas.

"Not *actual* Toss," said Eddy, loving the ranges up ahead, bare and singed. "My feelings about him. Sadness, guilt, fury. All that shit." He felt almost elated, saying those words.

"So it built up," said Boo. "Like a pressure cooker."

"Yes," said Eddy.

"And then Delphine with the carol."

"Yes."

"That was the valve blowing."

"Yes," said Eddy. *"That yongë child."*

51

"Tell me about that carol," Sue had said in the garden.

"But we'd practiced that carol for two weeks," said Boo as they made the descent to Castle Hill.

"Yes," said Eddy. "But it was something about that night, hearing her voice, that glassy sound, and watching her, and remembering Toss singing it when we did *Ceremony of Carols*. And missing singing with Toss. And I realized, I mean I knew this, but I realized *properly* that Delphine reminded me of Toss. The way she claims you. Her relentlessness. Plus, you know, all the *drink*, to quote Ginge. And Toss in my head going on about Gashlycrumbs."

"What are Gashlycrumbs?" said Boo.

Eddy explained about *The Gashlycrumb Tinies*, the Gothic abecedary: twenty-six kids, all meeting macabre deaths that were somehow also very funny. *A is for Amy who fell down the stairs. B is for Basil assaulted by bears. C is for Clara*—but he had cried when he'd told Sue, because Clara had *wasted away*.

At Cass, he and Boo stopped and walked to the railway station, in honor of Rita Angus, and sat on the rail platform for a few minutes.

"I know you couldn't stand him," said Eddy.

"But why did you?"

Eddy considered the tracks, gleaming in the sun, the worn sleepers, the gravel, the dry grass, and his bare feet, the tan lines from his sandals. Perhaps he would never be able to explain Toss. Toss was an acquired taste, he'd told Sue. He'd acquired it young. And it was a habit. But that was insufficient.

"I got the best of him," he said to Boo. "I know he was impossible. But he made me laugh. He read stuff no one else did. I could tell him anything. And singing . . ." He trailed off. It was all true, but somehow a hollow reckoning.

At Arthur's Pass Village they stopped again, for coffee, and saw a kōtare on a streetlamp, which Boo said was certainly good luck.

Good luck for Boo, wondered Eddy, or for him, or the two of them together? In the days after his wig-out, things had been difficult between them. They had lain far apart in the spare bed at the Mulhollands', newly strangers. For some reason he could not touch Boo. He felt like an invalid. He couldn't imagine having sex.

"Are you embarrassed about what happened?" asked Boo, her voice small in the dark.

Not sure, he thought. But he knew he must say something. It was his new promise to himself. He must *say* things.

He told her he felt fragile and, and *crumbly*.

"Like a soft biscuit?" said Boo.

In the morning, still half-asleep, they made their question-mark cocoon and said nothing. They had been kind with each other since then, but it was different.

"The brain-crypt," said Boo as they entered the Taramakau valley. "Did you put me there, too? After we broke up? And the not-baby?"

"Yes," said Eddy, determined to be honest.

The sprawling river winked in the sun, mild-mannered. *Pacific*, thought Eddy. He'd like a bit of that.

"I was in the brain-crypt with Toss for three months," said Boo. "Ewww."

They laughed all the way to Jacksons. Perhaps it would be okay, thought Eddy.

52

Eddy and Brain ate two scones apiece under the walnut tree.

"Four months since Marley, B," said Eddy. "To the day."

"I was thinking that," said Brain.

"Would you consider a kitten?" said Eddy, surprised to say this.

"You've been talking to Ginge."

"No."

"There's a tabby at Cats Protection. He showed me a photo. Lovely."

"So?"

"Shall we think on it?"

Of course. No hurry. Slow and steady.

But Eddy felt a new kindliness toward Brain's adagio mode. Brain who had watched him—watched *over* him—after Toss's death, had accepted his silence, had not pushed or prodded, had not forced him to do that which he couldn't yet face.

They had talked into the night on New Year's Eve. It had been just the two of them—astonishing in itself, since in previous years Eddy would rather have stuck pins in his eyeballs than be home alone with Brain on New Year's Eve. But he'd had no desire to do otherwise. He wasn't up for a party. In his new rinsed-out, clear-seeing incarnation, he wanted to talk to his uncle about everything.

"Everyone is different, of course," said Brain. "But I recognized how you were feeling. It was the same when Vincent died. I was too shocked to make sense of it. I parked it. It was a long time before I talked to anyone. You want to try this?" He held up the customary bottle of whisky the Modern Priest had given him for Christmas. An unimaginative present, Eddy had always thought. But Brain enjoyed the reliability of the gift—a new label each year. He made the bottle last the full twelve months.

"No thanks," said Eddy. He was never drinking again. Or at least, not for a month.

"And then it happened unexpectedly. You started school. And I was curiously upset saying goodbye to you in the classroom. A small loss, I suppose," said Brain, looking at the whisky in its cut glass, seeing that day, perhaps. Eddy had no memory of it. "And you looked so like your father at that age. Fearless like him, too, excited. I came home and rang Bridgie. She was very kind."

They sat in the living room as it got dark and the Christmas tree lights began to wink, and Brain talked about Vincent, and Eddy talked about Toss. And Eddy saw that Brain was uniquely placed to understand.

"You were each other's brother," he said simply. "You loved him and he loved you. And he was always there. Until he wasn't."

"I'm sorry I've been such an arsehole," said Eddy. It was past midnight by then, the new year had begun. He was glad the old year was done with. Good riddance. He wanted this one to be different.

"No, no," said Brain.

But he *had* been an arsehole. Impatient and brusque and withering and passive-aggressive. In the tradition of sons and fathers.

"No, but seriously," said Eddy. He wanted to apologize for the last three years, the school debacle, his war with the Modern Priest, his moodiness, his silences, his absences, his entire personality.

"Ed," said Brain. He traced the channels of the cut glass with his middle finger. "You're a young man. You're finding your way. I have great faith."

Eddy looked at his uncle now, full of scone, pleased with his day's efforts. His hand was no longer swollen, the wrist was mending, but he was tired every afternoon.

"Bit of a nap?" said Eddy. He was planning a lie-down himself, on the bench. More reading and dozing.

"Twelfth day of Christmas," said Brain. "Theoretically, it's the day the tree should come down."

"No, it's the day *after* the twelfth day of Christmas."

"You sure?"

"No doubt whatever," said Eddy. He was almost sure.

"I will have a nap, then." Brain stood and brushed the scone crumbs from his front. "Ham for dinner, I suppose. Every man for himself?"

"Roger," said Eddy.

53

Delphine got a phone for Christmas. She texted Eddy at 6 a.m. on Christmas morning. He stuffed the phone under his pillow and tried to get back to sleep, but it continued to beep and ping, so he turned it off. At 7:30 he gave up, crawled out of bed, and went to the kitchen to make coffee.

MERRY CHRISMAS, MR. K, said Delphine's first text. *HAS BRAIN OPEND HIS PRESENT YET? XX*

I JUST OPEND YR PRENSENT! said the next one. *THANX MR. K! XX*

Eddy had made Delphine her own Maud Island frog. For Jasper: a lesser short-tailed bat (pekapeka; *Mystacina tuberculata*)—a little crepuscular cave joke. It was a fiendish job on account of the snout and ball-bearing-like eyes and the folding wings. He'd written "Handle with Extreme Care" on the present tag.

WHAT R U HAVNG 4 XMAS BREAKFAST? XXX, said the third.

WERE HAVNG CRUSSONTS. XX

R U STILL ASLEEP. GET UP! XX

OK YOU MUST B ASLEP

Berry Kringle, Eddy texted at 10:30. *No presents here till after Xmas dinner. Enjoy your ice cream cake.*

ME & JAS R PLAYNG NANAS. I'M CHEETING! XXX

BOO TXTD. SHE GT A BCK PCK 4 HER TRAMP XXX

GIV BRAINA HUG FRM ME XXXOOOO

AND GINGE AND BRIGIE XXX

SAY HELO TO THE MINISTER GUY IF HES THER XXX

At midday, Eddy walked to Edgeware for cream. Unaccountably, Brain had not bought sufficient for the brandy snaps and the meringues. A grave oversight.

WHAT R U DOING NOW? XXX

I'm walking to the dairy to get extra cream. And possibly a gum alligator.

YUM! ME & JAS R WALKNG TH DOGS. JAS IS HOLDNG TH LEASHES SOI CN TEXT XXX

DID U GT TH GUM ALLIGATER? WOT COLOR I WD GT YELLOW XXX

JASP SAYS HE WD GET GREAN XXX

PS MUM & GRAN HVE HAD 2 FITES

At 3 p.m. Eddy made a spinach salad with toasted walnuts while Brain roasted capsicums and chopped several hundredweight of herbs. Eddy called Boo. They traded Delphine texts. Boo had received seventeen so far.

At 4 p.m. Sue Lombardo texted to say happy Christmas and a peaceful 2013. She was having Christmas dinner with three other nuns, two ex-priests, and Beate Lund, a Danish Lutheran bishop. She had received several texts from Delphine.

At 5 p.m. Ginge, Bridgie, and the Modern Priest arrived.

HAVE U HAD CHRISMAS DINNER YET? XXX

MOTHER HAS BEEN GD. JAS FED HER A CHRISMAS PRES
BANANA XX

MUM SAYS MEERY CHRSMAS. XXX

Having dinner any minute. I'm signing out for the night. Tell J only one banana per day for Mother. They're constipating x

54

It had been a good Christmas in the end. The usual suspects. But by then the beneficiary of several illuminating conversations with Sue, Eddy had felt a measure of detachment, was able to look the Modern Priest in the eye for the first time in years and respond civilly when Cristoforo asked him how he was.

"Better," said Eddy, which was only the truth.

"If you ever want to talk," said the Modern Priest, presuming too much as usual.

Fat chance, Eddy did not say, but having looked at the guy for the first time in so long, he suddenly saw him properly. He seemed smaller, despite the little tum, and he'd aged: new liver spots and lines on his face. His dial was turned down that day. He was slightly less irritating. "Thanks," said Eddy, offering him a blini with cream cheese and thinly shaved gherkin.

At the dinner table, they pulled a Christmas cracker. The Modern Priest ate the chocolate-covered apricot inside and read the Surprising Fact aloud: *"Bats always turn left when they leave a cave."* Thank you, Brain. He unfolded the green and gold crepe paper crown, stared at it, and finally stuck it on his head. He looked like a twat, but so did they all. Except Eddy. He never wore the paper crowns. He drew the line.

After dinner they sat around nursing their full stomachs. The Modern Priest suggested charades because he always won. By now Eddy was feeling so Zen, he wondered if the wig-out had short-circuited the part of his temporal lobe that controlled affect and emotion.

Nobody guessed the Modern Priest's charade. It was "Jesus Wants Me for a Sunbeam," a children's hymn. He was roundly abused for this nonsense. "Moreover," said Ginge, "the title is actually 'I'll Be a Sunbeam.'" The Modern Priest had used the first line. Technically, this was a disqualification and meant it was someone else's turn, but nobody except the Modern Priest could be bothered standing up and performing.

This was the secret to his success, Eddy thought. Having no shame. Also the reason for his downfall.

To be fair, though, Eddy owed him his latest job offer, a very good gig, indeed. House-sitting for a couple who were going to the UK for six months. They had two cats and the executive toy du jour: a large aquarium. He was thinking about it.

He guessed the Modern Priest's second charade in fifteen seconds. It came to him like a gift: the Koran.

"Huh," said the Modern Priest, baffled by this speed. "Your turn, then."

"No more charades," said Eddy. "It's time for Brain's present."

"Goody," said Ginge.

Eddy fetched the shoebox from his bedroom. He'd used the same one for the last eight years. It was wrapped in brown paper and tied with red string, also recycled.

"Any guesses?" he asked. They liked this part. He watched them trying to remember the Ark passengers so far.

"Kōtuku," said Bridgie. She'd been barracking for the kōtuku for years. It was on Eddy's list, but the heron's neck would be a major challenge.

"Stitchbird," said the Modern Priest. The hihi: nationally

vulnerable and definitely on his list. Lovely birdcall. But something about the bent beak and little black eyes reminded him of Doris's snark-face, so he was in no hurry.

Eddy handed the present to Brain.

"How many years for the string now, Ed?" asked Ginge.

"Eight," said Eddy. Holy God. Would he be using the same piece of string in twenty years? He could never not do it now; it was all part of the *ritual*. He would not ever be able to accidentally-on-purpose lose this piece of string and break out with another color. He would pick it up after Brain had unwrapped the present, wind it around his hand as he did every year, and put it away with the shoebox in his bedroom cupboard when the evening was over. For next year.

"You're calculating Christmases into the 2030s and beyond, aren't you?" said Bridgie.

"It is literally terrifying," said Eddy.

"Īnanga!" said Ginge. "Its time has come." Conservation status: at risk. Also on the list. But whitebait were so tiny, he'd have to do a swarm of pairs, and it would be a fiddle.

Brain did not hazard a guess. He was content to be surprised, to accept Eddy's choice. He declared no favorites among the foregoing twelve pairs, either. Maybe this year, thought Eddy. This year there was another layer.

The others stood around Brain's chair as he lifted the shoebox lid. With the utmost care, he unwrapped the tissue paper.

"Reptiles!" said the Modern Priest. "Haven't had a reptile in a while."

"Beautiful pattern," said Ginge.

"Chevron," said Brain. "From the French for building rafters.

Chevron skinks. Oh, very good, Ed," he said, smiling. "Very good, indeed."

"*One of our rarest and most secretive lizards*," read the Modern Priest, who had taken the little information card Eddy had written from the box. He included one every year, and Brain kept them in a small wooden box on the bookcase. A record of the progress and regress of Eddy's handwriting over the years, he said.

"*The distinctive teardrop shape beneath the eye is a pattern unique to each chevron skink and can be used to identify individuals.*"

Eddy had copied most of the information from the Department of Conservation website on vulnerable species.

"'*Lost' from science for more than sixty years before being discovered—*"

"Thank you, Mr. Grabby," said Bridgie, plucking the card from the Modern Priest's hand and giving it to Brain. "Whose present is this?" The Modern Priest gave her a distinctly playground pout.

On the other side of the card Eddy had written the full scientific classification:

Niho taniwha
Kingdom: Animalia
Phylum: Chordata
Class: Reptilia
Order: Squamata
Family: Scincidae
Genus: Oligosoma
Species: O. homalonotom

And one other thing:

"*The glorious king of lizards*"

"What's that last bit?" said Ginge.

Brain looked like his teeth had gone soft—Eddy's own four-year-old description for the feeling of immense happiness.

"A lovely thing," said Brain.

"Yes?" said Ginge. "Cough up."

"You tell them, Ed," said Brain. He looked at the skinks with wonder. So Eddy explained about the Christmas he was thirteen. His first time singing the *Messiah* with the Cathedral choir, the first time he'd ever looked at the libretto. How astonished he had been—and then astonishingly sheepish—to discover that in the chorus, "Lift up your heads, O ye gates," the repeated refrain was not in fact "Who is *the skink* of Glory?" It was "Who is *this King* of Glory?"

"*What?*" said the Modern Priest.

"Why would there be a skink in the *Messiah*?" said Bridgie.

"No reason!" said Eddy. "It's nuts. There's never a reason with mondegreens. They make no sense, yet you somehow accommodate them."

"True," said Ginge. "Remember *Warm sausage tea*. Instead of *Monstrosity*. I had some rationalization for that . . ."

"Yes," said Bridgie, "and *It's Miller* . . . but it was *Bismillah*—Arabic."

"'Bohemian Rhapsody,'" said Brain to the Modern Priest, who had no idea what they were talking about.

"That song's bonkers," said Ginge. "Anything could make sense. But skinks in the *Messiah*?"

"Well, Ginge," said Eddy, avuncular. "This depends on your capacity for lateral thinking. Here was mine: lizards, dry places, Old Testament, lots of desert . . . and also, could be some metaphor . . . God showing himself as a lowly reptile . . . you *know*."

"But wait," said Brain. "There's more."

"To wrap this up," said Eddy. "The real point is: when I told Brain about the mishearing and that fuckwitted rationalization, turned out he'd heard it *exactly the same way* when he was young. What are the odds?"

"I'd like to borrow that story for a sermon?" said the Modern Priest. "There's a metaphor there somewhere."

"No, there's not," said Eddy. "And no, you can't."

He was regretting the story. It was better just between him and Brain.

"Anyway, they're beautiful," said Brain, stroking a skink. "Best ever, Ed."

They all beheld the skinks, svelte and godly.

"I'm thinking . . . trifle?" said the Modern Priest.

55

"This trifle is basically just alcohol thickened with sponge and custard," said Bridgie later, on the couch. Eddy leaned his back against her right arm, so his head could loll on her shoulder. He was like a bookend.

"I actually look forward to it all year," she said. "I probably think about it a couple of times a week."

"Would you describe yourself as a voluptuary?" said Eddy.

"Yes," said Bridgie. "Dedicated to sensualism." She put the spoon down. "I think I'll lick the bowl."

"You and Boo," said Eddy.

"How is the adorable Roberta?"

"Not sure," said Eddy. "Enigmatic. Possibly fed up with me."

"How are *you*, George? Really."

How was he? What was he? A work in progress? A tabula rasa?

"Okay," he said.

"Are you still an agnostic?"

"Of course," said Eddy. "You?"

"Full atheist," said Bridgie. "Sometimes I miss believing, though."

Eddy knew what she meant. But then he thought about Toss, the distortions his belief had visited on him. He could think about this only sometimes, and not when he was alone. He looked over at Brain, empty dessert bowl in his lap, his benign resting face. Brain believed that music was the pathway to God. Or god. The Modern Priest believed in The Church, an altogether different proposition.

"I believe in nuns," said Eddy. "Modern ones." He knew the Modern Priest was listening, even as he rabbited on to Ginge.

"I've known a few good ones," said Bridgie.

Sue Lombardo had said she didn't believe in believing. That wasn't the point.

"What is the point?" Eddy asked.

"I don't know yet," said Sue. But she was thinking a lot about the motherhood of grace. Thank you, Julian of Norwich.

Sue had given Eddy a quote from Julian of Norwich for Christmas, written with fountain pen on creamy paper in her nunly hand. *Be a Gardener. Dig a ditch. Toil and sweat. And turn the earth upside down. And seek the deepness . . .*

"*Who IS the Skink of Glory?*" sang Ginge to the ceiling. "*Who IS the Skink of GLORY?*" Eddy looked up. No answer on the ceiling, just a house spider, speeding toward the north corner.

"I could believe in a Skink of Glory," said Ginge. He considered his nearly empty glass. "Secretive. Rarely seen."

Yes, thought Eddy.

56

After they'd all gone, Brain in bed and the house quiet, Eddy turned on his phone to see if there were any messages. It was 12:45 a.m. There was one from Jasper: *Cool bat. Thanks a lot. JM.* One from Boo: *Happy Boxing Day Mr. Ed x*

She had stopped calling him Mr. K. He didn't know how to interpret this.

There were seven messages from Delphine. All bonkers.

Toss's last text to him had been the day before he died. Eddy was on his bike, heading into the southerly. He pulled the phone from his pocket and read as he pedaled, a perilous maneuver. *All the girls: Barbara Allen, Annie Laurie, Jeannie.* Their song list for when he arrived home.

It was still there on his phone. He looked at it sometimes, to see if it told him anything new.

He watched the Christmas tree lights blink through their cycle. Nine days since his wig-out beside the tree, though it felt like months. Time had behaved so oddly this last year. Sometimes it seemed just last week that Toss had died, other times decades. No Toss in his head since the wig-out. He should probably stop saying wig-out. His unconscious had been placated by all the talking with Sue. Toss was no longer immured. But now, no longer keeping him at bay, Eddy fully missed him. Another paradox.

These nights, before sleep, he sometimes listened to Toss singing. In his head. "Steal Away." Their song, ha.

He closed his eyes and listened now: *Steal a-way, steal a-way, to Jesus. Steal a-way, steal a-way home, I ain't got long to stay here . . .*

His phone buzzed. Delphine, what was the bet?

GOOOOOOOD NIIIIIIIIIIIIITE XXX.

Boo

I went on about Eddy from the Smoke-ho car park, up the Croesus Track through the beech and podocarp, then all the way along the zigzag to the ridge between Blackball Creek and Roaring Meg Creek. Two and a half hours. How did Carys not push me off the ridgeline and into the Roaring Meg?

On the one hand, going on and on took my mind off the new pack strap digging into my shoulder, doubtless making a blister. On the other hand, I missed seeing the pair of whio waddling beside the Roaring Meg, because I was looking at my boots as I walked, ignoring nature, and trying to explain my fear that Eddy and I had only ended up back together because he needed something to blot out the awfulness with Toss.

"Hmmm," said Carys. But weren't motives usually mixed? Wasn't it possible that Eddy really wanted to get back together, for all the right reasons, whatever right was—attraction, love, rewriting the past, having a good time, etc., etc., etc.—but also found it a good distraction from Toss? Carys is a clear thinker.

I decided to stop obsessing about Eddy. I knew what the problem was. The problem was that I didn't know—what would happen with us, what the future would be, *where* the future would be. I have always hated not knowing.

The track climbed quite sharply after that, so we didn't talk as much. It was a warm, clear day. We could see Lake Brunner, navy blue and brooding, in the distance. Kōtuku Whakaoho. I thought of my

Christmas present from Eddy. A clay model of a black robin, kakaruia. Maybe the sweetest bird in the world. Eddy had chosen it because of *Old Blue*, a book about the last Chatham Island black robin we'd both had as kids. I'd knitted him a scarf. At Knit World, the one place you can knit on the job. Black merino silk. "For next winter," I said. We were thinking the same thing. Next winter? Who knew?

It was only 3:30 when we arrived at the hut. We shrugged off our packs and decided to do the side trip to Croesus Knob. It was like floating, without that pack. And the view at the top! Out to the Tasman Sea and all the way south to Aoraki. The world seemed big— and expanding. Eddy Smallbone would love me or he would not.

And then Carys told me an extraordinary story.

It was because we were looking at Aoraki. It made her think of the alpine fault line and the man from Mt. Cook.

On the day of the February quake, she was at the Fine Arts school, a holiday research job. It had been terrible of course. The building pitched and jerked, as solid as a rag doll. People froze or ran nowhere, shouted and cried. Then they were at the evacuation zones, milling aimlessly, constantly checking their phones though the servers had crashed, or listening to radio reports and retelling the news to each other every few minutes.

"Long story short," said Carys, "I went to a friend's house nearby, to write up this abstract. Amazing I could concentrate. I left just after dark, wheeled my bike out onto Clyde Road. It was gridlocked, the traffic was mad—the first day of our new traffic lives. I kept walking with the bike, don't know why, there was liquefaction everywhere. I got to the intersection of Clyde and Fendalton and Memorial, and there was the craziest thing. In the middle of the road, one of the cleaners from the Arts building was playing traffic cop. I knew him; I'd talked to him that morning. In his fifties maybe, solid guy, weathered, and tall. He's got fluorescent green plastic gloves on and the white cleaning coat, and he's *directing the traffic*. The real thing—he knew all the hand signals; it looked totally professional. It was, I don't know, *comforting*. He was imposing, authoritative. The traffic started to loosen up, flow better, and he was in his element, hand up stopping one line, ushering another through with wide arm sweeps. Unbelievable. And the green gloves! I couldn't take my eyes off them. People were tooting thanks, leaning out their windows, cheering him, giving him the thumbs-up. It was something else. I realized I was crying. This terrible day—we'd heard so much by then, the collapsed buildings, the deaths, the injuries—the world had changed. But here was this guy, the cleaner from Mt. Cook, at the helm.

"I stayed there," said Carys, "watching him until the traffic cleared, ages. But I wanted to talk to him. He was parked on Clyde, and I followed him to the car to say hello. Don't know why, to finish the story or something. I asked him how he knew all the signals. And he's taking off his gloves, folding his coat and tucking it into a bag, and he just laughs and says he'd always wanted to be a traffic cop, since he was really young. He'd wished they lived in a city because there were no traffic cops in Mt. Cook Village, it was too small. But he got a book on the signals somehow and learned them, and his mother bought him white cotton gloves. His day job now was in electronics; the cleaning was extra, he needed it for retirement. He never applied to be a traffic cop, but suddenly, here was this moment on this crazy day—and he went for it. Then he got in his car and I got on my bike and that was it. Took forever to get home, the traffic and everything."

We went back to looking at the grand landscape. Down the island to Aoraki with its patchy summer snow, and westward, tracking the sun as it crossed toward the Alps. Under the range was the great fault line—the one that should have ruptured. It was biding its time.

"I don't really know what that story means," said Carys as we started back to the hut. "I want it to mean something."

I didn't know what it meant, either, though I understood why she'd cried. The sweetness of that guy's moment, his bold move. The steady signaling amidst the chaos.

Then I thought of Eddy on the morning he found Toss More dead beside him.

At first he was dumb and dazed; he couldn't get his thoughts together. He sat in his boxers on the other side of the bed and stared at his feet, whitening with the cold. Time paused.

Eventually, he stood up, slow and stiff, like an old man. He found his phone fallen behind the bed and rang Brain. After they'd talked, he put on his jeans and T-shirt and sweater. Brain would get a taxi. He would be there in twenty minutes or so.

Eddy didn't want to leave Toss alone in the bed all that time; he would be cold. He found the remote and turned on the heat pump: 80 degrees. Then he got back into bed and pulled the duvets straight, over Toss's hands and chest, smoothing them under his chin. He lay down close to Toss, his front against Toss's side, his arm across Toss's middle, and his face tucked into Toss's neck. He closed his eyes and waited for Brain.

ACKNOWLEDGMENTS

Loving thanks to:

The Henderson Trust for the wonderful residency that enabled substantial progress on this novel.

Barbara Larson for her continuing generosity, editing, and wise counsel.

Jenny Hellen for great patience and support.

Emma Neale for her fine editorial judgments.

Julia Anderson for 136 Bishop Street.

John Peter Mullins for the New World history.

Clare De Goldi and Ewan Cameron for help with streets and trees.

Rina van Bohemen for her excellent ear.

Barbara Smith for her valuable forensics.

Bella Foster Lowe for teeth gone soft.

Glenn Busch for the astonishing traffic cop.

Gerald Kember, whose visit to the vet thirteen years ago began it all.

And Bruce Foster, without whom . . .